PAYING THE FERRYMAN

A Naomi Blake Novel

Jane A. Adams

This first world edition published 2014
in Great Britain and the USA by
SEVERN HOUSE PUBLISHERS LTD of
19 Cedar Road, Sutton, Surrey, England, SM2 5DA.
Trade paperback edition first published in Great Britain and the USA 2015
by SEVERN HOUSE PUBLISHERS LTD.

British Library Cataloguing in Publication Data

Adams, Jane, 1960- author.
   Paying the Ferryman. – (A Naomi Blake mystery)
   1. Blake, Naomi (Fictitious character)–Fiction.
   2. Ex-police officers–Fiction. 3. Blind women–Fiction.
   4. Murder–Investigation–Fiction. 5. Detective and
   mystery stories.
   I. Title II. Series
   823.9'2-dc23

ISBN-13: 978-0-7278-8424-4 (cased)
ISBN-13: 978-1-84751-532-2 (trade paper)
ISBN-13: 978-1-78010-576-5 (ebook)

All Severn House titles are printed on acid-free paper.

Severn House Publishers support the Forest Stewardship Council™ [FSC™],
the leading international forest certification organisation. All our titles that
are printed on FSC certified paper carry the FSC logo.

Typeset by Palimpsest Book Production Ltd.,
Falkirk, Stirlingshire, Scotland.
Printed and bound in Great Britain by
TJ International, Padstow, Cornwall.

PROLOGUE

Sarah was woken by angry voices from downstairs and the sound of her little brother crying in the next room.

For a moment she was disoriented. Her mum and stepdad never yelled at one another like that and then never left Jack to cry. Vic, her stepfather, would occasionally growl a bit but he was the most even-tempered person Sarah had ever known – which, she'd always figured, was one of the big reasons her mum had fallen for him.

Another moment and she recognized the third voice rising up to her from the room below.

'Shit!' Sarah said. What the hell was he doing here? In that moment, she was absolutely convinced that the voice belonged to her father.

Sarah pulled on her dressing gown and slippers and padded quietly into the next room. Fifteen-month-old Jack raised his arms to her and she picked him up, found a tissue and wiped away the snot and tears from his face and dressing gown collar. Her mum always put him to bed in his dressing gown. He was such a wriggle-wort that he always managed to throw the covers off and then he woke up cold. He snuffled against her shoulder and then stopped crying as she hugged him tight, stroking the fluffy blond head.

'There, that's better then,' Sarah said softly, soothing the little boy. She had been listening hard to the continued friction downstairs. Her dad hadn't been around in years, thankfully, but she remembered the last time she'd seen him. The threats, the violence, the police.

They'd moved just a little while after that – then moved again and again – and then . . . and then good things had begun to happen. Her mum had met Vic and, after a very cautious start, had fallen for him big time, and for once in her life she'd made a good decision.

So what the hell was her father doing here now? He sounded, even to Sarah's ears, madder than ever.

She crept out on to the landing and stood at the head of the stairs, listening.

'What kind of mother keeps a father away from his kid?'

'A mother who wants to keep her child safe,' Vic told him. He still wasn't shouting, Sarah noted, but he sounded angry, tense and – scared.

Vic never sounded anxious or scared.

Something else was said, but Sarah couldn't catch it. The voice had lowered and the words were lost.

And then she heard her mother scream and her stepfather shouting, 'Run, Sarah, run! Just run!'

And then two loud bangs that seemed to fill the house.

'Mum!' Sarah cried out, but she knew. Her mother was gone, Vic too, and there was only one thing left for her to do. Obey her stepfather's final words and run.

The toddler had begun to whimper again, scared by the noise and by Sarah's sudden tension. What to do, what the hell should she do?

She could hear his footsteps in the hall; another moment and he'd be coming up the stairs. Sarah backed away looking for a way to escape. There was no way she could climb down from the window with her brother in her arms. She had to find some means of getting down the stairs and outside.

He was on the stairs now and Sarah did the only thing she could think of: she dodged into her parents' room and hid behind the half open door, willing her little brother to stay silent and still.

The slow tamp of footsteps rose up the stairs and on to the landing. Her father never said a word. As he came on to the landing she could see that he was still holding the gun she had heard fired downstairs. It gleamed in the light coming from Jack's bedroom, his little plug-in night light turning the harsh metal a soft, petal pink. Sarah dared not breathe.

Please, go into my room, she prayed. Go into my room. It was the furthest down the hall and would give them just a little time to get to the stairs.

So little time.

She wasn't sure whether her father intended to kill her or abduct her – Sarah wasn't sure which was worse – and then there was Jack to think about. Her father had killed Jack's parents without a second thought. There was nothing to make her believe he would spare the child.

Sarah had been unable to help her mother or Vic but she was not about to let this man hurt Jack.

Her breath hurt in her chest. Slowly, she exhaled and then cautiously drew the air back into her lungs. She was certain he would hear her.

He moved along the landing towards her brother's little room. Surely he must realize they weren't there, Sarah thought. Or did he no longer think logically? Did someone who had just killed two people really even think?

Through the crack between door and hinges on her parents' bedroom door, she saw him go through the half closed door and then push it wide. Then her father stepped inside and Sarah knew it was now or never. He might move down the hall to her room but he could just as easily turn the other way and that would be an end of things. She just knew it.

Moving as softly as she could and just praying that Jack would stay quiet, Sarah stepped around the door and out of the room. She could not see her father and guessed he must be standing somewhere in the middle of the room or maybe even by the window. She kept close to the wall, away from the creaky floorboards that Vic was always trying to silence by adding more nails.

She made it to the top of the stairs and now she could see him, a shadowy figure standing beside Jack's empty cot and looking down into it, the gun still in his hand. Sarah moved on to the stairs, hurrying down them as fast as she could on slippered feet. He only had to turn, now, and he'd have a clean shot at them.

Her heart hammered, breath rasping as she tried hard to control it. Jack now felt very heavy in her arms. They were half way down the stairs when she heard the shots.

Sarah couldn't help herself. She screamed, and only as the sound escaped did she realize that though the shots had come from Jack's room they were not aimed in their direction.

Not yet.

As she leapt down the last two steps she heard him come out on to the landing and start down the stairs.

Sarah's thoughts seemed to come very fast. The front door? No, he'd have a clear view of her and the bolts were heavy and difficult to move.

The back door then; hope her mother hadn't locked up for the night.

Sarah charged through into the kitchen, slamming the door closed behind her, even while a little bit of her brain laughed that it was hardly going to be able to stop a bullet.

The key had been turned in the back door lock but had not been removed. She turned it, glancing down to ensure the bolt had not been thrown, thankful beyond words to find it hadn't. Jack was yelling now and she yanked the back door wide just as the man with the gun came into the kitchen.

Out into the garden. Rain pounded down fierce and cold and she held Jack tighter, screwing up her eyes against the force of it. She pulled the garden gate wide, then Sarah ran and ran.

Behind her a shot blasted through the cold night air and the pouring rain and she felt the pain of it. Sarah staggered, almost hit the floor. Jack was quiet now, still heavy in her arms. She tightened her grip; her side was on fire and her right arm didn't want to work. Somehow, she stumbled on.

Lights came on behind her, but Sarah was unaware of them. Reality, consciousness, for her it was all about putting one foot in front of the other and keeping Jack safe. But she knew where she was going now.

The house backed on to fields. The fields belonged to a farm. Across the fields was a barn. She lost her slippers in the sucking mud of the ploughed field but somehow made it into the barn.

Hay bales and farm equipment. Faint light from outside filtered in and memory supplemented it. She had been here several times, been chased out by the farmer more than once. She could just make out the massive thing with hooks that she had seen the farmer drag behind his tractor: spikes that looked like weapons, that looked like defence . . . A tarpaulin tossed beside the bales looked like potential shelter. Sarah crawled behind the machine and laid her brother down. Jack didn't move and Sarah could just make out the dark spread of blood staining the pale blue of his dressing gown.

She looked down at the crimson stains on her own and prayed that all the blood was hers. That Jack was all right.

She thought she heard a sound coming from outside. Her last act as she lost consciousness was to pull the tarpaulin across them both. Then she heard nothing more.

ONE

They brought the bodies out at dawn. The rain had ceased and the sunrise lit a pale scene, washed down with grey and bleakly cold.

Figures in white overalls handed over to men in black suits. Together they wheeled the gurneys with their weight of soot-dark plastic out towards the waiting cars. The gurneys were collapsed, body bags were slid inside, the doors were closed.

He counted them.

Only two. Only two bodies, he thought. Did that mean . . .? But he'd seen no ambulance arrive, heard no sirens, and no one had spoken of living victims being taken away.

A little cluster of people huddled at the end of the street behind the cordon. Those who had not been brought out by the rumours of gunshots had been evacuated by the police. An emergency shelter had been provided for them at a nearby church, but some had wandered back, curiosity and concern dragging them here to the end of their little road. One of them voiced what he had been thinking.

'Only two bodies. Does that mean the kiddies—?'

'Oh, God willing. Poor little buggers. He's such a little mite.'

'And she's a lovely girl. Always polite, always with a smile. I see her go off to school of a morning and she always waves.'

'The mother's a nice woman. I don't know him more than to say hello to, but she's always got a word, you know.'

'And they've not been here five minutes. Such a terrible thing.'

Three years, he thought. *They've lived here for three years.* Sarah had come to his school just after. She'd been a nervous little first year then and he'd been in the year above. She was now fourteen and Joey was just over a year older.

He stood a little apart from the rest, separated by his youth and by the fact that he didn't live in their street. There was curiosity about this teenage boy in his Puffa jacket, jeans and trainers who had arrived a couple of hours before and not moved since.

His bare hands were thrust into the depths of his pockets and he wished he had the nerve to ask the neighbours more about what had happened, but that would draw even more attention his way and there was enough of that already. Instead, he sank his chin further into his collar, tried to ignore the raging earache he now had – he'd rushed out without his hat – and watched intently, expecting other bodies to be brought out of that red front door, to be slid so quietly and efficiently into the waiting mortuary cars.

He heard the engine start, and a police officer walked up towards the cordon to open it for the vehicle to pass through. The officer eyed the watchers with that strange mix of criticism and compassion the boy had noticed earlier. He didn't approve of the gathering, but he understood it, and Joey wondered if he'd have joined them had it been his street.

The officer glanced his way. Joey's youth and stillness and silence were marking him out from the rest and Joey knew this was perhaps his only chance.

He took a hesitant step towards the policeman, breaking the habit, if not of a lifetime, then certainly of years. Policemen were not people he would usually talk to. 'The girl,' he said. 'Sarah. Is she OK?'

The officer scrutinized him. 'And you are?'

'A friend. She's my friend.'

'And your name is?'

He thought about lying, but the little knot of locals had turned their attention towards him now and he just knew that at least one of them would know his dad. Everyone knew his dad. 'Um, Joey,' he said. 'Joey Hughes. I go to school with Sarah.'

The mortuary car prowled up to the cordon and the police officer waved people aside. Joey thought that would be it. He'd get no response now.

'Christ sake, Matthew,' one of the neighbours said. 'Tell the boy. It'll all come out soon enough. Is the lass dead or not?'

The officer called Matthew scowled. 'There'll be a statement later,' he said.

'I'm sure there will, lad, but you've been asked a civil question, and times were you'd have given a civil answer. Just because you've got a uniform doesn't mean we don't all know you.'

Joey glanced gratefully at this unexpected ally, an elderly man with a raincoat belted tight over his pyjamas and dressing gown and a woollen hat tugged down over his ears.

The scowl deepened, but Matthew, as the speaker had pointed out, was a local boy and the influence of his neighbours was still ingrained. He glanced back towards the house and then at the man who had spoken to him.

'The kids weren't there,' he said. 'Look, you didn't hear this from me, but it looks like the girl took the baby and they got out when the shooting started. That's all guessing and we don't know.'

Joey's heart leapt and his throat tightened. Sarah wasn't dead. Sarah got away!

'There was blood,' the police officer called Matthew continued. 'So, we don't know—'

A collective sigh of relief transformed into a hiss of anxious anticipation.

'Best thing you can do now is get yourselves fed back at the church and then, if you want to do something, they'll be putting out a call for bodies to help with the search.'

'Where and when?' a woman demanded.

'We'll be using the church as an incident room,' he said. 'You'll be told more in about an hour, I reckon.'

'Thanks,' Joey said to the old man; then he turned and walked swiftly away. There was a chance Sarah and her little brother were still alive. There was going to be a search. He could help. He could find her. She was going to be all right.

He stopped in his tracks, the horror of it all suddenly overwhelming. His friend Tel, who lived in the next street, had texted him in the early hours.

Something going on at Sarah's.

So the text had said.

Police everywhere.

So Joey had slipped from the house and run to Sarah's place only to find that his friend was right. There *were* police everywhere. The street had been cordoned and some of the residents, those in neighbouring properties, evacuated while a search went on. He glimpsed armed officers, saw an ambulance standing with its doors wide; then the doors closed and it left, empty.

And now he knew. Sarah's mum and stepdad were dead. Sarah and her little brother were God knows where and the policeman had said . . . had said there was blood. Did he mean Sarah's blood?

Joey bent over, suddenly overcome by nausea and pure, cold sweat terror. He thought he was going to puke, but somehow managed to fight the cramping in his belly.

He had to go home, tell his mum what was going on, grab some stuff and then join the search. She'd be mad at him for sneaking out, but she'd want to know what was happening and she'd understand.

At least, he hoped she would.

He tried to think if his dad would be home yet. His mobile phone told him it was after seven, so it was likely, but he might be lucky – maybe his dad had not come back off his shift yet.

Joey sighed. He straightened up, the sudden cramps receding. He shivered despite the thick jacket. His legs and head and feet were freezing. Reluctantly, Joey headed for home.

'Where the fuck do you think you've been?'

So his dad was home then, Joey thought.

'None of your fucking business.'

A swift backhand aimed in the direction of Joey's head. He ducked, but it still caught him a stinging blow on his cold ear.

'Steve, please—'

Joey's mother stood in the kitchen doorway wringing a tea towel between her hands.

Steve, please, Joey thought. When did his dad ever take notice of 'please'?

'I said where have you been?'

'And I said it was none of your business.'

'Talk to me like that, boy, and you know what you'll get.'

Joey knew all too well. But somehow knowing didn't, couldn't, change the way he behaved. Joey would not bow down to this man. Not any more.

'Fuck you!' Joey said. He leapt past his dad and headed for the stairs, taking them two at a time and racing ahead of the steel hand grasping at his back.

'Joey!' his mother's voice was pleading. Scared now, both for him and for herself.

Joey felt a second or so of remorse, knowing what he was leaving her to face, but he pushed it aside. He was through the door just before his dad got to it. The bolt was drawn and the heavy chest of drawers slid into place as his father started bashing against the wooden panels.

Joey was well practised in this scenario. He knew he only ever delayed the beating, never avoided it, but for now that was enough.

He grabbed the backpack out of the bottom of his wardrobe. It was already partly packed. Joey kept it that way.

He grabbed a thick sweatshirt and a few other bits he thought might be useful to him and then opened the window and stepped outside. They had a flat roofed kitchen extension at the back of their house and so did their neighbours, and this had been a regular escape route for Joey, even though the neighbours objected loudly – though only when his dad wasn't in earshot – and his dad was wise to it now. Joey could hear that he'd abandoned the assault on the door and was now thundering down the stairs ready to intercept his son. He burst out into the yard just as Joey crossed the boundary between the houses and then leapt down into his neighbours' garden. He could hear his mother screaming and his dad's threats, but Joey knew he wouldn't be followed once he'd made it past the gardens and on to the allotments beyond. His dad, for all his vice-like hands and fists like hammers, was also fat and slow. While it was true the extra weight put power behind his fists it also prevented him from running much more than the length of the yard, and for that Joey was grateful.

Joey finally paused once he'd put the allotments and a couple of streets between himself and his parents. He turned then and headed back towards Sarah's street, pausing to call at Tel's house.

'So, what's going on?' Tel demanded. Joey could see Tel's mum hovering in the background, also anxious to know. He spoke to both of them, glancing at Tel's mum from time to time, hoping such inclusivity would earn him some breakfast and a chance to get warm – it often did; Tel's mum knew all about the Hughes family.

'Sarah's parents. They're dead,' Joey said.

'Dead? You're sure?' Tel's mother asked, her face reflecting the horror and doubt Joey himself had felt.

Joey nodded. 'They brought out body bags. Two of them. The neighbours say they heard shooting.'

'Shooting? What, guns? Here?'

Joey nodded again.

'And what about the children?' asked Maggie, Tel's mum.

Joey shook his head. 'No one knows. The policeman said they weren't there.'

'Well, thank God for that!'

'But there was blood.'

'Oh, good lord.'

'They'll be looking for volunteers to search. Everyone's meeting at the church. St Barts. The policeman said it would be a . . . an incident room.'

Tel's mother made up her mind. 'There's tea in the pot and there's bread for toast. Grab yourself something, Joey, while I get some warmer clothes on. Then we'll all go down. The more people volunteer, the better, I reckon.'

She paused as she passed Joey and inspected the blackening bruise on his ear and head. 'You need to report that bastard,' she said. 'I don't care if he is your father, you don't report him, Joey Hughes, and I damned well will.'

Joey believed her. He also believed that his dad would just be able to talk his way out of it, like he always did, like all the times the police had come when neighbours reported Joey's mother screaming, only to find themselves scuppered by her lack of cooperation. He'd heard that the police could now prosecute even if his mum didn't want them to, but he only half believed that. None of the officers that had turned up at their door so far had managed to make any fucking difference.

Tel's mother often said he could come and stay with them, but if he did then his mother really would be alone and he couldn't bear that. He knew what would happen to her.

Tel's mum had once said that Joey's mother was an adult, that she needed to think for herself and ask for help. That Joey couldn't be responsible for a woman who should be responsible for herself.

But Joey knew he'd not been supposed to overhear that conversation. That she'd been angry on his behalf and just let rip. He felt no ill will towards Maggie for it, even though it did prove to him just how little she really understood.

He knew his way around Tel's kitchen though, finding a mug and pouring himself some tea, adding three sugars while his friend operated the toaster.

'Your dad was home, then,' Tel said.

Joey shrugged. 'One day I'll kill him,' he said, and Tel just nodded.

'You want jam on your toast?' he said.

TWO

A large crowd gathered inside the church. The WI had convened and were serving tea and a local bakery brought fresh bread that more volunteers were turning into toast. Joey and Tel followed Tel's mother into the throng. Maggie left them for a moment while she found out who was in charge and what was going on. She returned a few minutes later holding three mugs of tea.

'Someone's coming to speak to us in a few minutes. They're bringing the search dogs in and going to divide the volunteers into teams. Thank the lord it's stopped raining,' she added. 'Last night's weather was vicious for a while.'

'Do they know . . . anything?'

'No, not really. Apparently there was some blood on the back gate, but most of it was washed away by the rain.'

'They'll be frozen,' Joey said. 'Maggie, can't we just get started? Get out there?'

'And do what? Look, sweetheart, I know what you must be feeling, but we've got to wait, let them organize us. We'll do a better job if we all work together.'

'I should have started looking for her last night,' Joey said angrily. 'I could have found her.'

'You didn't know Sarah and Jack were missing last night,' Maggie pointed out.

'Look,' Tel added. 'Last night you thought they were both dead. Or might be.'

Reluctantly Joey nodded. He clasped his mug tight, not sure

he wanted more tea but grateful for both the warmth and something to hang on to. He kept one eye on the door. Not really expecting his father to show up, but you never really knew what that man might do and Joey was always on watch. Always trying to keep one step ahead.

'If I can have your attention, please.'

A man had taken up position in the pulpit. He didn't look very sure of his right to be there, Joey thought. He was a big man, broad and bear-like, with hair that reached to his shoulders and a curling beard. He didn't, to Joey's eyes, look like a policeman. He was surprised to find that he recognized the man, though he had never spoken to him. Sometimes Joey went to a youth project set up on wasteland a couple of miles down the road. They had trials bikes there and Joey had started to learn. He'd seen this man chatting to some of the older members, helping them work on the bikes, sometimes even wielding a spanner himself. He hadn't realized this man was a police officer.

Tel had recognized him too. 'That's that older bloke from down the club.'

Joey nodded, not sure what he felt about that.

'My name is DI Steel and, for the moment at least, I'm in charge here. Thank you all very much for turning out.

'Now, I know there are a lot of rumours flying about, so let me tell you what we know. At about three thirty this morning there was an incident at number twenty-seven Hughenden Road.' He paused and pointed in the approximate direction of the street, just in case anyone should be in doubt. 'We're still trying to piece together what happened, but at about three thirty neighbours reported shouting and arguments, and a few minutes later they reported hearing what sounded like shots. Two, and then two more. A fifth shot was fired outside the property, by which time neighbours had called the police.

'My colleagues arrived to find two people shot dead within the property. We believe them to be Victor and Lisanne Griffin. I'm sure they are known to some of you.'

'And the kids?' someone in the crowd demanded.

'As I say, we're still trying to piece together what happened, but we think Sarah Griffin and her little brother, Jack, somehow managed to get out of the property and that the final shot was fired at them as they escaped; we believe that one or both of them was hit. We've had people out searching the alleyway behind the house and the field beyond but, frankly, the pouring rain and the dark haven't helped. So far, we've not found either of them.

'Our priority, now, is to get people out there looking. Now you all know the area better than most of my officers do, so . . .'

Tel, Maggie and Joey found themselves assigned to a team of twenty, headed up by an officer with a very large dog. He led them down the narrow path that ran behind Sarah's house and through a gap in the hedge that the farmer used to get his tractor into the field.

Maggie had vouched for both of the boys. Taken charge in such a way that the police seemed to assume that they were both hers. Joey got the impression that really no one cared. Someone had asked their ages, checked that they were both sixteen, and Maggie had fudged her reply, then hustled them away before further questions could be asked.

They were here to look for Sarah and little Jack. That was all that mattered.

Slowly they spread out and began to move across the sodden field. Eyes down and in close formation. Joey kept thinking about her. Seeing her face, remembering the first time he had seen her and how he'd felt. It was like being hit between the eyes by something hard and heavy. Something hard and heavy that burned its way in. She wasn't like the other girls. Her skin was the colour of milky coffee and her hair, slightly crinkly and very full, was tied back off her face in a red band.

Her mum was white, she told him, her dad mixed race. *Dual heritage*, she called it, with a sly grin that told him she didn't really think labels said very much. And she had these deep, dark eyes that sparkled when she laughed, and she blushed so dead easily, pink colouring the coffee cream of her cheeks.

He hadn't expected her to take much notice of him. He was just another awkward teenage boy, a year above her in school and distinguished neither by academic ability nor sporting achievement; not even geekiness. He was just . . .

Nothing . . .

At least that's what his dad kept telling him.

But Sarah didn't see it that way. This last year, after he'd finally summoned the courage to talk to her, she had become almost as close to him as Tel was. Soon she was even closer than Tel had ever been, and friendly enough to his oldest friend for Tel never to feel left out. Or at least not often.

And Sarah understood what he was going through with his dad. She'd been there. She'd seen it for herself, before her mum had done something about it.

'Vic's all right,' Sarah said. 'I like him. Love him, I guess. He's been a good dad and Mum's been happy. He's great with Jack. Just so . . . gentle.'

Sarah valued gentleness, Joey thought. What other people might think was soft and soppy, Sarah liked because she'd seen so much of the other. The violent, the cruel, the hurting and the hitting, and Joey knew where she was coming from. He just wished his mum would do what Sarah's had done and get them both away.

'Any idea what we're looking for?' Tel asked as they paced in line across the sodden field. Above them a heavy sky threatened another downpour.

'Anything that shouldn't be here,' Maggie said. 'Any trace of Sarah.'

'Have they checked the barns?' Joey asked, looking across at the farm buildings across the fields.

'I think they did that first,' Maggie said. 'But if she was hurt, well, that seems a long way for her to go. And she had Jack with her. He's no light weight.'

Joey looked at his phone. It was almost nine o clock. That meant wherever she was she'd probably been there for the best part of five hours.

'She'll be frozen,' Joey said. 'And Jack. He's just so little. They'll be wet, and—'

Maggie laid a hand on his arm. 'Look how many people there are out looking for her,' she said. She pointed towards the other groups stretched out across the fields, moving slowly in long lines.

'We will find her, Joey.' She reached out and embraced him in a quick hug. They moved forward, Joey trying to focus on the ground beneath his feet, constantly distracted now by the other searchers, by the sight of the police officer with the dog. They were moving across the field at a diagonal to the main line, the dog with its nose down, the officer following at the end of a very long lead.

Had it found something? Joey couldn't tell. Abruptly the dog changed direction, tracked back across the field, then turned again and stopped dead, hovering at a clod of mud. Then it lifted its head and sat down. The policeman held a large paper bag in his hand. He opened it and lowered the open bag towards the dog. It sniffed, then took off again, casting back and forth across the field.

Joey glanced back towards the houses. He could see Sarah's gate. Would she have come across here? Joey wondered. Across this way? If she'd come from her house, wouldn't she be closer to the field edge?

He watched the policeman and the dog again, willing it to pick up a scent. Closer to the wood and the barns another dog cast back and forth across the field, a line of searchers following behind.

'Are you sure they checked the outbuildings on the farm?' Joey said again.

'Joey, they've checked, and I've no doubt they'll check again. She can't have got far.'

'Not unless someone took them both,' Joey said, the possibility dawning on him for the first time. 'What if they were taken? What if they weren't, and the police think they were and so don't look in the right places?'

Maggie hugged him again. Maggie probably hugged him more than anyone, Joey thought. Anyone except for Sarah, and that was different. 'No one is going to stop looking,' she said. 'We'll all look and look and look again. Sarah and Jack will be found.'

'I love her,' Joey said, so quietly that Maggie almost didn't hear.

'I know you do,' Maggie said. 'And Sarah knows it too. She knows you'll come for her.'

THREE

The Griffins' home was last but one at the end of a row of larger Victorian terraced houses. Small wooden gates led through to tiny front gardens and then, at this house, three steps up to the front door. The added height gave the initial impression that there might be a basement, until you looked back down the row and realized that the house at the far end had no step and the last in the row had four. The added height was simply dictated by the lay of the land. It gave the row an imposing air though, Steel thought. A sense of being set back from the road and somehow rising above the rest of the street.

The door was red with an inset glass panel decorated with a stylized flower. DI Steel decided it dated from later than the house, but was still old. The sort of thing a conscientious resident might choose to buy from a reclamation yard. The clear fanlight window above the door suggested a much earlier building style, as did the sash windows, but he glanced down the row and decided that both were original.

Steel liked architecture.

'In here, sir.' A voice drew him into the hall where a young woman in uniform directed him into the room that led off to his right. The stairs were directly ahead and beyond them a short passage led to the kitchen.

Original tiles in the hall, he thought. Blue, red, cream and black, laid out in a geometric pattern. So many people covered up their tiles, and that was a shame. He thrust his massive hands into the pockets of his waxed jacket, flexed his shoulders. Outside the day had turned chill and the damp ate its way into everything. Inside the house was warm; a massive cast iron radiator filled the space beside the front door. He followed the directions to the living room and stepped inside.

The wooden door had been stripped and waxed and the floor-boards exposed and covered with brightly coloured rugs that picked up the shades of the tiles in the hall. The walls were cream; plain, but well hung with pictures. And there were books in the alcoves. A deep, comfortable chair in the shallow bay window. Heavy curtains.

The people who lived here were comfortable with themselves, Steel thought. Only the four locks and the heavy chain on the front door gave any indication to the contrary.

'What can you tell me?'

Sergeant Willis came to stand beside him. She handed him a sheaf of newly printed photographs and Steel riffled through them, reminding himself of the crime scene as he had first witnessed it. Before the bodies had been moved.

'Victor Griffin, and his wife Lisanne Griffin. Lived here for three years and according to neighbours were quiet and friendly. No one recalls them mentioning family and they had very few visitors. They seem to have had most to do with the elderly woman in the last house in the row. Mrs Ball, a widow. Apparently Lisanne Griffin used to take her shopping sometimes and the girl, Sarah, used to check in on her regularly and run errands. She seems to be genuinely fond of the family and I think is most likely to know about their background. The doctor gave her something to help her sleep though, so you'll have to wait. She was distraught, kept asking who could have killed such a lovely family. I think she assumed the kids had been shot too.'

'We don't know that they weren't.'

'True.'

Steel crouched down where the body of Lisanne Griffin had lain and studied his photographs. In the pictures she lay on her back, arms out to the side as though she had just fallen back. A blossom of red blood on her chest told him where the bullet had entered, and blood flowed outward from beneath her body, staining the wooden boards and the edge of the rug. Not so much blood, though; her heart had stopped when the bullet hit. Blood had exited under the influence of gravity, not been pumped by a dying heart.

Close by, Victor Griffin had lain on his side, and in the photographs the track of the bullet was less cleanly delineated. It seemed to have entered his body from the left side, Steel thought, shattering ribs, stopping the heart, then exiting somewhat higher on the right side, if the blood pool was any indicator.

Steel eased himself upward. He ached. Lack of sleep and a sudden urge to join the gym a couple of weeks before were really taking their toll. He tried to convince himself he'd eventually feel better for it.

'So,' he said, 'perhaps the wife is shot first, and then the husband as he turns towards her?'

'Has some logic to it,' Willis agreed. 'The angle of both shots is strange, though. It's like the shooter is below the victims. Victor Griffin . . . it looks as though the path of the bullet starts from below the ribs and exits under the opposite armpit.'

'So, maybe the shooter was sitting?' He pointed to a chair,

one of a pair either side of a matching sofa that was too bright and modern for Steel's taste. Its contemporary redness seemed out of place with the rest of the more restrained, period features.

'Which implies guest rather than assassin.'

'Maybe. A guest that arrives in the early hours of the morning?'

'Either someone very well known or someone they don't want seen hanging around on their doorstep.'

'An interesting thought,' Steel agreed. 'Either way, they weren't expecting him. Always assuming it was a him. They were both clearly dressed for bed.'

'So someone they didn't feel the need to get dressed for, or someone, as I said, they want to get off the street quickly before anyone sees them.' Willis shrugged. 'Or who came in the back way, of course. The front door was still fully locked when we got here.'

'And the back?'

'Wide open. Come on, I'll show you the rest of the house.'

Steel nodded. He enjoyed working with Willis. She was never afraid to speculate; never worried about getting it wrong – not that 'wrong' happened very often. He knew they presented an amusing pair. Sophie Willis, small and slight with dark brown skin and relaxed black hair, was a sharp contrast to Steel's height and bulk and pallor – even though he spent a good deal of his life outside, his skin rarely seemed to tan.

He told the crime scene manager that his people could go back in, and then followed Willis into the kitchen.

'Back door was open when we got here. There's a key in the lock, bolts top and bottom. All the windows have locks on them and there's an alarm, which wasn't set when we arrived.'

'So, security conscious. The crime rate round here is low; maybe they expected trouble?'

'Or maybe they'd just got used to hearing the statistics.'

He glanced around the kitchen. The cabinets looked modern and quite new but not expensively made, he thought. The centre of the kitchen was occupied by a large table with a fifties-style Formica top and lacquered black legs. Matching chairs with red seats and a high chair at one end, reminding him – if reminder were required – about the missing children. The kitchen units, he guessed, had been replaced ready for the house to be sold.

They had that bland 'it'll do' look that went with magnolia paint and white gloss. The table, on the other hand, suggested a love of retro and colour, as did the brightly coloured ceramic bowls on the counters and the red kettle. This was a home still in the making. Was that significant?

He peered out through the open back door.

'You want to look upstairs?'

Willis nodded, and he followed her back out into the hall.

Steel stared down at the little cot.

'Two shots,' Willis told him. 'Fired straight through the blankets and the mattress.'

'But anyone could see the bed was empty,' Steel commented. 'Why shoot into an empty cot?'

'I don't know. It's just possible it was for effect, maybe to scare Sarah or because the gunman was angry that the kid was not there, or . . . I don't know. You don't suppose there were two of them? That he came upstairs and fired the shots so someone else would hear and think—'

Steel was looking at her and she laughed self consciously. 'I know. Speculation. No evidence of anyone else.'

'No, but keep the thought in mind. Keep everything in mind. At the moment one idea is just as good as any other. Show me Sarah's room.'

Steel didn't go into the girl's room; he stood on the threshold and reviewed it as though, Willis thought, it was a stage set for some odd, avant-garde play. 'It all looks normal to you, does it?'

'It looks like a teenage girl's room, if that's what you mean. I don't think anything has been touched.' She paused, knowing that look. 'Something strike you as odd?'

'Only the fact that it's tidy. But then I only have my sister and her two girls as a frame of reference. Martha is anything but tidy even now. She calls it "creative clutter", or something.'

'The parents' room is down at the end, there, next to the bathroom.' She led Steel along the corridor. This time he did go in.

The duvet had been pushed back on both sides of the bed as the occupants had got out. Both the victims had been in nightclothes and dressing gowns. Vic Griffin had worn slippers;

Lisanne had not, but a pair of pink mules sat beside the bed waiting for their owner to return.

'Can't stand mules,' Willis commented. 'They just fall off my feet, especially when I'm hurrying to get somewhere.'

'So she may have rushed down the stairs to answer the door and left them there.'

'Maybe. A lot of people just don't like anything on their feet.'

'Then why would they be by the bed?'

Sophie Willis shrugged. Anyone else, she thought, and this would seem like irrelevant time wasting, but Steel noticed things. Random things, and nine times out of ten they turned out to be important.

'So, she jumps out of bed, rushes to the door. The baby's room is at the top of the stairs, she'd not want him woken up. So, are we assuming someone leaned on the doorbell or rapped on the back door? I think the neighbours might have heard the knocker and no one reported having done.'

'She opens the door and is convinced it's OK to let the visitor inside. Her husband follows her down.'

Steel frowned. 'And later, Sarah hears sounds from downstairs. Hears something that scares her enough to get Jack out of the cot and make a run for it.'

'Which suggests there was no second visitor in the house,' Willis speculated. 'I can just about see her getting out past one killer, but a second? No. That can't be right.'

'Baby monitor,' Steel said. 'Did they have a baby monitor?'

'Well, there's nothing here,' Willis said.

'No, but as you pointed out, Jack's room is next door. If he'd cried, they'd have heard him. Check downstairs and I'll look in his room.'

'I still don't see—' Willis shrugged and made her way back down the stairs. The crime scene manager pointed to a little white box with a flashing red light, sitting on the bookcase. Moments later, Steel joined her downstairs.

'So what's important about the baby monitor?'

The CSI laughed. 'It's like having a bug in your house,' he said. 'Especially the slightly older ones. They've got a transmission range of several hundred yards.'

'Really? So you're suggesting—'

'It strikes me as unlikely anyone would fire two bullets into an empty cot,' Steel said. 'But I may be wrong. It may be an irrelevance. What is relevant is that anyone downstairs would probably have heard Sarah, if she went into Jack's room.'

His mobile rang, and Steel listened.

'They've found Jack and Sarah,' he said.

FOUR

As Steel and Willis made their way across the field, they could see the search teams being pulled back towards the church. The kids had been found now. The searchers would be needed again later, but their function had changed; they needed tea and biscuits and fresh instructions.

An ambulance siren wailed from somewhere behind the hedge. Sarah and her little brother being taken away.

It took them several minutes to reach the barn and Willis found herself imagining having to do this at night, in the pouring rain and carrying a frightened, cold and heavy child. The mud dragged at her shoes and she slipped twice, almost losing her footing. Steel strode ahead, seemingly oblivious of both mud and difficulties in walking, his long legs eating the distance. He waited for her at the barn door, talking to a uniformed officer that Willis didn't know.

'I thought this place was searched early this morning?'

'It was, but it was pitch black and chucking it down with rain. There are no lights and no windows. The farmer and two of our lads came in and looked around best they could but they didn't see nothing. I think they figured the girl would shout out or the little lad might be crying.'

'Where were they?' Steel wanted to know.

They followed the officer into the gloom of the barn. The beam from his torch did little to alleviate the grey. From the dimness, shapes appeared. Machinery Willis could not guess the use of but which bristled with spikes and blades.

'We figure she must have known her way around here,' the

policeman said. 'The farmer says he has to chase the kids out
from time to time, but he's had no real problem with any of
them. He reckons most of the local kids find their way in here
and the other barn sooner or later and he only bothers because
they smoke. He's worried about the hay bales catching on fire.'
He shrugged. 'Kids will, I suppose. But she must have been here
before – otherwise in the dark she'd have got herself trapped in
something.'

Willis nodded even though she was bringing up the rear and
no one could see her. To her eyes this vast space looked like a
death trap but for Sarah, it seemed, it had spelt at least temporary
safety.

'Behind there, look,' the police officer said. 'She pulled the
tarp down over them both and then she must have passed out.
Me, I can't figure out how she managed to get here. She was
covered in blood.'

He stood aside and Steel moved over so that Willis had a view
of the space behind a particularly vicious looking piece of farm
equipment.

'She'd crawled into that space there.'

Willis crouched down and took a small Maglite from her
pocket. Straw bales had been stacked behind the machine and
against the barn wall. A small space stained heavily with blood
showed where the children had lain. A grey tarpaulin partly
covered the machine. It had been folded back and blood was
clearly visible on that too.

'The little boy was dead before they got here?'

'Almost certainly. From the look of it the shot went through
his sister and into him. Poor little blighter didn't stand a chance.
We found her curled up with baby Jack in her arms. The para-
medics were already on standby at the church, so we got them
in as fast as we could. One of them took pictures of the scene
while the others worked on the girl. They thought we might need
a visual record. I think the camera went back to the church for
the CSI to log.'

Steel nodded his shaggy head. 'Good. They say what her
chances are?'

'No. Wouldn't commit. They said she was cold. That in a way
that might have saved her because it slowed the bleeding down,

but that she'd not have lasted much longer. The cold or the blood loss would have got her.'

Willis straightened up, sensing that Steel was ready to leave. 'In the end, how was she found?'

'Farmer and one of the constables came back for another look. Brought better torches. The farmer saw the tarp had been disturbed and he crawled down behind the bales, found her there. Her and the baby. He's really cut up about it. I think, like the rest of us, he just wanted to find them alive.'

FIVE

Steel did not speak as they returned to the house. He paused outside the back door to scrape the mud from his boots and Sophie Willis did the same before removing shoes and replacing them once more with the crime scene bootees. A CSI appeared in the kitchen doorway and handed Sophie a couple of evidence bags. 'Shove your footwear in these,' she said, 'then you can leave them on the doormat. We're fighting a battle with the mud.'

'Anything useful turned up yet?'

'Possibly. We found an address book in a drawer. What's the news on the kids?'

'The girl's been taken to hospital. The little boy didn't make it,' Steel told her.

'Poor little sods. Will the girl pull through?'

'We don't know yet. Address book?'

'In the front.'

Steel and Willis returned to the living room. Willis glanced over to where the bodies had lain. Blood had soaked into the wooden floor. The blood pools were smaller than might be expected, given the severity of the wounds; testament to the fact that death had been swift. Willis remembered the blood on the floor of the barn and on the tarpaulin. Did Sarah Griffin know that her family had been wiped out? Did she know that her little brother had died in her arms as she carried him away?

Sophie Willis felt her heart go out to the girl. Both she and Steel had close families and she did not dare to imagine how she would feel if a similar tragedy struck at her own door. It was beyond her willing comprehension. Somehow, to imagine it seemed to invite it to happen – so Sophie did not. Could not. Would not.

Steel was looking at the address book, turning the pages with gloved hands. It had been kept in a drawer alongside other paperwork – bills, bank statements and the like.

'There's a list beside the phone,' the CSI told them. 'With numbers like the school and the doctor and so on. This has most of the same numbers and a few more, but with addresses added too.'

'But nothing looks old,' Steel commented. 'Almost all of the addresses are local. Doctor, school, nursery. If you look, most of the information is added using the same pen and in the same hand.'

'There was just one thing that stood out,' the CSI said. 'Almost at the back.'

Steel flicked through. Under Z there was no entry but a business card had been slipped between the pages. It was creased and coffee stained and had the look of something that had spent a long time in someone's pocket.

Willis leaned in to look more closely. 'DI Naomi Blake,' she said. 'Maybe she had some dealings with the family before they came here?'

'Maybe you should find out,' Steel said.

SIX

'Is that Inspector Friedman? Alec Friedman?'

'This is ex Inspector Friedman, yes. Who is this?'

'Sorry,' she said. 'They told me you'd both left the force, but . . . anyway. I'm DS Willis, Ferrymouth CID. I wonder if I could speak to your wife?'

'What seems to be the problem?' he asked.

'It's about an old case of hers. At least, we think it is.'

Alec hesitated, then said, 'OK, I'll hand you over. But you do know that—'

'That your wife had to resign on health grounds. Yes, your old colleagues filled me in.'

Alec could hear the smile in her voice as she added, 'They made me jump through a fair few hoops before I could get your number.'

Alec covered the receiver and explained to Naomi who the caller was and then handed over the phone. He sat back in the chair by the window while Naomi listened as Willis told her about the Griffins.

'I don't recognize the name,' Naomi said.

'She'd probably remarried since you gave her the card, but we don't know what her original name might have been. Her first name was Lisanne. It's unusual enough—'

'That I might have remembered her. Sorry, I don't recall anyone of that name. Is it possible she changed her first name as well? How far back do you think we're going?'

'I don't know. That's just it. The family moved here three years ago but we know absolutely nothing about them before that.'

Which in itself is strange, Naomi thought. Ferrymouth was, what, seventy miles away? Eighty, perhaps. 'You want me to come over?' she asked.

'Well, we did wonder if you would, but . . . look, usually before we inconvenienced you, I'd send some photos over, but . . .' she broke off, suddenly embarrassed.

'Send some over anyway,' Naomi said. 'Alec worked some of the same cases; it's possible he would remember her. I'll give you his mobile number.'

'What's all that about?' Alec asked.

'A double murder. Ferrymouth CID are having trouble contacting next of kin and they found an old business card of mine tucked into an address book. They hope I might be able to help out.'

'Bit of a long shot,' Alec said. 'We used to hand those things out like—'

Alec's phone beeped and Naomi listened as he opened the message.

'Well, I'll be damned,' he said.

'You recognize them, then?'

'The woman, yes. The man looks familiar, but I'm not sure. Six years, maybe seven years ago we finally managed to put her husband away. He'd been beating seven shades out of her and the kid for years. They moved up here from London, the Met asked us to keep an eye – he was a suspect in an armed robbery. She testified, finally, but not just for the domestic. You remember the Baldwins? Thea and Terry Baldwin.'

She heard him returning the call. 'DS Willis? Yes, right. The woman was Thea Baldwin. Married to Terry Baldwin. Went down about six years ago. History of domestic abuse, but what he was finally put away for was, among other things, the murder of an associate. If I remember right there was a falling out over the proceeds of a robbery.'

He paused. 'Yes, that would be it.'

Naomi heard him pause again. She listened, straining her ears but unable to catch the other side of the conversation. Napoleon, her big black guide dog, rubbed his nose against her hand, sensing her sudden change of mood. She stroked his ears. Yes, she remembered the Baldwins, Thea and her little girl. Naomi had been the one who had finally convinced Thea to shop her husband.

'So,' Naomi demanded when Alec had got off the phone. 'Are we off to Ferrymouth, then?'

'The Baldwin case was one of the last—' He broke off.

'One of the last before my accident,' she finished for him. 'It's OK, Alec. I can face my old life, you don't have to dance around it. You of all people should know that by now.'

'I'm sorry, love. You're right. I think the truth is, you handle it better than I do.'

'I came to the court to give evidence,' she recalled. 'About a week after I'd been discharged from hospital. Everyone was pushing for an adjournment, but—'

'No one thought it was fair that you should be dragged up to testify so soon after you'd come out of hospital.'

'I think it was good for me,' Naomi said. 'I think it reminded me I could still do something, even if my old life was over. I think I needed to know that.' She paused, then asked, 'So what are we doing once we get there, then?'

Alec laughed. 'I don't expect they'll want much from us; we

can take some time and have a look around the area. Its years since I was over that way. Best pack your thermals, though, the wind really howls in off that bit of the coast.'

'When are we going?'

'They want us to drive over later today. DS Willis is fixing up a B and B for the night. That OK with you?'

'So long as it's dog friendly. I've done it before. I'll get a bag packed,' Naomi told him. 'Then we can remind one another about the facts of this old case of ours.'

DS Willis found her boss mooching about in Sarah Griffin's bedroom, still searching for anything that would give them clues as to family. 'I called the hospital again,' Steel said. 'She's still not conscious but they've got her warmed up and she's showing signs of recovery.'

'The bullet wound?'

'Was a through and through. Caught her in the side and smashed through a lower rib. It hit the little boy on the way out and then passed through Sarah's arm as it exited, but didn't hit any of Sarah Griffin's vital organs. She's lost a lot of blood but it was the cold that almost killed her. Another hour at most, they reckon, and we'd have been burying her too.'

She nodded. 'I finally got through to Naomi Friedman – as she is now. They're coming this afternoon; I said I'd get a room booked for them somewhere. She left the force on health grounds just after they put Lisanne's husband inside.'

'Oh?'

'RTA, apparently, left her blind. So her husband is driving her over, but as he worked the case too . . . if they know the background we might start to understand why the Griffins were here and what happened after Lisanne left her husband. Find anything on family yet?'

Steel sat down on Sarah's bed and looked around. 'Nothing. There are a few photos from when she was younger, but nothing written on the back to tell us who was who. She kept a sort of diary but it seems to be mostly song lyrics and poems.'

'Hers?'

'Well, I think some of them are, but I'm not up on popular music, so I doubt I could tell.'

Willis smiled. Steel was strictly classical when it came to music. It was all Radio Three when she was in his car.

'She mentions friends.' The journal was on the bedside cabinet and Steel picked it up and flicked through the pages.

'"Went to the cinema with Joey and Evie. Saw Joey and Tel last night. Funfair with Joey and Tel. Stopped the night at Evie's." Joey seems to figure a lot.'

'So does Tel. One of them might be a boyfriend.'

'I'll get someone round to the school, talk to her teachers.'

'It's worth talking to the search teams,' Willis said. 'There were quite a few youngsters out there today. I'd guess about a dozen or so that should have been in school.'

'Good idea. I'm heading across there in a few minutes. What puzzles me is that there's nothing here from before they came to Ferrymouth, at least not that I can see. My sister's kids, you look at their rooms and there's birthday cards and school books and posters dating back to when they were embryos, and that doesn't include all the junk she manages to keep.'

'It's called sentiment,' Willis told him.

'Well, I must have had a bypass. Anyway, there's none of that here, not in the girl's room, not in the rest of the house.'

'Well, having spoken to Alec Friedman I may know why that is,' Willis said. 'Sarah and her mother had to start over with their lives about six years ago. She testified against her old man and changed her name thereafter.'

'And?'

'Lisanne Griffin was Thea Baldwin. I called up the case notes and had a quick skim. Lisanne was her middle name. Baldwin went down for eighteen years: sexual assault, aggravated burglary, armed robbery and a murder to top it off, not to mention domestic violence. Naomi Friedman was the one that persuaded her to testify, after which Thea Baldwin dropped off the planet. Until now.'

'And this Baldwin, he's still inside?'

'Apparently. Thugs like him have a long reach, though. He could have put out a hit on them.'

'So he could,' Steel agreed. 'But the one thing that still puzzles me is the angle of those shots. Unless the forensic reports come back different, I'm still betting on the shooter being seated. You don't invite a stranger into your house at three in the morning and then sit down for a chat until he produces a gun. Do you?'

'Not unless it's a stranger you think you can trust,' she said. 'And there are not many that fall into that category, especially given the time of night.'

'So who would seem legitimate, if they called round in the early hours of the morning?'

'Only one I can think of,' Willis said. 'Given this Thea or Lisanne's background, she might just be willing to open the door to a copper. Especially one that had something to say regarding her ex. I can see that just about being possible.'

Steel nodded. 'I've been thinking along the same lines,' he said. 'And what you've just told me about Baldwin reinforces that. She'd always be expecting that knock on the door, no matter how far she ran.'

Joey badly wanted to go to the hospital, to try and see Sarah. He knew Maggie was right when she kept telling him that no one was going to get in to see her, not unless they could prove they were family. But he couldn't shake off the need, the overwhelming desire just to get on a bus and go to the hospital and wait for as long as it took until they let him in.

Then the policeman arrived, the one called Steel who was in charge, and he asked for anyone that knew the family well to come and talk to him, and Joey and Tel found themselves dragged forward by Maggie and brought to his attention.

Tel wasn't sure he liked that, but for Joey it was almost akin to torture. The only dealings he'd had with the police was when his dad kicked off and they came round to sort him out. The one good thing about the police, Joey thought, was that they sometimes hauled his dad off for a night in the cells. He always made up for his absence once he'd come back, but Joey had come to cherish those few, safe hours, even if they were only the calm before a usually massive storm.

The policeman led them through into what Maggie called the vestry and they all sat down.

'That's Sarah's book,' Joey said accusingly, as the policeman produced the little red diary.

'It is, and it mentions both of you,' DI Steel told him.

Joey bristled. 'You shouldn't go through people's private things.'

'We're trying to find family. Next of kin. We've had to look through a lot of things.'

'I don't think they had any,' Maggie said. 'Joey, did Sarah ever mention family?'

He shook his head. 'She said her dad had gone to prison. That he beat on her mum. Like . . . well, anyway.'

DI Steel waited, but Joey didn't go on. He spoke to Maggie. 'So you're Tel's mother?'

She nodded. 'Joey and Tel are best friends. Always round at our place, aren't you, Joey? Sarah came over a lot too. She's a lovely girl. Do we know—?'

'The hospital says that the signs are good' he said.

Joey leaned forward. 'She'll be OK?'

'They believe so.'

He looked, Steel thought, as if he was about to cry.

'I'm sorry about Jack, though. She loved Jack.'

'We think she was trying to keep him safe.'

'She would do. She'd try.' Joey fidgeted awkwardly in his seat. 'I want to see her,' he said.

'She can't see anyone just now,' Steel said. 'But I'll see what I can do, OK?'

'Joey's not family,' Maggie said. 'Will they let him in? You shouldn't make promises – even half promises – you might not be able to keep.'

Steel raised an eyebrow at the reprimand. Then he nodded. 'As I say, I'll see what I can do. We're trying to find next of kin but it doesn't look as if the Griffins have had any contact with anyone, former friends or family, since they moved here. I think Sarah will need her friends around her when she wakes up.'

'But she will wake up?' Joey insisted.

Steel's gaze flashed briefly across to Maggie as though mindful of her warning.

'The doctors think so,' he said. 'I can't tell you any more than that right now.'

Joey nodded, but he didn't look convinced.

'What can we do to help?' Maggie asked.

'You can tell me all about the Griffins. Anything you can think of. Who their friends were, who they associated with. If they mentioned anyone from their past. Tell me what Sarah liked to do, who she saw after school, where she went. Just talk to me.'

Maggie, Joey and Tel exchanged looks and Maggie shrugged. 'Where to start?' she wondered.

'Sarah's best friend is Evie Watts,' Joey told him. 'They sit together in class. She didn't like talking about "before". That's what she called it, when they still lived with her dad. He was violent. Her mum told the police and she went to court and they put him away. Sarah didn't like to talk about it. She said they'd got away from him and that was all that mattered.'

'And her stepdad. How did she get along with him?'

'She loved him,' Joey said simply. 'He was kind, gentle, she said. Never yelled or got mad with them. And she loved her little brother. It's going to tear her up, you know, when she knows he's dead. When she finds out they're all dead.'

Silence crept into the room and remained, settling between the policeman and the teenagers and Maggie. It was Maggie who finally broke it.

'Who would do a thing like that? It seems . . . impossible. Especially in a place like this.'

'It's all about "before", isn't it?' Joey said. 'About what they were running away from. All about the stuff she didn't like to talk about. It came and caught up with them, didn't it?'

Steel nodded slowly. 'It looks that way,' he said.

Joey sniffed hard, trying not to cry. He looked down at the scuffed red top of the vestry table. He wanted so much to help Sarah, to help this Steel to catch whoever did this to her and her family. His black hair needed cutting and it flopped down into his eyes. Impatiently he pushed it back and raised his head to look at Steel.

'She had an auntie,' he said. 'She was the only person from before that Sarah talked about. I don't think she was a proper auntie, not like a relative.'

'And did she have any contact with this auntie? Did she tell you where she was? Her name?'

Joey thought about it. One day in the summer they'd crept into the barn with a bottle of cheap cider Joey had pinched from his dad. They'd sat with the barn doors open, sun streaming on to the hay-strewn floor, and shared it – or some of it anyway. Neither of them had dared turn up at home drunk or stinking of booze, though their reasons had been very different. Joey didn't want his dad to have anything more to punish him for and Sarah just didn't want to upset her mum and stepdad.

But they'd drunk enough to loosen tongues. Joey had told her about his life. About his hatred for his father. About his wish that he could just leave and keep on going until his dad was just a memory disappearing over the horizon, and Sarah had finally talked a little about 'before'.

'Trinny,' he said. 'Aunt Trinny. She said she was a neighbour who lived a few doors down. Sarah said she was always kind, that she looked after Sarah and her mum when . . . you know, when her dad kicked off. She said she was the one person she wished she could still keep in touch with.'

Steel was watching him intently and Joey found himself returning that look. For a moment it was as if there were only the two of them in the room.

'And did she make contact?' Steel asked.

Joey shook his head. 'No, but I know she told her mum how she felt because she told me she had. I told Sarah she should talk to her mum about how she felt.'

'And what happened?' Steel asked gently.

Joey broke contact, looking away from him. There was a lump in his throat that seemed to be big enough to choke him. The words could hardly come out. 'Sarah said her mum reckoned they could risk sending her a birthday card,' he said. 'It was her birthday in October, I think. Sarah was really happy about it. She said that friends should know you'd not forgotten them.'

Steel sat back in his chair.

'Do you think that might have given them away?' Maggie asked. She sounded awed. 'Do you think Sarah's father caught up with them or something? My God, to even think of doing that to your own child.'

'I don't know,' Steel admitted. 'We need to be careful about getting ahead of ourselves. But it's a start. Thank you, Joey, you've been a big help.'

'What else can we do?' Tel asked.

Steel smiled at him. He was clearly feeling left out. 'The three of you can start by making me a list of names,' he said. 'Anyone Sarah might have been close to. And places she liked to visit, things she liked to do or that she told you her family liked to do. Anything you can think of, OK?'

Three heads nodded. Maggie and the boys rose to leave. At the door, Joey turned back to look at him. 'I've seen you before,' he said. 'You go to the bike project.'

Steel raised an eyebrow and then nodded.

'You promised,' Joey added. 'About Sarah. About trying to get me in to see her.'

'I'll do everything I can,' Steel said.

SEVEN

T he tide was out when Alec approached Ferrymouth. The road wove narrowly between open fields and marsh which, some distance away, gave way to mud flats and narrow beach and then estuary.

'It's going to rain again,' he told Naomi. 'The sky is damn near black.'

'What's the view like?'

'Flat and muddy. Beached boats waiting for the tide to come in. It's all marshland between here and the sea, cut across with dykes and run-offs. I think it's some kind of bird sanctuary, if I remember right. I've not been here for a long time.'

Back the way they had come the land rose, cliffs faced out to sea, rich farmland beyond, but for this brief stretch the topography slid downward, flattened out, marinated itself in mud and peat and salt. Someone had once told Alec that this had been forested land a few thousand years before and you could still find semi-fossilized trees in amongst the peat. It had never been more than sparsely inhabited; you couldn't farm the land and the fishing was scant and hard. The small town of Ferrymouth had grown up because of the need of folk to cross the estuary. The ferry was long gone, replaced a century or more before by a narrow road bridge some miles further down the river and more recently by a suspension bridge that Alec could see even though he knew it to be ten miles or so away, the land was so flat here.

They had arranged to go to the incident room set up in the town and Alec had been given the post code for a place called St Barts church that was apparently being used. He soon realized that they needn't have worried about being lost; Ferrymouth was just one main street with a plethora of smaller ones leading off. A market square in the centre with what looked like a town hall occupying one complete side. St Barts was on the way out of town. Red brick, Victorian, the building looked functional, fitting into a street of Victorian terraced houses and a couple of little shops.

Alec pulled up in front of the church, not sure where he should park. Naomi had called ahead a few minutes before when they'd first entered the town and told Sergeant Willis where they were. Alec guessed that the woman waiting for them at the church door was probably her.

'Well?' Naomi asked.

Alec laughed. His wife had him well schooled. *We reach a place and you describe it to me.*

'Terraced street,' he said. 'Though wider than most. It's a continuation of the main road. The rest of the road is cordoned off and there are access only signs and a couple of uniforms. Red brick church, mid-nineteenth century, I'd say, and what looks like it might have been a school behind. There are separate entrances for boys and girls. Our guide – at least I'm guessing that's what she is – is about thirtyish, pretty, black and very slim.'

'Best pull the stomach in, then,' Naomi teased.

As they got out of the car the young woman came to meet them. 'You must be Alec and Naomi? I'm DS Sophie Willis. Thank you very much for coming. The boss has just gone to the hospital. Sarah Griffin woke up a while ago.'

'She'll be all right?' Alec asked. 'I mean, as much as she can be.'

'As all right as she can be. Yes. Come along inside.'

It had begun to rain again.

She led them through into what Alec realized must have been the school house. The church itself had been taken over by officers in uniform. The investigation had set up shop anywhere they could fit a table and a couple of chairs, and local people sat in the pews waiting to make statements while others milled around grasping mugs and chatting in slightly hushed tones. Someone laughed and the sound ricocheted around the nave. Conversation was suspended as everyone turned to look.

'We're using the old school as the major incident area,' Willis said. 'The hall is our assembly point.' She pointed through a door as they passed and Alec gained a swift impression of maps and more people. 'We're using that space to organize search teams and collate anything they find.'

'Will there be much to find?' Naomi asked.

'Probably not, but people want to be involved. You know what it's like. And you never know, we're woefully short of personnel, and extra bodies are very welcome just now.'

Naomi nodded.

'We've been promised more officers this afternoon, but this morning we had to make do with anyone we could rustle up from the local constabulary and the TA. We're a rural force, low crime rate, scanty population.' Willis shrugged. 'Actually, all the reasons I like being out here, but when you do need the extra manpower, it can take a bit of time to arrive.'

'I can imagine,' Naomi said. 'So how can we help you?'

'That's the big question, isn't it? Look, best thing is to take you over to the Dog and Gun; they've opened up a room for you, and Douggie, the landlord, he does good food. We can get a decent cuppa and something to eat and I'll bring you up to speed. My DI would like to keep your presence under the radar. We're already starting to fall over journalists every time we move. I'm sure you'd like to avoid that.'

'Sounds good,' Alec said. 'Lead the way.'

EIGHT

'You can have a few minutes, no more. She's deeply distressed and the doctor's given her a sedative so I doubt she'll stay awake for long.'

Steel nodded. 'I've just got a few questions,' he said. 'Does she know about her family?'

'That her mother and stepfather are dead, yes. And about her baby brother, though I'm not sure she's taken it all in. Have the relatives been informed? When can we expect someone to come and be with her?'

Steel shook his head. 'So far we've been able to find no one,' he said. 'The family moved to Ferrymouth only about three years ago, but they seem to have cut themselves off from everyone when they did.'

'And why on earth would they do that?'

'I don't know, yet,' Steel told her. 'She has good friends, though. I said I'd ask if they could visit.'

'Not yet.' The sister sighed. 'Poor little girl. Look, you see if you can track down some relatives and I'll see about letting her see her friends, if she's ready, maybe tomorrow. She could do with someone she knows.'

Steel nodded and decided not to push things further. He was determined to get Joey in to see Sarah and figured that Maggie would be willing to come along and ease the way. He liked her instinctively and liked Tel and Joey too, though he sensed that Joey had problems of his own.

'I'll come in with you,' the sister told him. 'At least she knows me.'

Steel nodded and they pushed through the double doors. A female officer sat beside the bed, Sarah's hand clasped tight in her own. The girl looked so small, Steel thought, propped up on the pillows with her hair spread out like a curly halo. She had been crying; her eyes were red and sore and she looked exhausted. The nurse hovered at the end of the bed and Steel sat down on the side opposite to the female officer.

'Sarah, my name is Inspector Steel. Ryan Steel.' He smiled at her and tried to look non-threatening, acutely aware of his height and size and the fact that, as Sophie Willis often said, he looked more Yeti than human.

Sarah turned her head in his direction. He was struck by the grief and pain in the girl's eyes.

'Sarah, I'm so terribly sorry about your family.'

Tears welled again. A box of tissues stood on the bedside table and he grasped a bundle of them and handed them to her. Sarah hesitated and then took them.

'What happened last night? Can you tell me anything?'

'I heard them shouting. Vic and Mum, they didn't shout. And Jack was crying. I went to him and picked him up. Then I heard . . . I heard . . .'

'You heard what, Sarah?'

'Vic must have known I was in Jack's room. The baby monitor. He'd have heard me talking to Jack. He knew I was up and he shouted to me to run and then I heard the shooting.'

'You knew it was shots?'

She nodded. 'I knew.'

'And then what?'

'I hid. With Jack. I heard *him* coming up the stairs and I saw him go into Jack's room and then I took Jack and sneaked down the stairs and out the back. But he must have heard me because he ran down after and as we got through the gate he shot at us. He killed Jack.'

The flow of tears had become a flood and the nursing sister looked meaningfully in Steel's direction and jerked her head towards the door. He held up a hand, gesturing for a moment more.

'Sarah, I know this must be terribly hard, but just tell me one more thing. Did you hear the gunman speak? Was there anything distinctive about his voice?'

He saw the police officer shift in her chair and guessed that Sarah might already have told her something that there'd been no time for her to relay. He raised an eyebrow, but Sarah was ahead of them.

'I *know* who it was,' she said, and her voice was fierce. 'It was *him*.'

'Him?'

'My fucking dad,' Sarah spat the words. 'He'd come back, just like he said he would. He came back and he killed them all.'

Steel waited outside Sarah's room until the young officer could extricate herself. Through the glass panels in the doors he could see the nurse trying to comfort the distraught child and the officer gradually easing her hand free of Sarah's death grip.

'I'll buy you a coffee,' he said as she joined him. 'There's a café downstairs.'

'I don't know if I should.' She glanced anxiously over her shoulder. 'I said I'd stay with her. There's a vending machine just down the hall.'

'That will have to do, then. What's your name, by the way?'

She laughed. 'Right. I'm Stacy. DC Stacy Woods. I'm from Cauldwell, came over this morning when you put out the call for backup.'

Steel nodded. 'She'd already told you about her father?'

'Just before you arrived. She's sure it was him.'

'Well, so far as I know, he's in prison, but . . . anything else?'

'Not a lot. She woke up, heard arguing downstairs, and Jack was crying. She got out of bed and went to Jack and then realized there was someone else arguing with her parents downstairs.'

'And she's convinced that someone was her father. She's sure she recognized the voice?'

'Seems to be, but I wonder if it's more what the man said. She says it's been something like six years since she spoke to her real father, so she might have been confused. I don't know.'

'And what did he say?'

'Something about what kind of woman keeps a father from seeing his child,' Stacy told him. 'Apparently Vic, the stepdad, then said something like "a mother who wants to protect her kid" and then shortly after that Victor Griffin yells at Sarah to run and then there are the shots.'

'She seemed very quick to realize what had happened,' Steel observed.

'She said she'd heard gunshots before. I just figured her stepdad must have sounded scared enough that she didn't question anything, she just took Jack and tried to get the hell out.'

Steel fed the vending machine with coins and handed hot chocolate to Stacy, deciding to follow her example. Vending machine coffee never tasted of anything much in his opinion; chocolate stood at least a fighting chance of having a flavour. There were chairs nearby and they sat down, Stacy checking her watch to see how long she'd been away.

'Has she mentioned anything else?'

'Only that the rain was cold and the mud made it hard to run. She took Jack into the barn and she said it was really dark, but that she could remember what had been there from before. She'd apparently been inside a few times. She remembered the farm machinery and thought it would be a good hiding place. She said she felt like she was going to pass out and it was a struggle to get to the barn. The doctors had to give her a transfusion; she'd lost a heck of a lot of blood. She crawled into the space and pulled the tarpaulin down over herself and Jack. She's pretty sure she heard a sound outside, like maybe the gunman had followed them. If so, then she was doubly lucky. If he'd gone inside—'

'Why didn't he?' Steel wondered. 'That's assuming she did hear something. And if not, why didn't he follow them? Though presumably he ran because the shots had attracted the neighbours and the lights were coming on. But he didn't go out the front; the door was still locked.' Steel shook his head. He needed to go back and look at the house again.

'It was chucking it down with rain last night,' Stacy said. 'I came off shift just after midnight and I had my windscreen wipers on full and I still couldn't see a damn thing.'

'Good point,' Steel said, then 'Midnight? So you shouldn't have been at work at all this morning. Have you had any sleep?'

She shrugged. 'The call came in at six, my boss phoned me just after. I'm fine.'

Steel nodded again and Stacy got up, ready to return to Sarah. 'I'd best get back.'

'And I'd best get to the school before they finish for the day.' He handed her his card. 'If she says anything more or if she wants to talk to me, just call. And I'll see to it someone comes to relieve you later this afternoon.'

She shook her head. 'I can sleep in the chair for now. No rush. Sarah seems to like me and I'd sooner be with her until you find some family to come and be with her.'

'The way things are going, that might take some time,' Steel said.

NINE

'But why a croft? I mean, what do you know about farming? Or sheep?'

'I don't have to keep sheep. And I don't intend to farm. I might dig a bit. Grow something. Keep chickens.'

'Now I know you've lost it.' Nathan grinned at his friend. 'You need something to keep you busy, and I don't mean feeding chooks or planting carrots.'

'I'm not sure I want anything else. I like it up here.'

Nathan looked around with a considering eye. True, it was wildly beautiful. The sky had cleared and was crisply blue, though the sea still churned and roiled below the cliff. And it was bitterly cold. 'No trees,' he said.

'True. I might miss the trees. I could fish?'

Nathan wasn't sure how that observation connected to trees. 'I'm not sure your boat would like it up here,' he said. 'She's always struck me as a southern sort of girl.'

'Maybe.'

'It's also bloody cold.' Nathan shivered and adjusted his scarf and hat. He hated being cold and since he'd been shot last autumn his body didn't take kindly to the tension that went with such buttock-clenching, belly-tightening chill.

Gregory looked at his younger friend with concern. 'We'll get you back into the warm,' he said. 'Get some grub inside us. Then I think I'll take a walk.'

Nathan groaned. 'Well, I hope you don't mind if I settle in by the fire with a good book. Even a bad book. I've been blown off my feet enough for one day.'

Gregory nodded.

'Food sounds good, though.'

They walked back to the hotel in companionable silence. Gregory had been very quiet of late, even by Gregory standards, and Nathan was concerned for him. He recognized the sense of dislocation, of not knowing what life could or should bring next, but this trip up to the Scottish Isles in the middle of winter seemed symptomatic of an even more powerful sense of confusion than Nathan had reckoned on.

Both men had led dangerous lives, though until recently, Nathan Crow, the adopted son of the hugely powerful diplomat and spymaster Gustav Clay, had managed to stay approximately on the right side of the law. His association with the enigmatic hit man Gregory Hess – along with other circumstances – had changed that forever. When Nathan had been shot a few months before, while helping Naomi and Alec rescue a kidnapped mother and child, Gregory had rescued him. And, while Nathan was recovering, Gregory had taken care of him. Kept him safe, brought him back from a very close brush with death.[1] As Nathan got back on his feet – literally and figuratively – Gregory had ensured he rested, exercised, ate, kept his mind busy, knowing just how frustrating the long convalescence would be. Nathan was grateful. Gregory had been both father and brother these last months but the truth was, Nathan was better now. Not healed, not back to what he had been before, but well enough now for Gregory to require another outlet, another interest. Something else that could consume his time and energy. Gregory, Nathan had discovered, needed to be needed. He'd spent his life *doing*. He couldn't just stop now, no matter what he said. And buying a croft right up in the North of Northness was not the answer.

The previous year, their friend, Alec Friedman had gone through a similar dilemma. Had found himself sunk into a deep depression when he'd retired from the police force and suddenly felt himself cut adrift and utterly purposeless. Nathan and Gregory might be on a different side of the law to their friend Alec, but Nathan recognized that the problems were identical. If you'd spent most of your adult life with a sense of direction, a purpose, then it was nigh on impossible to settle for a life that had no direction and no perceptible purpose either.

'Maybe, if you want to buy land, you could look at something in East Anglia, or the West Country. Your boat would like it better there. Find a pretty harbour or some exclusive little marina?

[1] See *Gregory's Game*

Seriously, Gregory, I can't see you living in a house anywhere, if I'm honest.'

'I had a house, once.'

'True.'

'And a cat.'

'That didn't like you and moved next door.'

'I think it liked me,' Gregory objected. 'But I was rarely there. My neighbour fed it when I went away. Being a cat, it just went to where it knew the food was.'

'Why did you get a cat anyway?'

'I was trying to fit in,' Gregory said. 'To be normal. So I bought furniture and I bought cushions for the sofa and I bought a cat.'

Nathan tried not to laugh, then gave in and laughed anyway, stopping only because it hurt his still tender abdomen. 'Sorry,' he said. 'Did it have a name?'

Gregory shrugged. 'My neighbour thought so. The cat and I were never convinced.'

They had reached the hotel and Nathan stepped gratefully over the threshold and into the warm bright welcome of the bar. He knew that they had attracted a great deal of curiosity – two men, of different ages and not obviously related – and with Gregory determined to be at his most taciturn, it had been left to Nathan to deflect the inquisitiveness of the locals. The little hotel was not fully open this early in the year, but the owner's wife had provided some fine meals and, as Nathan had observed earlier, there was always a fire lit in the bar and they were welcome to sit even when the pub wasn't open. In the evening many of the locals crowded into the warmth, and twice now there had been music. Nathan had enjoyed it. Gregory, while he hadn't passed comment, had appeared to enjoy it too.

At any rate, he hadn't walked out.

He'd seemed content to sit in the corner, nursing his beer and watching – though Nathan was not convinced that what he watched was in the same room or even the same time as the musicians playing by the bar. He wondered how Alec and Naomi were doing, and Patrick and his father, Harry. When he'd been shot, they'd helped to shelter and protect him, hiding him from the storm breaking over his life, and he'd come to know Alec and Harry a little. Harry was Naomi's oldest friend; she had known him since childhood, when he'd been the big brother to her best friend. Harry was divorced and had raised Patrick alone; he'd done a good job, Nathan thought. Patrick was a gentle soul, but he'd proved his courage more than once – helping to protect Gregory, and also saving the life of a little girl. Gregory was very fond of the boy, Nathan realized. Patrick intrigued him.

'He's like me,' Gregory had once said. Nathan had laughed at that too.

'No he's not. You'd be hard pressed to find two people more different.'

Gregory had let it pass; dropped the conversation, and for that Nathan had been sorry. Gregory rarely committed himself in words but when he did it was because what he had to say mattered, and Nathan was sorry now that he hadn't asked more about why Gregory had come to that strange conclusion. Patrick, eighteen years old, gentle, artistic, a little lost when it came to social interactions, seemed so different from Gregory, twice his age and with an entire lifetime of violence left in his wake. But Nathan had wondered about it afterwards and thought he now understood. There was, about both of them, a sense of otherness, of dislocation. Of watchfulness.

'Had a good walk?' Mrs Gornal, the landlady, asked them. 'It's a bit brisk out.'

'It's freezing,' Nathan said.

'The winds come straight off the Arctic Circle,' she said. 'Nothing in the way to stop them. Lunch is about ready. You want to eat it in the bar? The fire's just been banked up, but she'll be blazing again in a minute or so.'

'That sounds wonderful,' Nathan said fervently. He went through and dropped into what had become his favourite chair beside the fire, aware only after he'd shed his coat and scarf that Gregory had not followed him. Leaning forward in his seat he saw that the older man was still standing in the entrance hall, coat still on, peering at his mobile phone. Something in his look and stance alerted Nathan. Trouble, he thought, and the newly healed wounds in his side and back stabbed at him in anticipation. The truth was, Nathan had endured his fill of trouble; he wasn't ready for more.

Gregory mooched over, a slight frown creasing between his eyes. Nathan looked at him expectantly.

'From Patrick,' Gregory said.

'Oh?'

'Sent me a link to a news website. Naomi and Alec are off chasing a murder, or so Patrick says. According to the news, it's a double shooting. Patrick says it's linked to an old case they worked on.'

'That's bad,' Nathan said cautiously. 'And he sent you the link because?'

Gregory shrugged. Nathan watched as he fiddled with his smartphone, called up the website and read. Nathan leaned across so he could see too. Patrick and Gregory communicated most days, he knew. Random things mostly; on Gregory's part, since they had been up here, it had often been photographs of scenery he thought the boy might like to use as references for his artwork. Patrick's communications had been brief observations on his day, maybe things he had learnt from Bob Taylor, the artist he worked for, or expressions of disgust at what his latest uni assignment entailed. Nathan knew that Patrick was only really sticking with his course because that had been the deal he had made with his mentor, Bob, and Patrick's father, Harry. Harry badly wanted his son to have some proper qualifications, though privately Nathan had to agree with Patrick and Gregory that Bob Taylor could probably teach him more that was actually relevant to his own process than his professors ever could.

'Seems there's a bit of a mystery about who the dead couple were,' Gregory observed.

'So how do Alec and Naomi know they were linked to their investigation?'

'Don't know. Patrick didn't say. Presumably the local force made the connection and contacted them.'

Nathan nodded. He could see Gregory was itching for more intel and wondered why.

Gregory handed the phone to him so he could read the article for himself and follow the links to other reports. None of it told him much more. This was still breaking news and most reports rehashed what was probably an early press bulletin. 'Poor sods,' Nathan said. 'I hope the kid makes it through.'

Gregory considered and then nodded. 'On balance I agree,' he said. 'She's still young enough to recover, I suppose.'

Nathan had many such experiences on his CV and had learnt

to live with the impact. But then, he'd been practising such skills since he'd been fourteen years old. The same age as they said the girl who had been shot was. There was speculation about another child. A baby. Reading between the lines, Nathan concluded that one was already dead.

It was different for him. Wasn't it?

'That was a long text.' Nathan smiled.

'Short text, telling me to check my email. Long email.'

Lunch arrived, steaming plates unloaded from large trays.

Nathan realized how hungry he was. 'I'm going to miss the food,' he said, 'when we leave here. We could catch the morning ferry.'

Gregory, fork raised, frowned. 'I'm that easy to read?'

'Of course you are. Look, we leave tomorrow. Drop me off in Edinburgh; I'll get in touch with Jackie and set up a bit of a control post for you. Manage the intel side. We've still got friends and resources we can tap into so I can provide backup. Go, see if you can help out with whatever they're doing. Discreetly, mind.'

'I'm always discreet.'

'Don't make me laugh. It'll be like old times, but hopefully with less of the shooting.'

Gregory nodded and dug into his pie. Nathan watched him for a moment. Good, he thought. It didn't really matter if this all came to nothing and it turned out that Naomi and Alec had only gone off to answer a few questions about a previous case. Gregory had something to think about again and, Nathan thought, they could finally get away from that bloody wind.

TEN

Douggie had installed Alec and Naomi in a tiny room that he referred to as 'the snug', tucked at the side of the bar. He brought them tea and coffee and sandwiches and then left them in peace with instructions to ring the bell if they needed anything else.

'He's a good sort,' Willis said. 'Ex boxer, so's his head barman. You don't get much trouble in the Dog.'

'You live round here?' Alec asked.

'Two villages down. I bought a place with my partner last year. Property's cheap round here, comparatively speaking. It's isolated and there's no way you can commute to anywhere. And it's bloody cold in the winter.'

'What does your partner do?'

'She's a GP and yes, we did raise a few eyebrows. We became the only gays in the village. I also became the only black person in the village. But we've settled and become as much a part of the community as you can be when you've not lived here for at least three generations.'

Alec laughed. 'Do you think the Griffins had the same problem? Not being local?'

'I wouldn't have thought so. Ferrymouth gets its share of tourists and there's even a few holiday cottages up by the creek and a little caravan site. Most of the local pubs have a room or two they let out in the holiday season and so it's opened up a bit. The kids get bused across the Kingsmere when they turn eleven. Ferrymouth is almost what passes for cosmopolitan in these parts.'

Naomi had noted the fondness in the woman's voice. 'You really like it round here, don't you?'

'Apart from the cold, yes I do. I like the sense of community, I like the flat land and all the birds and I like the quiet. The job, too. It's too easy to get lost in the job in a big city. Out here you actually get to know people, you've at least got the illusion that you make a difference.'

'Illusion?'

'Ignore that. I'm feeling particularly jaundiced today. A triple murder is not the norm for Ferrymouth; for anywhere round here. It feels like . . . I don't know, like an invasion. Like the outside world suddenly came visiting.'

Naomi sipped her coffee and nibbled at a sandwich. 'So, what can we tell you?' Alec asked.

'Well, you can start with family. There's no reference to anyone at the house and our colleagues in London can't tell us anything about family we might actually want to bring here. Terry Baldwin's lot seem to be out and out trouble and no one has any record for the mother. Lisanne Griffin – Thea Baldwin as she was, of course – married Terry when she was twenty, and no one knows about parents or siblings. Terry Baldwin's lot, of course, are mostly either banged up or trouble. And we don't have a clue about Victor Griffin so far.'

Naomi nodded. 'We got involved with the Baldwins when Terry moved north here about a year before his arrest. He was suspected of having taken part in an armed robbery in Luton. Two people died and another was badly injured. Terry was supposed to have been the brains behind the operation and several other similar robberies across the Home Counties.'

'I remember it vaguely,' Sophie Willis said. 'So he went north to get out of the way?'

'His father thought it would be a good thing to get Terry out for a while. Not just because of the bank jobs. Terry Baldwin had a short fuse, and he'd got into a fight with the son of another local hard man, Ray Tobias. Terry had beaten seven shades out of him in some really stupid argument over a round of drinks. He spent three weeks in a coma, nearly didn't make it and, from what I've heard, never made a full recovery. Of course, no one admitted to seeing a damn thing, even though the pub was full that night. The two had supposedly been close friends prior to that. Ray Tobias was also suspected of being involved in the bank job.'

'So Terry was sent away—'

'Because Tobias senior threatened a more permanent departure if he wasn't. Terry was furious that his old man hadn't stood his ground but if he had there'd have been a full-scale turf war. Traditionally the Tobiases and the Baldwins rubbed along together most of the time, alibied one another on occasion. Don't get me wrong, they were never major players, either of them, but the families had danced attendance on the major gangs in London for so long they were accepted as part of the bigger scene. Both families could be counted on to provide extra bodies for the bigger players when necessary and they acted as managers, shall we say, for drugs, prostitutes and some of the street crime.'

'And an extra level of security for the big players.' Willis nodded. 'So how did Terry Baldwin and Thea hook up?'

'She said they met in the West Country somewhere. Terry was on holiday, she was living down there, they met at a hotel she was working at and the holiday romance turned into something more permanent. He brought her back to London, she got pregnant, they got married. Terry's dad was oddly proper in some ways. Sarah was born and Thea found herself well and truly trapped.'

'Terry Baldwin was mixed race?'

'Um, yes. Baldwin senior had a wife but he also had other women on the side and Terry's mum was one of them. The women came and went, but the wife was a fixture and, oddly, so were the kids. He made certain that they were raised as Baldwins. Most followed him into the family business.'

'And was he a violent man too?'

'I don't know; there were never official complaints. Terry's father, old man Baldwin, he died just after Terry moved up north. Terry was always convinced someone helped him on his way but the official line is that he suffered a heart attack. Terry's elder brother took the reins and Terry was told he could go back for the funeral, that there was an amnesty for that, but that he'd better get himself lost again afterwards.'

'He can't have liked that.'

'Oh, he didn't. Took it out, as always, on his wife and kid, and that's when we were first involved. Local police called out to a domestic. It was only when he was put into the system that he was flagged up as being a person of interest. We contacted the Met.'

Sophie smiled, grimly. 'The joy of integrated computer systems, eh?'

'When they work,' Naomi agreed. 'So we contacted our colleagues in the Met and paid a bit more attention than a simple domestic would usually warrant.'

'Isn't that the truth? Unfortunately. You know I read a report once that reckoned up to seventy per cent of call outs were essentially domestic incidents.'

'Wouldn't be surprised. Anyway, the Met also told us that this wasn't the first time he'd taken his frustrations out on his family. There was history. They'd also not known where he'd disappeared to, so we began to cooperate. At that time I was back and forth to London on secondment anyway. I'd been thinking about what next – you know, looking at the future. I was offered an opportunity to shadow a DI in the organized crime unit and that led on to other things and, well, I used the contacts I'd made down there.'

'Ambitious,' Willis commented.

'You'd better believe it,' Alec said. 'Naomi was headed for the top. She'd got far more fire in her belly than I ever had. Me, I was comfortable at Pinsent. Big fish in a fairly small pond, but that suited me just fine.'

'And yet you left?'

'And yet I left. Let's just say that while I was busy trying to avoid the world, the world was busy trying not to avoid me.'

Sophie cast him a curious glance but didn't ask for more. 'So, you started to cooperate,' she said. 'And—'

'And I decided that Thea Baldwin was my best lever. It wasn't that I didn't care about her – though actually, I'm not certain that I really did care about her at first. But as I got to know her and Sarah I did start to care. I got drawn in. I wanted her to flip on her husband. I was sure she knew enough about his activities to turn informant – and I was right, and eventually she did. But I did feel sorry for her in the end and I did try to help. I put her in touch with someone who gave her an escape route and in return she gave me the information we needed to put her husband away.'

'So she was pivotal.'

Naomi nodded. 'I think the Met would have put a case together eventually. They'd have applied other pressure, elsewhere. Once Terry's father had died and his son Roddy took over there was some considerable amount of scrabbling about in the lower ranks for whatever crumbs might have been dropped. There's a good chance someone would have squealed on Terry eventually, but this way was quicker, cleaner and seemed like it solved the problem of Thea too. She got away. Or so I thought.'

'Seems she thought so too.'

Alec poured them all more drinks. 'Wasn't there an aunt?' he asked. 'Married out, cut herself off from the family and went to live in . . . Kent? Ipswich? Somewhere like that.'

'Like Kent and Ipswich are next door to one another,' Naomi laughed. 'Ipswich, I think. Her name was . . . Madeleine. Madeleine Jeffries, or something like that. She married a teacher. All I really know about her is that when she married she didn't invite any of her family. Terry sent a card apparently threatening what he'd do to her and her husband should they ever come anywhere near the rest of the family. It was in the file.'

'And was that it?' Sophie asked. 'He doesn't sound like the type to stop at a casual threat.'

Naomi shook her head. 'Truthfully, I have no idea. It was a side issue. We got Thea and Sarah away, charged Terry and brought him to trial, and the trial had just begun when I had my accident. That was it.'

'So, we should maybe try and track down this Madeleine Jeffries. Just on the off chance she might still be interested in her niece. Also on the off chance that someone is settling scores and she's also on the list.'

Naomi nodded. 'I thought afterwards that the one really good thing that came out of the case was that a woman and child were safe. That they'd been given a second chance. Now I find out that was wrong.'

Sophie looked at Alec and then at Naomi, not sure what she should say. 'This must be hard for you,' she said.

'Not hard. Sad. And strange. I've given them no thought in years. I did the job, and when I came out of hospital I gave evidence. I made sure that word was sent to Thea that she was safe. Free to make her new life for herself and her daughter.'

'You kept in touch with her?'

'No, I managed to persuade the contact I had to pass the message along. I had no idea where they'd gone, what name they were using, anything. That was the way it was done and that was what happened. I just . . . I don't know. She'd put so much trust in me in the end, I didn't want to let her down. I wanted her to *know* that I hadn't let her down, you know?'

Sophie Willis nodded and then remembered Naomi couldn't see. 'Well, thanks,' she said. 'I'm glad you're here and we're grateful you could come. The boss will want to have a chat later.'

'That's fine,' Alec said. He took Naomi's hand and squeezed gently, sensing her renewed feeling of loss.

ELEVEN

'What I can't understand is how you could possibly fail.'

'I didn't fail. The woman and the man, they're gone. I did the job.'

'And left the kids behind.'

'I told you, the girl did a runner, took the baby with her. I couldn't hang around.'

'And just how did she manage to do a runner, as you put it?'

'He shouted, didn't he? She must have heard us downstairs and got nosy. Then he shouts up to her and she takes off, with the little kid.'

'And you let them get past you.'

'I didn't let them—'

'But they got away. The contract was clear. You take out the adults and you get rid of the kids. If you had qualms about that, maybe you should have said something. There's plenty lining up behind you. Plenty who aren't so fussy. Plenty who wouldn't mind finding you on their CV.'

'I told you. She ran, the lights came on and it was chucking it down with rain. I couldn't see bugger all. Next thing I know there's sirens everywhere.'

This might have been a slight exaggeration. He'd been long gone before the two local constables arrived, realized this was too big for them to handle alone and finally summoned the cavalry.

'So you said.' The voice on the other end of the phone didn't sound convinced. In fact, sounded dangerously unconvinced.

'So what now then, you want me to find the girl? I know I winged her.'

'You winged her. So that makes it all right then. You'd best come in, we'll sort this out.'

The call ended and he listened to the silence for a moment or two before slipping the phone back into his pocket.

'Come in?' he said. 'Fuck that for a game of monkeys.' Ricky could go and talk to the boss if he wanted, but Tommy was damn sure he wasn't going to risk it.

He called Ricky and relayed the gist of the conversation. 'So, up to you, my man. But I'm out of here.'

'Seriously? You want to make him madder than he is now?'

'Seriously. You decide for yourself, but I'm gone.'

Ricky was quiet, considering. 'Never understood why they wanted the kids dead,' he said. 'What do they know?'

'The little one? Fuck all now. The girl, I don't know, Terry had a bee in his bonnet about her overhearing something or other. But even if she did, she wouldn't know what it was, would she? Anyway, like I say, up to you.'

Tommy rang off and took the SIM card out of his phone, then crushed it beneath the heel of his boot. He had a suspicion that Ricky would make a beeline for the boss, try to get back into his good books, remind him that all *he* did that night was drive the car.

'Yeah, right.' That would really work. Tommy turned and walked back down the road towards the train station. Like excuses would get him off the hook now. Like anyone would care. Tommy was pretty sure he'd be reading Ricky's name in the obituary column inside a week. He sure as hell wasn't going to stick around to share the same fate. He had some cash on him and he had plenty more he could lay hands on and no one he cared enough about to worry about leaving them behind.

Know when to walk away, his dad had always told him. Know when enough is enough.

Strange to think Ricky had the same father as Terry Baldwin. Tommy grinned. One thing you could say about the old man. He'd known how to spread it about.

TWELVE

Students were leaving for the day when Steel arrived at Marion Deans Comprehensive just after three. The head teacher met him in the foyer and took him through to her office. 'I've asked three of the girls to stay and talk to you,' she said. 'Evie Watts is waiting for her mother to arrive. Susan Pierson and Tania Hayes are with Mrs Hayes. The Piersons are happy for you to speak to their daughter if Mrs Hayes is present. Shall I get them in?'

'In just a moment, that would be great,' Steel said. 'I just want a quick word with you first and with Sarah's class teacher—'

'On hand and waiting to see you. I thought we should deal with the students first. What else did you want to know?'

'Sarah seems to be close to Joey Hughes and Terrence Clarke. Can you tell me about them?'

Mrs Preston's eyes narrowed. 'And why would I do that?'

'For no bad reason. I met Tel and Joey today and Tel's mother, Maggie. I imagine the boys should have been in school, but they joined the search teams, with Tel's mother.' He paused, but it seemed Mrs Preston wanted more.

'They struck me as bright boys,' he said. 'And both care a great deal for Sarah.'

Mrs Preston leaned back in her chair and steepled her fingers. Steel was suddenly twelve years old and in the headmaster's office.

'Terrence Clarke is a very nice boy. His mother is an active member of the parent-teacher committee and helps out whenever we have functions. She has a husband, but he works away most of the time and the impression I get is that they are marking time until Tel is old enough for a painless divorce. I don't think there's any real acrimony, just no real intensity either. But,' she added sternly, 'they do both love their son.'

Steel nodded, considering himself told. 'And Joey?'

'Joey Hughes,' Mrs Preston sounded as though she was chewing on his name. 'A troubled family. The father is a bully who can't control his fists and the mother is a downtrodden little ghost of a woman. She managed to come to one parents' evening. Looked terrified every minute of it. The Hughes family are well known locally and for all the worst reasons. I know your colleagues are regular attendees at the Hughes' residence and I also know that he hits the boy. I've reported it, my staff have reported it.'

'And nothing has been done?'

'That man. That man is as slippery as . . . well, anyway. *She* won't do anything and Joey won't do anything for fear of things getting worse for his mother. I know he spends a lot of his time with Terrence and his mother.'

'And did the Griffins know that Joey and Sarah were seeing one another?'

'Knew, disapproved. Not of Joey himself, I don't think. He's a good kid and he's doing his best. But I think they felt it could never end well, and I suspect Mrs Griffin had history? Violence in her past?'

Steel nodded slowly. 'And you think that because?'

Mrs Preston sighed. 'Because when Sarah came to my school the head of her primary school came and had a quiet word. She told me that I'd find Sarah's records a little patchy. That the family had relocated under difficult circumstances and that social services were aware and were supporting them.'

'Sarah and her mother had a social worker?'

'I think so, though not by the time she came here or I'd have been made aware. I didn't pry and I made sure everything was handled carefully. But in my experience, that's the sort of conversation I have when there's been a history of domestic violence. Given that, you can understand their wariness when Sarah got involved with Joey Hughes.'

'But Joey isn't violent.'

'Joey?' She laughed. 'No. Mostly he just wants to be left alone, I think. He keeps his head down and tries hard. I'm not saying he's the brightest kid in the class. Far from it, but he's a trier and that, in my book, counts for a lot. And this year he's started to show a real ability in his science classes. We're doing all we can to encourage that.'

'You seem to know your students well.'

She shrugged. 'Not all of them. But there are those who come to your notice for whatever reason and I do try to be as familiar with my pupils as I can. It's not a massive school and that does help, but . . .' She got up. 'Shall I fetch the girls in for you?'

Steel nodded and thanked her.

Susan and Tania told Steel very little that was useful. No, Sarah didn't talk much about before she'd come to Ferrymouth. No, she'd not seemed worried or said anything unusual. They were both clearly upset and also, Steel suspected, a trifle miffed that they were not considered Sarah's *best* best friends, but only her next best.

'She's a lovely girl,' Mrs Hayes said. 'It's a terrible thing.'

Steel nodded and sat back to wait for Evie and her mother to be ushered in. Mrs Preston resumed her seat at the back of the room, quietly present.

Evie was devastated; Steel could see that immediately. Her mother was also deeply shaken.

'We were going to come and get Evie out of school,' she said. 'But Mrs Preston said we should wait because the police would want to talk to her, and anyway they were offering counselling and suchlike and she'd be better here with her friends.'

'She was probably right,' Steel soothed.

'Sarah stays over at our house. Once a week, maybe. She's a sweet girl.'

Steel nodded. 'Evie, did you stay over at Sarah's house?'

She shook her head. 'Not often.'

'Any reason for that?'

Unexpectedly, Evie blushed, embarrassed. 'I liked Sarah's mum and her stepdad,' she said. 'But the truth is, I'm not that keen on little kids. Jack was cute, but little kids . . . well, they're always kind of sticky. You know what I mean?'

Steel nodded solemnly.

'I know that sounds horrid,' Evie said. 'I did like Jack, I just—'

'Small children *are* kind of sticky,' Steel said gently. 'My sister has two girls. I love them dearly. I also carry wet wipes in my pocket when I'm with them.'

Evie laughed, and her mother gave him a look that was half grateful, half oddly resentful that he should make her daughter laugh at a time like this.

'Did she talk much about her past? About her father, maybe?'

Evie shook her head. 'No. Only that she hated him. He was violent and she and her mum left. I think they lived in a shelter somewhere for a while. She said once that they hid from him. But her mother didn't like her talking about it and so she didn't. I think she wanted to forget about it, you know?'

Steel nodded.

'Do you know who did this? Who would do a thing like this?'
Evie's mother asked.

'As yet, no.'

'But what if they do it again? What if they target other families?
What if it was random?'

'Mum!' Evie looked horrified.

'We have no reason to believe that might be the case.'

'You had no reason to believe someone might go and shoot
the Griffins. That poor little boy. Who'd shoot at children?'

Steel didn't reply. Nothing he could say would make this better.
He caught Mrs Preston's eye.

'Would you like to speak to Sarah's class teacher next?' she
said. She rose and gently eased Evie and her mother from the
room, returning a few minutes later with a young woman and
two mugs of strong tea. Steel thanked her.

'This is Arlene Thompson,' Mrs Preston said. 'She looks after
Sarah's group.'

Steel rose and shook her hand. Arlene Thompson was a tall
woman and very thin. She had, Steel thought, a plain face with
a somewhat large nose, but when she smiled it was oddly
appealing and she had a direct way of looking at him that he
rather liked. 'I'm pleased to meet you,' he said.

'Likewise. Though sorry about the circumstances. How is Sarah?'

'Distressed, as you can imagine. The hospital staff say she'll
recover; we're still trying to track down some family.'

'Hmm.' Arlene Thompson pursed her lips. 'I don't think you'll
have much luck there.'

'Oh? Did she speak to you about them?'

Arlene sipped her tea while she measured her response. 'It's
more what she didn't say. Look, we regularly do local history
projects and also family history stuff. It's something separate
from the actual curriculum; we feel the students need to have
projects that don't have to attract grades and judgement, you
know?'

Steel nodded.

'Well, because there's not a lot of free time, these projects tend
to span the school year. We put on an end-of-year show for the
parents and the project work forms part of the display. Anyway,
to cut a very long story short, I'd got the class researching their

family trees and Sarah was pretty upset about doing that. It's not uncommon these days for there to be gaps or for families to be estranged and not know exactly who went where, so we usually discuss a work-around with individual students, fill in what they know and speculate about the rest. For example, if the family is local, we look at local people from the past with the same family name. If they're from elsewhere we learn about their town or their country of origin, that sort of thing. Well, Sarah was different, you know? She talked about her mum and her stepdad and her little brother and how her stepdad was a manager and her mother a receptionist and what she hoped to do when she got older, but beyond that she was very reluctant even to speculate about her family, certainly to talk about them.'

'So what did you do?'

'I had a quiet word and told her to make it up if she wanted to. Mrs Preston explained when I spoke to her that Sarah and her mum had a difficult past, so that seemed like the easiest solution. It wasn't a major problem. Sarah was really happy to do the local history research. I just wanted her to have something down on paper so the other kids didn't start asking questions.'

Steel nodded.

'Can't you just ask Sarah?' Mrs Preston said. 'That would seem to be the best solution.'

'I have an officer on duty who will do just that,' Steel said. 'I'm more concerned—' He paused, wondering how to phrase it. 'I'm more concerned that we don't bring the wrong people to her door. Sarah's mother was very eager to escape her past. The last thing I want is to hand her daughter over to the people she had run away from.'

Having satisfied himself that nothing further could be learnt from the school, Steel left and prepared to turn his car back towards the hospital. There had been no strangers hanging about, no phone calls with enquiries regarding Sarah Griffin. No sign that Sarah was worried or upset. Willis had sent a message that the Friedmans had arrived and she'd had a preliminary conversation with them. He called her now.

'Anything useful?'

'Well, they remember Thea Baldwin, as she was then. Naomi was instrumental in getting her to testify and Alec became involved in the case – or rather cases – when Naomi went on a three-month secondment to the Met. He did all the pre-trial prep. According to them the wife and child were taken into protective custody. Even Naomi didn't know where. The mother handed over evidence that was instrumental in charging Baldwin with both the robberies and the attempted murder. He was never charged with the domestic; she'd gone by then and everyone agreed it was better to get him on the bigger charges even if that meant losing out on the lesser. And then she quietly disappeared. To be honest, I think the Friedmans had other things on their minds then anyway – though this was before they got married. When she was still Naomi Blake. Naomi had her accident just before the trial began. Multi-car pile up on the M-One. She was badly hurt. She came through it but, as you know, was left blinded.'

'So she was off the case when it came to court.'

'Well, yes, but no, not really. She'd been out of hospital a week when she testified, regarding the regular beatings Baldwin was giving his wife and kid and also the attempted murder. She'd been involved with that from the start and was instrumental in persuading Thea to hand over evidence that broke the case.'

Steel was silent for a moment. Thinking.

'You still there?'

'Yes. Look, I'm going to check in with the hospital while I'm over this way. Then I'll go and talk to the Friedmans.'

'Right you are. See you later,' Sophie said. 'I like them,' she added. 'And I think they'll be useful. Douggie's keeping them away from the journalistic hoards.'

'Good for Douggie. I'll speak to you in a little while.'

THIRTEEN

I t was after five by the time Steel got to the Dog and Gun to meet with Alec and Naomi. The Dog was a popular local pub, just on the outskirts of Ferrymouth, that had a couple of rooms it let out in the tourist season. Willis had called in and asked the landlord if he'd consider opening up for a few days and providing some meals. A couple of ex police officers, she'd explained, who had come over to help with the investigation because they knew the Griffins. Sophie Willis had, with Steel's approval, decided something close to the truth would be the best option – local gossip would be rife anyway, and it was Steel's view that a bit of truth kept people on side much better than a barrelful of lies and supposition. He'd grown up round Ferrymouth and knew better than to try deceit where none was necessary.

Steel drove through a town already transformed by the police and media. The cordon was still in place and residents had been given passes for themselves and their cars so they could get through. Anyone else, Steel had given notice, must be vouched for by either a senior officer or a resident, and *they* must come and collect their visitors from the cordon.

The locals, he was glad to say, had taken this in very good part. Still twitchy and anxious about the deaths in their quiet little street, they were, for now, happy to have some sort of barrier between themselves and the threat of the outside world, even if that barrier did comprise only of a length of flimsy tape and a couple of local constables.

Steel had promised a press conference at St Barts just after six, even though he knew that would annoy the editors, who'd want it before the hour so they could make the evening schedules. He hoped his conference would be billed as 'breaking news', knowing that ultimately the impact of that would be greater and more memorable than a simple scheduled headline. Steel wanted his message to get out there, as widely and as loudly as possible. Someone had come on to his patch, his quiet, uneventful, low crime stats patch, and shot three people dead, including a toddler, and tried for a fourth. They were not about to get away with it. Steel was personally affronted.

He found Willis and the Friedmans in the snug. He paused to speak to the landlord and thank him for his help and cooperation. The Dog had not yet opened up for the evening.

'You'll get a lot of media people in here this evening, Douggie. Town centre is full of them.'

'So long as they behave themselves. They can use the bar and the lounge. I'm saying the snug's closed for a private function.

There's a back door and a bit of a hallway, Sophie will show
you where. Your lot and Alec and Naomi can come and go just
as you like and the Friedmans can get to their room through the
back way too.'

Steel thanked him.

'I hear the little lass has woken up?'

'She has. She couldn't tell us much we hadn't worked out,
though.'

Douggie nodded wisely. 'Her mam and dad used to drink here
sometimes. Our Sal used to babysit from time to time. She did
a bit of a cleaning job at the doctors', so she knew Lisanne.
Sophie's already had a word with her but I've told her you'll
maybe want to talk to her as well.'

Steel had no idea who 'our Sal' might be but assumed Willis
would fill him in if it mattered. 'Thanks,' he said. 'You've been
really helpful.'

'Community spirit,' Douggie said, and Steel had a sudden
anxiety that he might be about to be on the receiving end of a
lecture on the subject. Fortunately, Douggie noticed the time and
decided he'd best 'get another barrel on' ready for the expected
influx of extra customers.

'You'll find tea and coffee and sandwiches in the snug,' he told
Steel, and then disappeared down through a hatch behind the bar.

Steel went through to the tiny room at the side of the bar. A
notice had been plastered across the door which announced that
the snug was closed for a private function. Three people sat
around a couple of round tables, eating their way through a
mountain of sandwiches and shop-bought cake.

Willis looked tired, he thought, but then she'd been on scene
as long as he had. She smiled at him as he ducked his head under
the low door and came inside. Steel knew he must look as though
he could fill the little room all on his own.

The strangers looked his way as he entered. The man stood
and extended a hand to shake. The woman faced in his direction,
her gaze almost but not quite on target.

Introductions were made, hands shaken, then Steel grabbed a
plate and joined them at the feast, suddenly aware that he'd not
eaten since the couple of slices of toast one of the volunteers
had given him at the church that morning.

'I called the prison,' Willis said. 'Terry Baldwin is still under lock and key. Sarah was definitely mistaken about hearing her father's voice.'

Steel nodded, gestured for her to go on. 'I spoke to both the doctors at the surgery where Lisanne Griffin worked as receptionist. The Pauleys are husband and wife. Been here for ever and the practice was his father's before that. She'd been recommended to them by someone from the Winslow Trust. It's an organization that helps the families of prisoners relocate, find work, accommodation, that sort of thing. It also helps women whose partners were convicted of violent acts against them or their children and who want to make a fresh start.'

'Have you spoken to anyone from the Trust?' Steel asked before taking another ravenous mouthful of cheese and pickle and thick crusty bread.

'Not yet. I've left a message with the contact the doctors had but they've warned me that the Trust security is on a level that MI Five would be proud of. It might take a while before Lisanne Griffin's friend – they call their caseworkers "friends", apparently – will get in touch with us.'

'I had dealings with the Winslow Trust once or twice,' Naomi said. 'Not just over Lisanne Griffin – or rather Thea Baldwin, as she was when we knew her.'

'What can you tell me about them?' Steel asked.

Naomi gathered her thoughts. 'It's an old organization, got charitable status back in the eighteen hundreds, I think, and I think it was originally for the rehabilitation of sex workers—'

'It was a Quaker thing, wasn't it?' Alec asked.

'I believe so, initially, yes. They don't advertise their activities and they don't encourage any kind of publicity. If I remember right, the first time I heard of them was when a prison chaplain I knew introduced me to a woman called Jessica Spence. I needed somewhere for a woman and two kids to go very quickly and very discreetly. The woman's old man was coming home and she was petrified, knew he'd find her in any of the local shelters because he had before. The chaplain suggested the Trust might help.'

'And they did?'

'They were startlingly efficient,' Naomi said. 'I got a card from the woman a few months later. Just a thank you.'

'And the second time?'

'Jessica Spence gave me her card and told me I could contact her direct. The one rule – well, I suppose there were two rules, really. One was that I should never pass her details on, even to a colleague. *I* was her point of contact and that was that. If I broke that rule, she'd refuse to have anything to do with me. The second was that I should only ever call when all other avenues had been explored. The Trust isn't a first line of defence, it's the last.'

'And the second time you had contact with her?'

'Was a different situation,' Naomi said. 'It was a man this time. Do you know, there's not one dedicated shelter in the country for male victims of domestic violence?'

Steel nodded, then remembered she couldn't see him. 'It's largely unreported,' he agreed. 'Did they help?'

'They did, yes. I contacted Jess Spence again about a year after that when I needed help for Thea and Sarah. She was very ill by then and in a hospice, but she passed my details on and another woman contacted me. I never even knew her name. I just had a phone number and was told to ask for Jessica's friend. After that I had no further contact with the Trust.'

'Did the doctors Pauley say how they knew about the Trust?'

Willis nodded. 'Mrs Pauley is from a Quaker family. She said the request came via the community, but she didn't know much more than that. I think the whole point is that as little information as possible is passed on.'

'So . . .' Steel paused thoughtfully. 'We know who Lisanne and Sarah were and why they ran. Also how they stayed ahead of her husband or whoever it was that put out the hit on them. Was she actually married to Victor Griffin or did she just take his name? And what do we know about him?'

'So far, not a lot. They bought the house just over three years ago. We're still chasing down the estate agent on that. Victor Griffin got the job at Andersons a couple of months after that. He was the assistant manager there and apparently very well thought of.'

'Andersons?' Alec asked.

'Sells agricultural equipment and feed, that sort of thing,' Willis told him. 'They said he didn't socialize much but he and Mrs Griffin would turn up for the works Christmas do and the summer barbecue, which was a sort of local event for customers as well.'

Steel nodded.

'One thing that puzzles me,' Naomi said. 'Thea Baldwin was a city girl, grew up in south London. She didn't meet Terry there but she came back to the city when she married him. They settled back there. If she wanted to disappear, why not choose another city? Manchester, Liverpool, even somewhere in the Midlands. True, this is a bit off the beaten track, but it's also small, exposed.'

'And somewhere a stranger would stand out,' Steel said. 'You could argue it works either way. Once the Griffins got established here the community would be aware of anyone coming and asking after them. Maybe it felt safer. Maybe Victor Griffin has connections round here. Maybe it just happened to be where this Trust thought it could place them. Jobs where no questions are asked are not easy to come by.'

'And Victor Griffin?' Alec asked. 'Did they ask questions about him when he applied for the job?'

'Came with excellent references, apparently. From some company down in the West Country.' She flipped through her notes. 'Chambers and Son. Similar set up to Andersons from the look of it. Agricultural supplies. I tried the number but didn't get a reply. I've not had a chance to chase it.'

'The information is three years old,' Steel said. 'It could be out of date. We'll get the local force involved, see what they can turn up, but my guess is it'll turn out to be another dead end.'

He glanced at his watch and stood up, instinctively bowing his head in the low ceilinged room.

'You want me?' Willis asked.

'No, I want you to get back to the church hall, see what's happening over there, and then check in with the hospital. Then I want you to get off home and get some sleep. Meet me back here at seven thirty, we'll join Alec and Naomi for breakfast, if that's all right with them. Then I want to take Naomi with me, if she agrees.'

'Agrees to what?' Naomi said.

'To go with me to visit Terry Baldwin in prison. You put him there, it seems right you should be with me when I ask him about his wife.'

Naomi tensed, then nodded.

'You don't have to do that,' Alec told her. 'I could go. I worked on the same case.'

'Sorry, Alec, but by the time you came on board most of it was done and dusted. Baldwin was my last big job before . . . before I left. No, I'll go.' She smiled. 'Baldwin always hated the fact that it was a woman who brought him down. I can't imagine he'll be any more pleased to see me now than he was back then.'

FOURTEEN

Joey hadn't wanted to go home but knew he'd have to sooner or later. He hung around at Tel's place until he was fairly sure his dad would have gone out – first to the pub and then on to work – then took his leave of Tel and Maggie and walked slowly home.

Maggie had called the policeman earlier, that DI Steel that looked like a scruffy bear, and asked if there was any news from the hospital. He told her that he'd not forgotten his promise to get Joey in to see Sarah – and in Joey's mind the rather vague assertion that he'd try had solidified into just that – and that he'd call Maggie the following day.

He'd not suggested calling Joey, or coming and talking to Joey at his house either; that told Joey that this Steel knew all about the Hughes family, and Joey wasn't sure what to think about that. Whether to be glad that the Inspector had the good sense not to bring police business to Joey's door, or sad that his dad had such a crap reputation that even a man like Steel, built like a brick shithouse, as Joey's granddad used to say, was reluctant to cross the Hughes threshold.

Maggie had fed him and Joey was grateful for that. His mum might have cooked him something but that depended on how long his dad had been gone and what she'd managed to put aside and hide from her husband. Joey's dad always laid down the law when he'd had a run in with his son ('He doesn't show respect, he doesn't get fed') and though Joey's mum did her best to sneak food for him, Joey's dad knew, he reckoned, to the last slice of bread what was in the house.

Joey turned his key in the lock and stepped quietly into the hall, listening all the while and ready to make a run for it.

'He's not here, Joey. He's gone already.' His mother's voice came from the living room and Joey went through. She was sitting with the lights off, staring at the television. Joey turned on the lamp and came round to look at her. She'd got another bruise on her face and finger marks blackened her arm. She pulled down the cardigan sleeve to hide that but could do nothing about the mess on her face.

'God, Mum. You've got to do something about him.'

She shook her head. 'Like what, Joey?'

'Leave.'

'And where would I go? Who'd have me now?'

'Anywhere. We could go anywhere. We could get on a bus and just clear out. We could go to the police.'

'No police,' she said flatly. 'I don't trust the police.'

Joey sighed. 'And as to who'd have you, Mum, what kind of stupid question is that?'

She flinched at the 's' word and Joey immediately regretted it. His dad was always 'stupid' this and 'stupid' that . . . 'You don't need anyone to "have you". You don't need another man. Life isn't about having some man just so he can knock you about.'

She flinched again and in that moment Joey both pitied and hated her. Anger and frustration boiling up inside of him until he almost wanted to hit her too. He turned away, ashamed and horrified. One of his dad's other sayings was 'She asked for it. She just asked for it', and in that fraction of a second Joey almost saw what he meant.

'Want some tea?' he said.

'I'll make it.'

'No, you stay there. You had anything to eat?'

'I'm not hungry, Joey.'

'Did he tell you that? Tell you you weren't hungry? God, Mum—'

'I've been watching on the telly,' she interrupted and Joey, reluctantly, allowed her to distract him.

'I saw about that girl you like and her family.'

'Sarah. Her name's Sarah. Her little brother was called Jack. Her mum and stepdad were Vic and Lisanne. I liked them.'

He was driving the knife in again, Joey thought. Hurting her. Trouble was, he didn't know how not to hurt his mother and he wondered if she even knew how not to be hurt.

'Will she be OK?'

Joey sat down on the settee next to her. 'They think so,' he said. 'Jack was shot dead. She tried to get him away but she was shot and the bullet went through into Jack.'

That was what Maggie had told him the policeman had said. Maggie had told him that Steel was telling more than he should, probably, because he knew how Joey felt about Sarah. Joey wasn't sure any of that was true, but he liked the sound of it anyway. Liked that someone cared how he felt.

'Do they know who did it? The telly didn't say much. Did you go to school today?'

Joey leaned back with his eyes closed, the frustration building again. He'd run off that morning, not in his uniform, without his school bag, and not come home until three hours after school was over – though to be fair, that wasn't unusual – and she wanted to know if he'd been to school.

'No,' he said. 'I joined in the search. Tel did too. Maggie was there.'

'Maggie.' Joey's mum almost spat the word and he immediately regretted mentioning it. His mum knew that Tel was his best friend and she knew that Maggie fed her son, looked after him in a way, and that was the trouble, Joey supposed. His mum saw Joey's involvement with this other woman as almost as much of a betrayal as if his dad had found himself someone else to beat up.

'I'll make that tea,' Joey said.

They spent the evening watching television, Joey trying to catch every news bulletin and his mum fretting at the interruption to her programmes. They were her escape, she always said, though Joey could never see how; the soaps and dramas she loved seemed to be full of violent men and troubled women and people doing unspeakable things to others. He wondered just how any of that could be classed as an escape.

He went to his room just after ten and texted Tel. Joey's phone was an old one of Maggie's – and his mum didn't know about that, either. Maggie slipped him a five pound token every now and again and, as he only ever texted on it, Joey managed to keep it fed with credit. He charged it in the socket under his bed, hidden behind a box so neither parent could see the bright blue LED charging light. Not that his parents came into his room very often. The only time his mum bothered was to bring him the occasional cup of tea. His dad's only reason was to take some item of Joey's and deliberately break it when Joey had upset him more than usual, but the truth was the novelty of that was wearing off, simply because Joey didn't own very much.

You OK? Tel asked. *Is your mum OK?*

He hit her again. I told her she's got to leave to call the police or something but it's wasting breath.

Sorry. You heard anything new?

No. You going to school tomorrow?

Mum says I have to, she says she can't take more time off work anyway. She says you should come for breakfast.

Joey smiled. *OK thanks. See you tomorrow.*

He wasn't sure he wanted to face school, but there wasn't a lot else he could do. He and Maggie and Tel had rejoined the search teams that afternoon and stayed until it was getting dark but only smaller teams would be needed tomorrow and Maggie had told them that they should not lose more time from their studies. That it would be far better to keep their minds occupied than hang around brooding anyway.

Then she had called Inspector Steel and spoken to him and he'd made his promise.

Joey lay down on his bed and pulled the quilt up. He was still fully dressed but the room was cold and he could never be quite sure that his dad wouldn't make a surprise visit home between leaving the pub and going to work at eleven. Once that milestone had passed Joey felt more confident about undressing and getting to sleep.

He thought about what his mother had said, about not being

able to leave, and Joey sighed. He couldn't go on living like this; other people didn't live like this so why should he?

But he knew he couldn't leave either, at least not yet, and the reason was not just his mother. Sarah was hurt; Sarah was lying in a hospital bed because someone had tried not just to beat her but to take her life away, and the thought of losing her terrified him. He knew that few people took the feelings of a fifteen-year-old boy and a fourteen-year-old girl very seriously, but Joey knew that he loved her and the thought that he'd almost lost her was tearing him apart.

FIFTEEN

In her waking life, Naomi rarely spared time or regrets thinking about what she had come to regard as her previous self, but she had no such control over her dreams.

She drifted into sleep thinking about Thea Baldwin as she had been back then, so the fact that she found herself, somewhere between dreaming and waking, back in those few weeks before her accident, came as no surprise.

Thea Baldwin had been a pretty woman. Mid twenties, blonde and slim, with long, highlighted hair and blue grey eyes. Her little girl, though with coffee-coloured skin and faintly crinkly hair that spoke of her father's ancestry, still managed to look a lot like her.

Thea had been bright, intelligent, not what Naomi had come to think of as the victim type. Thea reminded her that anyone could become a victim; that there wasn't a type or even a situation.

How had Thea and Terry got together? Naomi wondered about that a lot. What had convinced this gorgeous, far from stupid woman to hook up with someone like Terry Baldwin? Phrasing it with a little more tact, she had asked her.

'He was charming,' Thea told her. 'Kind of a bit exotic. I'd never dated anyone like him before and he took me out, bought me presents, made me laugh.'

She had seen the scepticism in Naomi's eyes. 'Yes, really. Terry can be funny and kind and even gentle and that's the trouble, isn't it? If it was all pain and bruises and Terry when he's being . . . well, not the Terry I first got to know, then it would be easier to walk away. Wouldn't it?'

Naomi, who had seen her fair share of women in Thea's situation, wasn't so sure. Only a scant handful ever seemed to make it out of the front door without looking back.

'But he'd say he was sorry,' Thea said. 'And for a while it would be wonderful again, just like it had been, and then, of course, something would trigger it, set him off, and I'd be the punching bag.'

'What sort of things set him off?'

'Oh, he gets so jealous. You know, at first I found it flattering. This man was so proud of me, loved me so much he couldn't bear to think of me going off with someone else. But then it got oppressive. It wasn't because he cared about me; it was because he wanted to own me, you know. Like I was just his property and no one else could come anywhere near. I told myself he was just scared. Of losing me, but it wasn't that. Even after Sarah was born and we really started to drift apart. He just didn't want anyone else having what belonged to him, even if he'd lost interest. He liked having me around because he liked the way other men looked at me – just so long as I never looked back. It made him feel special. Successful, I suppose, and Terry liked to feel successful. Didn't matter if it was business or personal.'

'And is he successful? Business-wise, I mean?' Naomi had asked her.

Thea smiled at her. 'Ah, now we've reached the crux of the matter,' she said. 'The real reason Inspector Naomi Blake is spending time with poor little Mrs Baldwin.'

She held up a hand for silence when Naomi started to protest. 'Please, don't. We both want something out of this and hopefully we'll both get it. Let's not pretend. Truth is, I'm sick of games.'

Naomi held her gaze. She wanted to deny what Thea said, but knew instinctively that if she did the woman would dismiss her. She'd lose the ground she felt she had gained in the past days. 'So is he successful?' she asked again.

She remembered that Thea glanced out of the café window. Until that moment, Naomi, half asleep, had forgotten where the two of them had met up. Thea would leave soon, to get Sarah from school. These meetings, Naomi recalled, were always tense and hurried, never in the same location. Thea was careful to the point of paranoia, Naomi had thought then. But she had been proved right in the end, hadn't she?

'He is,' Thea said. 'He makes money. He could make more, but Terry is essentially lazy. I know that's a strange thing for me to say. But you ask anyone, they'll tell you the same. It's changing, though. He has something planned, but I don't know what it is. Just that it's big.'

'And how do you know that?'

Thea looked at Naomi and smiled. 'I'm not leading you on,' she said. 'I can get you proof of his involvement in at least three armed robberies and I can get you proof that he tried to murder Stevie Meehan.'

'His partner in the robberies?'

'Some of them, yes. There was Stevie Meehan, and Ray Tobias. You know what happened to him.'

Naomi nodded. 'Rumour is, Terry almost beat him to death. But the witnesses won't talk.'

'I kept his clothes,' Thea told her. 'And I kept the gun he used to shoot Stevie. His prints will be on it. And if Stevie knows he's safe, he'll give you all the evidence you need on the robberies.' She shrugged. 'Terry lost his phone a while ago, had to get himself another one. There were texts on the phone, between him and Tobias and Stevie.'

'Lost it?'

'I've got it safe,' Thea said. 'There's other stuff too.'

'Like what?'

'Like that'll have to be it. For now. You get me out and we'll talk again. Maybe.'

Naomi opened her eyes. They hadn't spoken again and, so far as she knew, no one had ever isolated what the 'something big' might have been. She'd put it in her report, but the consensus had been that Thea Baldwin was scared, she just wanted to keep Naomi on the hook. The evidence she had promised had been handed over on the day Thea had left and for Naomi that had been an end to it. Naomi's days on the force had soon been ended too.

She turned over and tried to get back to sleep, but the thought nagged. What if Thea Baldwin had been telling the truth about Terry's plans and what if that truth, even after all this time, had been what killed her?

SIXTEEN

Joey left the house before his father arrived home the next morning, his mother already up and dressed and getting ready to feed her man when he came in from work.

'Stay and see him,' she pleaded. 'It just makes him worse when you avoid him.'

'Worse than when I don't? I don't think so, Mum. Yeah, we could both go out today with matching bruises; would that make it better?'

She looked away, staring out of the window, blinking as though defying the tears. Joey sighed. 'I'm sorry, Mum, but the truth is there *is* no better. You've got to do something. Like not be here when he comes home. That's the only way there's going to be any better.'

As he walked down the street Joey could feel the tears pricking his own eyes as the slow realization that Maggie was right and there was nothing he, alone, could do to help his mother resurfaced once again. It hadn't really gone away these past weeks, since he'd overheard that conversation. Maggie, he knew, felt terribly sorry for Joey's mum and even more sorry for Joey himself, and for a while he'd resented what he read as pity. As time went on he realized that what Maggie was offering was simply friendship. Joey was her son's best friend and, fortunately, Maggie liked him. That made Maggie an automatic ally and he knew she'd do anything she could to make things better for him, just because that was the right thing to do. He wished fervently that there were more Tels and Maggies in the world. Come to that, even Tel's dad was OK, though you could see, just watching him and Maggie together, that they weren't in love any more. They seemed like good friends, Joey thought, but Tel had once told him that they had made a pact to stay married and sort of living together until Tel was old enough to understand – that had made them both laugh; like Tel didn't understand already.

He knocked on Maggie's door. Tel opened it, and to his surprise Evie was there too. She looked as if she'd been crying.

Joey's immediate thought was that Evie somehow knew something bad that he didn't.

'My mum's sending me away,' Evie said. 'She's been scared by the shooting so we're going to my gran's.'

Immediate relief flooded Joey, followed by pity and then annoyance at her mum. 'He's not going to come back,' he said. 'Why would he come back?'

Maggie poured water into the teapot and then put an arm around Evie's shoulders. 'It won't be for long, love, and we'll all keep in touch, make sure you know what's going on. The boys have your mobile number, don't they, and if you text me your gran's number when you get there I'll let them use the landline to call you. Or you could Skype?'

Evie nodded but she wasn't really consoled. Maggie had cooked scrambled eggs and streaky bacon. Tel was buttering toast and Joey was grateful to see that a place had been laid for him too. Evie agreed to a cup of tea and she nibbled a slice of buttered toast. Maggie left them to it and went off to get ready for work.

'Mum dropped me off so I could say goodbye,' Evie told Joey. 'I hoped you'd show up too. She wouldn't let me come to your house.'

Joey nodded. He was past being offended by that sort of thing. 'Is she coming to collect you?'

'Yeah, soon as she's finished packing. She was up all night, said she couldn't sleep, not with a violent criminal around.'

Tel laughed. 'She seen how many coppers there are in town, has she? Probably the safest place in the world right now.'

Maybe he could divert a few of them round to his house, Joey thought.

'Mum called that Inspector Steel this morning,' Tel said. 'He said the hospital told him that Sarah had a comfortable night, which Mum says probably means she was drugged up to the eyeballs.'

'She's getting better, though?' It was agony, not being able to find anything out for himself.

'Yeah. She'll be fine. She's got to be.'

A knock on the door announced the arrival of Evie's mother. Maggie ran down the stairs to let her in and Joey was glad to be concealed from view behind the kitchen door. Evie's mum didn't exactly approve of his friendship with her daughter and he was pretty sure she'd find a way of blaming his family for the shooting if she could. Evie came round and hugged him quickly, torn between friendship and parental disapproval. Tel, in full view of the front door, got a longer, more tearful hug. Evie's mother approved of him. Joey listened as the goodbyes were said, scooping up the last of his eggs and helping himself to the last slice of bacon. He sometimes wondered what he'd do if Maggie didn't feed him. He felt bad about it, but felt even worse those odd times that he dared to acknowledge that he loved Maggie maybe more than he loved his own mother.

The front door closed and Maggie, dressed for work, returned to the kitchen. She always looked so different in her work clothes, Joey thought. Today she wore a dark blue suit and deep red lipstick. Joey wasn't sure what she did. Tel had said she was a PA, which meant she organized things for some big boss. Occasionally she worked late and then Tel did the cooking.

'Got to go,' she said. 'Tel, did you pack your lunch yet? Joey, if you didn't get time to do yours you'll find bread in the usual place, and I think there's some ham left in the fridge.'

If I'd not had time, Joey thought. Like there had been opportunity – or anything to pack up anyway – but Maggie always tried to help out in ways that didn't make him uncomfortable – which in one way made it worse; it highlighted just how bad things really were.

'I should be home usual time. If I'm going to be late, I'll text you. Carol said she wasn't the only one sending her kids away,' she added. 'So there might be a few missing from your classes today. I'm not at all sure that's a good thing to be doing. Friends need one another at a time like this.'

She gave Tel a quick kiss and headed for the door.

* * *

Steel returned to the Dog and Gun for a breakfast conference with Naomi and Alec before going on to the church hall to speak to his team. News from the hospital was mixed. Sarah had had a good night and the prognosis for her physical recovery was good but doctors were worried that she was shutting down emotionally. The police officer he'd left with Sarah had been relieved in the late evening and sent home, but she'd been back before Sarah awoke though even she had been unable to get a word out of the girl for most of the time.

'I'm going back to see her later today,' he said. 'I want to take a couple of her friends in with me but I'm having a tough time getting that past the consultant at the moment. It might call for a few underhand tactics. I think I'll just have to be sneaky.'

'You're too big to sneak anywhere,' Naomi observed.

'And you know that, how?' He was intrigued.

Naomi laughed. 'Well, for starters, your voice comes from high up, like Alec's does, but I'm guessing you're taller than Alec. And you block out all the light when you come into a room. You create a very large, very solid shadow.'

'You can see light and dark?'

'Just a little. The light has to be very bright, but yes, there's just a bit of light perception left.'

'And I'm a big shadow. I shall have to remember that. You still up for our trip today?'

'I am, yes. But I'm not quite sure what you think it will achieve.'

'Maybe nothing,' he admitted. 'But you know Terry Baldwin, I don't. You might have a better chance of pressing his buttons than me. I think it's worth giving it a go.'

Naomi nodded.

'Can I say I'm not happy about this?' Alec asked.

'You can say it,' his wife told him. 'In fact I think you have, several times already.'

'Just so everyone knows. And what can I do?' he asked.

It was Sophie Willis who replied. 'I've sent for all the records from the Baldwin cases. They should be here sometime mid morning. Douggie's said we can use the second guest room as an office. It's secure and private, so you and I, if you agree, will be reprising the old case files.'

Alec nodded. 'From what I recall, it's going to take more than two of us.'

'Three of us,' Naomi said. 'I may not be able to read them but I can add detail. I lived and breathed Terry Baldwin for close on a year.'

'Then it's agreed,' Steel said. 'Naomi, I'm going to get the morning briefing done and then I'll be back to pick you up. It's a couple of hours' drive so we'll grab some lunch before we come back, should be here by mid afternoon. Sophie, anything comes up you can't handle, DI Rubin is on standby – and when I say *can't handle* I'm thinking media and politics rather than investigation, OK.'

Sophie laughed. 'Thanks, boss,' she said. 'I'll be sure to send all media queries his way. He can do the midday statements.'

'Oh, he'll enjoy that,' Steel said.

Naomi smiled. The banter reminded her of her days in the force. She missed the camaraderie more than anything else; that sense of belonging was a hard thing to replace. She and Alec went up to their room so she could get ready to go with Steel.

'Are you sure you're OK with this?'

'I'm sure. If you'd asked me a year ago if I was ready to face that man again I'd have told you no, but things have changed since then. I've changed. I'll be fine, Alec.'

He clasped her hand. And then kissed her gently. 'I am so very proud of you,' he said.

SEVENTEEN

'Whoohoo.' Terry Baldwin, sitting across the table, waved a hand in front of Naomi's face. 'Oh, sorry. Can't see me, can you? Couldn't see me in court, could you? One thing that really made my day, that was, knowing you'd got yours.'

Steel frowned, started to intervene, but Naomi interrupted him. 'And you're still locked up, Terry. Now that really does make *my* day.'

The chair creaked as Terry Baldwin sat back and crossed his arms. Somehow, Steel thought, his body language and demeanour were those of a rather immature teenager, not a man who would not see thirty again.

'You've heard about your wife and her family, I suppose.'

'I've been informed. Can't say I'm surprised. She pissed me off enough times, looks like she did it to someone else.'

'Someone else? You sure you didn't have a hand in this, Terry?'

'Like you said. I'm in here. She's out there – oh, but sorry, she's not any more, is she?'

'Her partner and her child were shot too, Terry. Though I don't suppose you know anything about that either. Your daughter survived, though. Lucky, that.'

'I wouldn't know. I don't care. That it? You got anything more to ask me?'

'You might have known her husband. A man by the name of Victor Griffin.'

'Never heard of him.'

'You sure, Terry? Well, we've got a picture or two to show you.' Steel laid out several photographs on the table top. They had been taken at the crime scene. In them Lisanne and Victor Griffin were very obviously very dead.

'Your ex.' Steel slid the photograph across the table towards Terry.

'Well, she certainly is now,' he laughed. 'Pity about the kid. My kid, I mean. Pity they *missed*, whoever it was.'

'And Victor Griffin. Take a good look. See if you recognize him.'

'Why should I?'

Steel slid the picture across and placed it in front of Terry Baldwin.

'Never seen him before. But he don't look well.'

'You sure, Terry? Take a second look.'

But Terry Baldwin was in no mood to cooperate. He shoved the pictures back across the table and leaned his chair rearward, staring at the ceiling.

He's rattled, Naomi thought. Something got to him.

They got little more out of Terry Baldwin after that, beyond a few mean comments about his ex wife and their child, but

Naomi could not shake the sense that he was less sanguine about events than he'd have liked them to think.

A few minutes later he demanded to be taken back to his cell and they let him go, Naomi certain that they would learn no more.

They stopped off at the governor's office before leaving. Terry had few visitors, they were told. But he regularly spoke to his elder brother by phone and received visits from a member of his legal team about once a month.

'Why?' Naomi asked. 'Are there charges still pending? New charges?'

The governor shook his head. 'Nothing,' he said. 'But he has the right to legal advice as and when he requests it. We, on the other hand, have no right to deny him access.'

'But you suspect that not all lawyers are equal,' Steel said. 'That some, shall we say, have less experience of the courtroom.'

'I can suspect what I like but it changes nothing. They have been cleared to visit and that's that, so far as the prison bureaucracy is concerned.'

'What's his position in the prison community?' Naomi asked.

'Not as influential as he'd like to think. His brother gains him certain kudos but I suspect most of his cohabitants think he's a bit of an idiot. On the up side, he rarely gives us any bother. He's noisy, but . . . empty vessels, as they say.'

Naomi nodded and they took their leave shortly after.

Naomi closed her eyes, remembering.

She had forgotten how much she had loved to run. Not in the gym, treadmill kind of way she did now, purely as an exercise in building stamina. No, this was the sheer joy she felt in knowing that she was fast and sure footed and fit. The feel of the ground, hard beneath her feet, or springy as she left the track and moved on to the short grass. The wind against her skin. The sense of her body moving as a coordinated whole.

Run, you bastard, she thought. You sure as hell aren't going to outrun me.

She could see him up ahead; he'd left the park and was now

cutting across between buildings. Her hearing and peripheral vision told her that a patrol car was screaming around the corner, blues and twos in full glare and cry.

Sod you, Naomi thought. He's mine, you wait your turn.

She knew, even as she remembered it, that it was a ridiculous thought, but at the time she had fully meant it. The bastard had run away from her. From *her*. She was going to be the one to take him down.

Where did that woman go to? the present Naomi found herself thinking. She was still driven, still unable to settle for anything less than whatever it was she thought she ought to be capable of, but that Naomi, her past self – she had verged on the obsessive.

No, she corrected herself. Not even verged. She'd tipped joyfully right over the edge and then kept on falling. Falling, and celebrating the fall.

She was aware that Steel was waiting for her to continue, wondering what was going on in her head. She smiled.

'I saw him run across the road and into a side street. By the time I'd reached the corner he'd disappeared but I knew he couldn't have gone far. I'd got a clear view of the whole road, down to the junction. I could hear the patrol car and I knew backup was on its way and everything that was logical said I should wait. You know when you've run so hard that when you stop your whole body is shaking with that mix of adrenalin and exhaustion?'

Steel laughed. 'I used to play rugby,' he said. 'I can probably empathize.'

'But I knew that if I stopped, it'd be a full stop. I wanted to finish it, you know? I wanted to be the first one there. I'm not saying that was right, I'm just telling you how it was.

'I started to jog down the road. I thought I'd spotted him cutting between two buildings and I was right. But he'd miscalculated. There was a high wall behind the shops and by the time I ran down into the alleyway he was looking for something to climb on to to get over the wall.'

'So, what did you do?'

'I shouted. I called his name. He turned and he laughed.'

A fucking woman, Terry Baldwin had said. *A fucking woman.*

'Laughed?'

'You saw him today. Cocky as hell. He doesn't care. I mean he really doesn't care. It's not something he even thinks about – prison, punishment, restitution. He laughed because it didn't matter; the only thing that bothered him was that I was the first on scene.'

And then he'd started to move towards her and Naomi had realized that he had a knife and she had no illusion at all that his threat to use it was an idle one. Terry Baldwin didn't do idle threats.

'He was holding a knife,' she said. 'A craft knife. You know, the sort with the snap-off blades.' Nothing big and brash, just sharp as hell.

'Most people slash with a knife rather than stab,' Steel observed. 'To stab someone you have to come in close; to slash you can keep at arm's length.'

'True. You know, I think the fact that it was such an everyday, ordinary kind of weapon made it more frightening in a way. We've all cut ourselves one time or another so we've all got an idea of how much it hurts. I read some research somewhere that said people are more likely to tackle a gunman than someone wielding a knife. They reckoned it was because of that. Because most of us don't know what it's like to be shot, but we all know what it's like to be cut.'

Steel laughed and switched on the indicator. 'We're off the motorway in a few minutes,' he said. 'I know a place we can stop for something to eat. That all right with you?'

'Absolutely. I'm starving.'

'I'm not so sure I've got a preference,' Steel said, referring back to her confrontation with Terry Baldwin. 'I've faced a few incidents, thankfully not alone. Only one of those involved a gun. So what happened then?'

'I told you we were in an alleyway at the back of some shops? Well, to cut a long story short, I floored him with an industrial sized wheelie bin.'

'Seriously?' Steel guffawed and Naomi felt the car shake. The man had a big laugh, she thought.

'Seriously. Believe me, I might have been keen, but I wasn't going anywhere near him. I knew backup was coming, so I grabbed the bin and swung it towards him. There was, like, this slight camber in the alleyway and the whole thing just kept travelling and . . . bang. Terry Baldwin on the floor, reinforcements arrive. Problem solved.'

'No wonder he hates the sight of you,' Steel said bluntly. 'Can't have done his reputation much good. Arrested by a woman and floored by a bin.'

'I was improvising,' Naomi said. 'Actually, my boss wasn't impressed. Said I should have held back and not gone in alone.'

'And he was right,' Steel told her.

'And he was right,' Naomi conceded. 'But what is correct and what is expedient don't always tally, do they?'

'No,' he said. 'Sometimes they don't.'

EIGHTEEN

Steel waited outside the school for Joey and Tel to appear and then got out of his car and called to them.

Joey turned guiltily; Tel just looked surprised. He saw Joey's expression turn from one of guilt to sudden anxiety as both boys hurried over.

'Sarah?' Joey asked.

'Is all right. Look, I've called Tel's mum to warn her you'll be a bit late back. I thought you might like to come with me to the hospital. I want to talk to Sarah again and I think she might be more willing to chat to me if she's got friends there.'

Joey was already opening the car door.

'Evie's mum has taken her away,' Tel said.

'So I heard. We'll be sure to tell Sarah why Evie couldn't be there.'

Steel had already spoken with Mrs Preston about collecting the boys but he was very conscious of the curious looks he was getting from members of staff and from the kids getting on to the school buses. He was not exactly inconspicuous. As Naomi had told him that morning, he did tend to block out the light.

'How was school?' he asked.

Tel laughed. 'It was school,' he said.

'Are you in your GCSE year?'

'Exams next year. Then I'm doing AS, or whatever it is by then.'

'University?'

'Mum wants me to. I think she fancies me being a lawyer or something.'

'And you? What would you want to be?'

'Well, I've kind of grown out of wanting to be a fireman and an astronaut. I wanted to be Indiana Jones for a bit but now I really don't know. I like sciences, but I'm not sure I'm good enough to do them at A level.'

'You get good grades,' Joey objected.

'Yeah, but not good enough. Not really. Yours are better.'

That was interesting, Steel thought. He didn't press the point. 'So if not sciences?'

Tel shrugged. 'I'm trying not to think that far,' he admitted. 'It's like we've got to decide on the rest of our lives, like in the next year. I mean—'

'Seems a tall order,' Steel agreed. Should he ask Joey what he wanted to do? He wasn't sure. 'And Sarah, what does she want to do?'

'Art and languages,' Joey replied without hesitation. 'She's brilliant at art.'

'And languages,' Tel added. 'In the top stream for French and German and they've let her add Spanish this year. She's doing Japanese at Summer School.'

'Talented, then,' Steel said. 'Me, I failed French. I went to night school to learn Spanish for a holiday I never actually went on.'

Tel laughed. 'Why not?'

'Well, I had this girlfriend. She wanted to go to Spain, wanted to get off the beaten track, so she said, so she reckoned we should take a language class.'

'And what happened?'

'She met someone else,' Joey guessed.

'Unfortunately, yes. She met him at the language class. They went off to Spain and I decided languages were definitely not my forte.'

The two boys laughed and then fell silent for a bit and then
Joey asked, 'Did you always want to be a policeman?'

'Always, as in when I was a kid? No. Not even later. I went
to university, did Politics, Economics and Modern British History,
then had to think what to do with that. The local force were
advertising a graduate recruitment programme and so I thought
I'd give it a go until I found something better.'

'But you liked it,' Joey said.

'Not at first. I hated the routine and the shifts and having to
get up early and all the stuff most people hate when they leave
uni for the real world. But I found I was good at it. I liked seeing
the connections, I liked the people. I liked the idea of maybe
making a difference. I mean to real people. So I stayed and
worked my way up and here I am.'

'You don't though, do you?' Joey said, and Steel heard the
sudden bitterness in his voice. 'Make a difference?'

'Why do you say that, Joey?'

No response. Steel glanced into his rear-view and looked at
both boys. Joey, sullen and angry now, staring out of the side
window and Tel, concerned and a little embarrassed, not too sure
what to say.

'The police round where you live have let you down?' Steel
asked.

'Of course they fucking have.'

Steel's eyebrow raised at the sudden expletive, but more at the
burst of rage. 'They come out and they talk to my mum and dad
and my dad sweet talks them and me mam, she just nods and
tells them what they want to hear. What he wants to tell them,
and then they go away again and nothing changes. You fucking
tell me how that makes a difference?'

'Joey, it's not *his* fault,' Tel said, gesturing towards Steel.

Steel said nothing. Joey needed this explosion, he thought.
Joey badly needed help too.

'But nothing gets done,' Joey went on. 'I saw on the news
that the police can prosecute now, even if the woman doesn't
want to. You could take him away. Lock him up, even if she
didn't want it. You could change it. But no one ever does.'

They had reached the hospital car park and Steel pulled into
a space. He cut the engine and turned in his seat to face the

furious boy. Joey was trying very hard not to cry. His face was set and hard and Steel suddenly glimpsed the man Joey would become if nothing was done for him.

'So, tell *me*,' he said. 'Let *me* try. Let me make it change.'

Joey slumped back and rubbed his eyes fiercely. 'I want her to leave him,' he said, 'but she doesn't know how. All she knows is him or some other bastard beating up on her, and you know what? You know what really scares me? Sometimes I feel so mad with her that I want to hit her too. I just get—'

Tel was staring at his friend as though suddenly seeing him in a new light.

'You don't mean that,' he said. 'You'd never hurt anyone. Except maybe your dad.'

Joey shrugged.

'What you're describing is very common, Joey. Both your mum's reaction and what you feel. Sometimes people get so worn down they can't see any other kind of life. But that can change too, with the right care and the right opportunities.'

'And who's going to give her those? She won't talk to you.'

'Probably not. But you just have, and that's a beginning. Your mother isn't the only victim here, Joey, and I don't just mean because your father hits you too. You're a victim of your mum's inability to act too. All the pain and the frustration that brings. It isn't fair, Joey, and it shouldn't be your responsibility either.'

Joey wiped his eyes again. 'I want to see Sarah,' he said. 'Now.'

Steel nodded and they all got out of the car. He could see that already Joey was regretting his outburst and he knew he couldn't just let this opportunity slip by.

'Sarah's mother lived with a violent man,' he said. 'I met him today.'

He had their attention now, Steel realized.

'What did he say?' Tel asked. 'Is he sorry? Did he do it?'

'No, he's locked up in prison. Sarah's mother managed to escape, with help. She made a fresh start here. Many people do.'

'Until someone killed her,' Tel said.

'Which is not the usual outcome when a woman, or a man for that matter, manages to get away. The odds that they'll be able to rebuild their lives improve with every day. The odds that

their partner will kill them also increase with every day they
have to remain.'

'You said men too?' Tel was a little shocked.

'Anyone can find themselves undermined and hurt,' Steel said.
'It can start with something very small. Little actions that bully
and diminish. Someone constantly telling you that you are stupid
or unworthy – that can be the start of things. Sometimes that's
all it is – if you can call it *all* – but when that erosion of self
belief happens over a long period of time it can destroy someone
just as surely as the beatings can. And it doesn't make any difference if it's a woman or a man or a child. It can happen to anyone
and when it does, it's always wrong. Something should always
be done.'

They had entered the hospital by the back door into the basement. 'There's a lot of media interest,' Steel said. 'I didn't want
you to have to face that out front.'

He took them up the back stairs and down a long corridor.
Despite what Naomi had suggested, Steel had been doing a lot
of sneaking about this last day or so. He guided the boys through
two doors locked by key codes and two security checks, then on
to the ward that Sarah was on. Two uniformed officers stood
chatting at the nurses' station and Steel paused for a word with
them before leading Tel and Joey into a side room. A woman
sat beside the bed and she rose with a smile as Steel entered,
then looked curiously at the boys. Sarah lay in the bed with her
eyes closed. Joey was awed. She looked so small and so fragile.
So un-Sarah. The woman stood and Joey took her seat, Tel moving
round to the other side of the bed. Joey could hear her talking
quietly to Inspector Steel.

He took Sarah's hand. 'Sarah?'

She turned her head and opened her eyes. 'Joey? How did you
get in here?'

For the first time in two days, Sarah smiled. Joey leaned
forward and laid his head on the pillow close to hers. 'I thought
you were dead too,' he said, and he began to cry.

Later, when the first flood of emotion had passed, Steel sat beside
the bed with Tel and Joey and DC Stacy Woods, and he told
Sarah about his trip to visit her father.

'Do you remember being Sarah Baldwin?' he asked.

'Sure. I was seven, nearly eight, the last time I saw him. I wasn't a baby.'

'And your mother told you that you were going to leave, change your names, live a new life?'

Sarah nodded, her eyes filling with tears again. Her mother was gone – the pain of that would be terribly raw for a long time, Steel thought. He hated having to scrape an already open wound, but he had no real choice.

'One day, it was a Monday, my dad left in the morning. He and Mum had had a terrible row the night before and he'd hit her so hard she'd fallen down and not been able to get up again. I was so scared. He just stood there, leaning over her, breathing really hard like he'd been running for miles. It was horrible.'

Joey gripped her hand even harder, his thumb stroking gently across her fingers. He looked very pale, Steel noted, and his eyes were very red.

'The next morning he left early and Mum said we had to go. Right then. She made a phone call and told me to grab a few things. Just a small bag, she said. Like my school rucksack and maybe a carrier bag with toys. I asked her what was going on and she said we were walking away and that we'd never be able to come back.'

'That must have frightened you a great deal.'

She shook her head. 'Not right then. I didn't realize what she meant by "never". I didn't really think about leaving our friends behind and never being able to talk to them again. Like my auntie down the road.'

'You sent a card to her,' Steel remembered.

She nodded. 'Mum said it would be all right so long as we didn't leave a return address and she got someone to post it from miles away when they went on a business trip.' Sarah turned to Tel. 'Your mum was going down to London with her boss. Maggie took the letter with her and posted it from there.'

'So Maggie knew a lot about your mum?'

'No. She knew a bit, guessed a lot more. Maggie doesn't need to *know* everything. She's nice. She just helps people because it's the right thing to do, you know?'

Steel nodded. Tel looked pleased, he noticed.

'And you went where?'

'I don't know. We went to this café I'd never been to before
and then a woman came and picked us up in a car. There was
another woman there, a policewoman. She'd been to see Mum
before. Mum had been really mad with her then but she wasn't
after, not in the café. She was just . . . just kind of determined,
you know?'

'Do you remember the names of the policewoman and this
other woman that picked you both up?'

'Naomi. The policewoman was called Naomi. I don't think I
knew the other one. She wasn't with us for very long.'

'And what happened then?'

'We were driving for a long time, then the woman stopped on
a road in the country and got into another car. Naomi didn't
come with us after that. She said goodbye and told my mum she
was doing the right thing and that it would all be OK and then
we got in this other car with another woman and we drove off
again. We stayed the night at this big house. It was on a farm, I
think, because we could hear cows, but it was dark when we got
there and not light when we left, and then the next day we ended
up at this seaside place and we stayed there for a few days.'

'And what did your mum tell you all that time? Did she say
where you were going?'

'Scotland,' Sarah said. 'We spent about six months there, somewhere near Aberdeen. I didn't go to school or anything. Mum
and a man called Tony taught me from home. Tony was married
to Greta, who owned the house we were living in. He helped with
my maths and stuff and they told everyone that Mum was a cousin.
She was calling herself Lisanne by then, but I stayed Sarah.'

'And a last name?'

'Kemp. It was Gran's maiden name. She died when I was
really little so I don't really remember her.'

'And then?'

Sarah thought about it. 'Mum got a letter and when she got
it she cried a lot, and I was scared at first because I thought all
the bad stuff was coming back but then she told me that my dad
had been locked up for a very long time and we didn't have to
be scared any more. That we could find somewhere to settle
down and be happy.'

Steel thought about it. That would fit with the length of the trial, more or less. That had lasted nearly seven months in total. 'And you left after that?'

'We stayed until Christmas and then we packed our stuff and Greta gave us a lift to the station and we left.' Sarah frowned. 'It got a bit confused after that. Mum couldn't seem to decide where she wanted to be and there was a whole load of B and Bs and cheap hotels for a bit, and then she rented a flat and we moved in at Easter.'

'And that was in . . .?'

'Peterborough. I liked it but Mum hated the one-way system. Anyway, I went to school and she got a job in a shop. It was all right for a while.'

'For a while?'

'Mum found it really hard to settle anywhere. She was always looking over her shoulder, I suppose. I didn't understand it at the time, but for a while it wasn't at all like she'd said. We didn't settle anywhere for long. She'd get a job and we'd find a place to live and then she'd suddenly decide we had to leave again. Then, four years ago, she met Vic and everything changed.'

'And where did she meet him?'

Sarah bit her lip. She'd been talking quite normally, as though the horror of the past couple of days had somehow receded. Now it returned, forcefully.

'They're really gone, aren't they? I mean really, like for ever.'

'I'm so sorry, Sarah,' Steel said. 'But yes. They really are.'

For a few minutes they all sat in a silence broken only by Sarah's tears and Joey's soothing noises. He talked to her as if she were a little child, Steel noted, hushing and holding and stroking like he would for a baby. It was so at odds with his outburst in the car that Steel was fascinated. He sensed that they were standing at a pivotal moment in two young lives. Joey could be redeemed, or he could turn out like his father – not because he wanted that, but because the dice might just fall that way – and Sarah . . . what would the future bring for her?

Had they been just a little older, Steel thought, they'd have been able to help one another through. Two whole, healed young people might emerge. But they were both just kids. Who would, could, ease the path for both of them?

'Do you remember where Lisanne and Victor met?' he pressed gently.

'It was in Bristol, wasn't it?' Joey said. 'You'd been down there three weeks and your mum had found a part-time job in a café near the docks and it was summertime and there were lots of visitors.'

Sarah nodded. 'And he was a customer. But that wasn't where they met. She'd met him before. Before she knew my dad, I think. She lived down there for a while when she was about nineteen. She'd gone to a festival and stayed on after, found some work at a local hotel. I think that was a happy time and that's why she wanted to go back.'

'And he just happened to come into the café?'

'He still lived down there. He'd never left.'

It was still a major coincidence, Steel thought. Though coincidences did happen.

'I liked him a lot, even at the start,' Sarah said. 'He was just so kind. Mum fell back in love with him and they got married and then we moved up here.'

'Ferrymouth is a long way from Bristol,' Steel said. 'What brought them this far north?'

'I'm not sure,' Sarah said. 'I think he was offered a job. We came up to look around and Mum liked it and so we decided this should be the real fresh start. Mum told me that if we moved here, I'd be leaving friends behind again and that it was like before, I'd just have to forget about them all. I'd kind of got used to doing that. I'd been doing it since I was seven. But I wanted this to be the last time, and Mum said she did too. She promised me, this would be it. If I made friends here, I wouldn't have to leave them behind.'

Steel thought about what Sarah had told him. While it was true that casual work and short-term lets were usually available, it sounded the way Sarah told it as though Lisanne had just hopped from place to place and job to job with very little trouble or intervening unemployment. That in itself was odd. Had she moved from place to place with the help of the Winslow Trust? If her last job had been found through their community, then it was obvious they'd not just let her go. They had continued to protect and help her even after the trial and that first move.

'Did Vic know all about her past?'

Sarah nodded. 'She told him everything when he asked her to marry him. She told me she was going to, that it was fair, that if he couldn't cope with it then she and I would just move on again.'

'He knew who your father was?'

'She told him everything.'

Steel shifted in his seat. Sarah was obviously tired now and he ought to get the boys back to Maggie's and then catch at least the tail end of the evening briefing.

'Sarah, did you know your mum's family at all? Anyone we can get in touch with for you?'

She shook her head slowly. 'Mum left home and she sort of broke contact, I think. I never really thought about it much. I met my gran once, I think, but I don't remember. Mum said she died. She didn't like it when I asked about them and my dad would just yell if he heard me anyway. I don't know what happened.'

Steel nodded. 'Sarah, you seemed really certain that you heard your father's voice downstairs on the night of the shooting. But we know that's impossible. We know that your father is still in prison. Do you have any further thoughts about that? Someone you remember from before who sounded like him?'

She shook her head. 'It was him,' she said. 'I mean, you're telling me it couldn't be, but it was him. I was sure of it then and I'm still sure of it now.'

Steel nodded and then stood, telling Tel and Joey that they really had to leave. They parted reluctantly, Joey holding Sarah's hand until the very last second. They were quiet as Steel led them through the back way to his car. Steel called Maggie from his mobile and told her that he'd be bringing Tel home and then dropping Joey off.

He listened. Joey realized that Maggie was objecting to the plan, telling Steel to bring Joey too.

'I'll see what he wants me to do,' Steel said. He hung up, then turned around in his seat. 'Maggie says you're welcome to have a dinner there,' he said. 'I told her I'd ask you.'

Joey peered between the seats to look at the dashboard clock. It was five fifteen. His dad would still be home.

'Um, I'd like to go home with Tel,' he said.

Steel nodded. Joey's pale face flushed with embarrassment. 'You and I should have a serious talk,' Steel said. 'This can't go on, Joey. You need someone to help you.'

'Know someone with a twelve bore, do you?' Joey said bitterly.

Steel raised an eyebrow and Joey shook his head. 'Sorry,' he said. 'But I can't say I don't mean that.'

'I'd be surprised if you could,' Steel said quietly. 'I also know that people like your father are not worth the trouble it would cause if you took that way out. Joey, will you let me help you?'

'Don't see what you can do,' Joey said. But Steel could see that he really wanted him to try.

NINETEEN

Alec and Sophie Willis had spent much of the day reprising old case files. Naomi had joined them when she returned from the prison. Alec could see she was blazingly angry, but her fury remained contained and secured until Sophie left them to attend the evening briefing over at the church.

All day the media crowd had increased in number, many coming into the Dog and Gun for lunch, and as Alec and Naomi made their way down to the snug they could hear the evening throng had begun to arrive.

Douggie intercepted them on the back stairs. 'I can bring food up to your room if you like. You don't have to come down to order.'

'Thanks, Douggie, I think that would be a good idea. We're going to slip out for a quick walk first. I've been inside all day and I think we both need a breath of air.'

Douggie nodded. 'When you get out of the back yard, turn left and about fifty yards down you'll see a public footpath; it leads off towards the river. It's a nice walk even this time of the year.'

He headed back towards the bar and Alec led Naomi out through the back entrance. It was at times like this that he wished they had brought Napoleon, Naomi's guide dog, with them, knowing that he gave her so much more a feeling of independence. But originally the idea had been that they'd stay overnight and then head back. Plans had changed and Alec wasn't sure how long they'd stay now. He'd called their friend Mari, who was looking after Napoleon, and she'd been happy to continue for a few days. Napoleon would be spoilt rotten, Alec thought.

He spotted the sign for the footpath and warned Naomi that there was a stile and that it would be slippy.

'You'll be OK in those shoes?'

'I will. I need to walk. If I ruin them I'll just have to get some more.'

Alec laughed. 'Oh, the hardship,' he said. 'I can just see a shopping trip with Sam coming on when we get back.'

'Oh yes. All day, so get your babysitting head on.'

They walked in silence for a few minutes as Alec admired the view and Naomi seethed. Scrubby grassland reached down towards the river. Beyond that more of the same, gradually dropping down and giving way to mud flats. Moored boats heeled over waiting for the tide to return, though he guessed the draught was shallow even at high tide. Wading birds patrolled the shallows and gulls shrieked overhead. It would be dark soon and a damp chill came in from across the water. Their walk would be a short one.

'It's the arrogance of the man,' Naomi said. 'It always was the thing that riled me most. How someone like that could even have a relationship – I mean who'd—?'

She broke off. 'Fuck him,' she said.

Alec smiled, glad for once that she couldn't see him. Naomi swore rarely and never did it very convincingly. 'Did you find out anything useful?'

She shook her head. 'I don't think so. He was adamant it had nothing to do with him. Not that he was sorry. He just kept referring to them as "that bitch of a wife" and "that whiny child". You know how with most people, no matter what they are or what they've done, you can usually find some tiny glimmer of a redeeming feature? Well, I never could with Terry Baldwin. I can't even excuse him by saying he's a sociopath because I don't believe he is. I don't think Terry Baldwin is evil or misguided or wrong in the head, I just think he's a scrote. He enjoys it, thinks it gives him some kind of kudos. Not that he's got two brain cells capable of talking to one another.'

She broke off and shivered. 'It's cold out here.'

'You want to go back?'

'In a minute or two. I want to get really cold first. I need the pleasure of getting warm again.'

Alec laughed at her but contented himself with standing at her side as the sky darkened and the chill from the seaward view crawled landward, condensing into a clinging, warmth-sapping mist.

'I'm cold enough, now,' she said.

'I'm glad about that. I'm hungry too. What do you think of Steel?' he asked as they turned back along the path. He was glad to be able to see the lights from the pub up ahead. It was getting truly, country dark and he'd neglected to bring a torch with him.

'I like him. He's funny and intelligent and cares about the job. I like Sophie too. Do you think anyone ever gets to use his first name?'

'What, "Man of"? No. Actually, I don't think he has one. Did you think Terry Baldwin was telling the truth?'

'I don't think Terry Baldwin would recognize the truth if it came and bit his face off,' she said bitterly. 'But unfortunately, I suspect he was this time. I've been rerunning the original interviews in my head. I can't read him in the same way now. I can't see him to do that, but I can remember his voice from before. I got so I could recognize when he was skirting round the truth and when he was out and out lying, and though it's harder now I can't see his face or read his body language, I can still hear the changes in his voice. I don't think he arranged the hit.'

'If you're right that puts everything back to square one.'

'It does, sort of. Not arranging it doesn't mean he didn't know about it and I'm not so certain on that score. But there's something else, and I don't know quite what it was that made me think it. Steel asked him about Vic Griffin and he just said he'd never heard of him. Then Steel showed him a photograph and there was just a moment – just that little hesitation, I suppose – that made me think he recognized the face.'

'You mentioned this to Steel?'

'Of course. Thing is, he'd picked up on it too. If that's so then it puts quite a different spin on things, doesn't it?'

TWENTY

Steel had been in two minds about where to hold the twice daily briefings. One sort of logic said he should call everyone back to headquarters and do it there. The other logic said that doing that meant an hour lost in travelling each way. Instead, he decided it would be far more practical to keep everything in the school house next to the church. Those few officers who might have been sent elsewhere could either check in by phone or be caught up with separately.

About fifty officers of assorted ranks and from various rural headquarters crowded into what had been the main hall. Joining them were local civilians who had been acting as liaison for Steel. He knew this was a move frowned on in some quarters but Steel had grown up locally, he knew the power of the vicars, the doctors, the established traders. They knew everyone, noticed everything and would be far more effective at organizing community efforts than any police officer, and so he had decided to include them in the evening briefing. They stood apart from their police colleagues, a little nervous, uncertain of what was expected or even their right to be there.

Steel thanked everyone for attending and for the day's efforts. 'The good news,' he said, 'is that Sarah Griffin is recovering well, physically at least. We still have nothing new on family, but I was able to take some of her friends in to see her today. I hoped she'd be able to talk to me more freely if she had familiar faces around and I have, as a result, gained a few more pieces of information.'

Steel explained that when Thea Baldwin had decided to testify against her husband she had been given a new identity and moved around a good deal. He deliberately didn't mention the Winslow Trust. He had spotted Doctor Eric Pauley, one of his chosen local representatives, standing at the back of the hall and decided that a private word, later on, would be a better policy.

'We know that Mrs Griffin took her mother's maiden name for a while and lived as Lisanne Kemp. We know that she and Victor Griffin had originally met when she lived in the Bristol area in her late teens. The relationship seems to have ended then, but she met Mr Griffin, by chance it would seem, when she and her daughter moved to Bristol about four years ago. Their relationship was rekindled. Their previous friendship may or may not be significant. Sarah assumed that their meeting was by chance, but it is possible that contact was made earlier. Again, that may be significant; as yet, we have no idea what led to their deaths and that of baby Jack, and we've got to keep all options open.'

He glanced at Willis and then continued. 'I visited Terry Baldwin in prison this morning. He denies any knowledge of the attack on his ex wife and her family but we are continuing to view his possible involvement as an important line of inquiry. Now, I know some of you have information to add, so,' he smiled wryly, 'if you'd like to form an orderly queue . . .'

He moved back to stand beside Willis while results of house-to-house enquiries, further searches of the fields and generalized bits and pieces of gossip and hearsay were shared with the group. Steel knew from experience that even what passed for tittle tattle could be significant, especially if it surfaced more than once. He encouraged his civilian helpers to have their say too but it soon became obvious that there was little of significance. To Steel's mind only two things really stood out.

PC Divers, a very young officer, spotty faced and sporting something that might one day grow into a moustache, took his place on the platform.

'I finally managed to have a proper talk to the old lady next door. Mrs Ball. She was still really upset but she told me a couple of things. One was that the Griffins had more visitors than usual in the ten days or so before they got shot. Two men, she said. Sometimes together and sometimes singly, but the same two men. She thinks they called about half a dozen times in all. At first she thought they were selling something and expected them to knock on her door, but they didn't.'

'Description?'

'One older than the other, both wore suits and ties, looked kind of official. She says she thought they might be God-botherers.'

Laughter in the room. Divers blushed.

'Then she says Mrs Griffin had a row with one of them on the doorstep, but she couldn't hear what was said. Mrs Griffin slammed the door and the man got into a car that had been parked across the road. A dark car, she says. The other man was driving.'

'Try her again,' Steel said. 'See if you can get anything more detailed on the description.'

Divers stepped down and another took his place. A woman who lived a little further up the road had noticed a dark coloured car with two men inside a few days before the shootings. She had not taken much notice, only that it wasn't anyone local, and it had only occurred to her it might be important afterwards when they were asked to report anything unusual. She had, as it happened, noticed the make. A Ford Focus, she thought, because it was like her brother's car, but that was all.

'I don't suppose there's any useful CCTV round here?' someone said. The question was greeted with general amusement.

'There's a CCTV camera outside the bank,' Steel said. 'And one in Robsons, the jewellers on the corner of the market square, but it shows very little of the street.'

'And there's a camera on the first set of lights, as you come into town,' one of the civilians standing at the back of the hall told him.

Steel realized it was Doctor Pauley who had spoken. 'I didn't know that,' he said.

'It's a school crossing. We had a child knocked down there a few years ago so, after a lot of noise, the local council agreed to install a traffic camera. I don't know if it's just triggered by speed or if it records.'

Steel nodded. It was worth checking out.

There was little more to be said and the meeting began to break up. A few people hung around to drink tea and exchange thoughts but most were eager to be off home. Steel caught up with Dr Pauley just before he reached the door.

'Mind if I have a word?' he said.

'About the camera? I don't know anything more about it, I'm afraid.'

'No. I want to talk about the Winslow Trust.'

'I'm sorry. That's all confidential. There's not much I can say.'

'No, I understand that. Look, how would it be if I ask you some questions and you respond to any that you feel you can? Three people are dead, and there's a young girl left who could do with some answers.'

Pauley smiled at him. 'I don't respond to emotional blackmail, Inspector.'

'And I don't expect you to.'

He waited while Pauley considered the options. 'All right,' he agreed, 'you can ask.'

Steel led the doctor through into the vicar's office and closed the door. 'As I said, I spoke to Sarah today. She described a life of being constantly on the move until her mother met Victor Griffin. New jobs, new homes. The impression I got is that Lisanne moved very easily from one job to another, one flat to another. I know the Trust asked you to employ her and I wondered if they had, shall we say, supported this constant travelling, constant change of jobs?'

Pauley scrutinized Steel carefully. 'You have to understand,' he said, 'that my only contact with the Trust is through my wife; her only contact is through the community she has been part of since childhood. We needed a receptionist, Rachel mentioned it to someone and the next thing I know, we're being offered someone to fill the job. Understand, she was interviewed and found suitable. We didn't just take her because the Trust asked.'

'Had you done this before?'

Pauley hesitated. 'A few years ago we were asked to look after a young woman for a few days, just until somewhere else could be found. She arrived one night, very late, and stayed three days. I think she was seventeen. I know she was very frightened. I didn't know where she came from or where she went to. We gave her a bed, fed her and listened when she wanted to talk, and my wife re-dressed the burns on her arms three or four times a day. That's all I know.'

'Who runs the Trust?'

'Ah, now that's a matter of public record. They even have a website. They run retreats and a counselling service for kids coming out of care and offenders leaving prison. They offer practical support and help in finding jobs and accommodation. I'm sure you're aware of the failings in the so-called care system; they are like a great many charities up and down the country who take up the slack in this age of the so-called "big society". I imagine there are others who, like the Trust, provide an escape route for the desperate, but I don't know.'

'And Lisanne Griffin?'

'Was pleasant, efficient and friendly. She was discreet and the patients liked her. We didn't see her much outside of work time but in a small community like this everyone tends to turn up at the summer fête and the school fund-raisers, that kind of thing. I didn't really know her husband other than to pass the time of day with. I gave the children their immunizations and prescribed antibiotics when Sarah got a bad chest infection last winter. Beyond that – I'm sorry, Inspector. We were happy with Lisanne and we thought she was happy in her job. The kids were well cared for and she and Vic seemed a good partnership. I don't know what else I can say.'

Steel nodded. 'Can you give me the address for the Trust?'

'Off hand, no. But if you Google it you'll find it.'

Pauley turned to the door, ready to leave. 'I hope you solve this quickly, Inspector. This is a resilient community, but you can imagine how shaken everyone is. We've always been a bit self congratulatory about the low crime rate and how safe we all are. This is seismic.'

'You off then, boss?' Sophie Willis grinned at him.

'I thought I'd go and take another look at the house,' he said.

'Any particular reason?'

He shook his head. 'Just want to have a think.'

'You want me to come?'

'No, you get off home. I'll see you tomorrow.'

He walked with her out to her car. 'Pauley tell you anything?' she asked.

'Only that the community is shocked. No, that's not fair; he told me a bit about the Winslow Trust and I think it's a lead worth pursuing, though the chances are they just acted like the charity everyone tells me they are, and won't be able to add much.'

'So, what's bothering you?'

'The fact that Thea Baldwin knew Victor Griffin way back when.'

'Actually, she'd have been Lisanne Kemp then,' Willis reminded him.

'She would, wouldn't she?'

'Not that it's significant, I suppose.'

'Probably not, but first thing tomorrow see what you can track down about her family from the old case files.'

Willis shook her head. 'First thing we did today, trying to find next of kin, remember? Maternal grandparents are both dead; there was possibly an aunt but no one had anything to do with her back then, no address in the files.'

'But now you aren't looking for next of kin. Now you're looking for connections.'

'To what?'

He shrugged. 'That, I don't know. Not yet.'

'OK, so first thing tomorrow Alec, Naomi and I will start looking for new connections to . . . whatever.'

'Night, Sophie.' Steel smiled at her.

She returned the smile. 'Night, boss. If you get an inkle as to what we're looking for, be sure to let me know, won't you?'

Steel walked slowly down the road to the Griffin house. It was only a few hundred yards from their centre of activity at the church and the street was already quiet and empty now his colleagues had departed and most of the media had also given up for the night.

Earlier that day the mix of TV vans and reporters hauling equipment after them had virtually blocked the street but in the usual nature of such things, they'd had a day of looking at a couple of police officers standing beside a plastic barrier of police tape and slowly their number had diminished. The shortage of accommodation in Ferrymouth had added to the attrition rate, as had the damp and bitter cold blowing in off the estuary. Now, at seven thirty, those reporters who had managed to find places to stay had returned to them, while others had retreated to nearby pubs and eateries and still others had returned inland to find the nearest chain hotel.

Two police officers sat in a car outside the crime scene. Steel had made sure they'd been fed and watered earlier and, glancing at his watch, realized that they only had about an hour of their shift to go.

One of them got out of the car as Steel drew level. He was clutching a newspaper and Steel glanced at the headline. 'Three Dead in Ferrymouth Shooting'.

'All quiet?' he asked.

'A couple of dog walkers, but I think everyone's shut themselves up for the night. You going in, sir?'

Steel nodded. He indicated the paper. 'Mind if I take a look?'

'Be my guest.'

Steel read the paragraph below the headline and then turned, as instructed, to page three. Both he and Willis had made statements to camera earlier in the day and Steel had repeated his media appeal for family of Lisanne or Victor Griffin to get in touch. The article made much of this.

> Police have taken the unusual step of releasing the names
> of the victims before family have been contacted. It is known
> that Lisanne Griffin lost touch with her immediate family
> and her daughter, Sarah, is now alone [. . .]

He handed the paper back. He knew he'd take some flack for revealing the victims' names, but local knowledge would have put them out there soon enough; Steel was just riding the wave. He wondered what it would wash up.

He made his way into the crime scene, stood in the hallway and listened to the sounds the house made as it settled for the night. He studied the assortment of locks and bolts that embellished the heavy front door. They had all been fastened when the police arrived, summoned by neighbours who had heard the shots. The first officers had come round the back, directed by those same neighbours, who said the back door was open. The killer had left that way, out through the garden and down the little path that led back to the road in one direction and into the fields in the other.

Had the killer come in that way too? Would you let someone in through the front door and then refasten all the locks and bolts, knowing that you'd have to unfasten them all in order to let them out again?

He went through into the kitchen, wishing he'd thought to ask Sarah which door the family most used. It was easy to get from the main road round the back of the house, or if they'd been across the fields on one of the public footpaths Steel had noticed earlier. Beside the back door was a shoe rack. Four pairs of wellingtons and a couple of pairs of trainers. Male slippers. There was an old-fashioned shoe scraper outside that looked as though it had been well used.

Bolts top and bottom, a deadlock, with the key left in place . . . Would a late-night visitor really come round the back? Perhaps, Steel thought, but they'd have to know the family, the house, the layout, perhaps. Sarah's room was at the front of the house and her parents' room and Jack's both at the back. Sarah might not have heard someone knocking at the door in the middle of the night but her parents would.

And they had gone down and let the killer in.

Why?

Steel left the back door and went upstairs. He stood in Lisanne and Victor Griffin's room and looked around once more. Like the rest of the house it was comfortable but still felt like a work in progress. He could almost hear Lisanne Griffin saying of the heavy wooden bed and the bright red rug, and maybe the floral quilt cover, 'These are what I want', and of the rather bland, flat pack wardrobe and chest of drawers, 'They'll do for now.'

He crossed to the window and looked down. He couldn't see the back doorstep, but once he cracked the window open just a little he realized he'd have a good view of anyone standing by the back door.

'So,' Steel said. 'He knocked, one of them looked down to see who it was, then went down to open the door. Wouldn't it be more normal just to call down to find out who it was first? Would you not tell them to go away and come back in the morning? Or did you not want the neighbours to hear?' Which they would, presumably, if you called to someone out of the window.

It came back to Willis's point that you'd only open the door at night to a select few people. A policeman, maybe. But how would you know it was a policeman? So, someone in uniform.

And how did that fit in with the men seen hanging around, the ones who had argued with Lisanne Griffin? Was this someone different? Or was it one of the men, but wearing a uniform and hiding his face by wearing a helmet?

Steel sighed and closed the window, suddenly aware that he was bone weary and needed to follow his own advice and get some rest.

Fact, he thought, as he went back down the stairs. Or at least probably fact: the killer came in through the back door. Fact: they didn't seem to have hesitated to let him in.

Fact: Sarah Griffin thought he sounded like her father.

Why?

Probably because of what he had said about keeping children from their father.

Would that be enough to convince her? Would she remember the sound of his voice, even after six years? Add to that the fact that she'd glimpsed him when he passed down the corridor and into her brother's room. So it made sense that he bore at least a passing resemblance to Terry Baldwin, if only in height and build. Enough that a child who had not seen her father for six years might be mistaken.

Maybe, Steel thought, you had to add to the mix the fact that Terry Baldwin had been the bogeyman in Sarah's life. The thing to be afraid of. What then was more natural than that she would superimpose one fear upon another?

Fact, anyway: Terry Baldwin was still locked up at Her Majesty's pleasure, so barring a massive conspiracy of governor and staff, it was safe to assume he had not been there when his ex wife, her husband and their baby son had been killed.

Steel left, pausing for a word with the new crew sitting outside in their car. He checked they had all they required and wished them good night. As he walked back to collect his own vehicle his mind wandered back to the visit he and Naomi had made that morning to Terry Baldwin.

'Why the hell should I care what happened to that bitch?' Baldwin had said. 'And the kid wasn't even mine.'

'Sarah is yours.'

'And?'

'So you might care.'

'He won't,' Naomi had said with a cold certainty that had surprised Steel. 'You don't, do you Terry? I don't think you're capable.'

He remembered how Terry Baldwin had laughed then, as though Naomi had told some really amusing story. Naomi had said nothing. Steel sat still, waiting for events to unfold.

'Why the fuck should I?' Terry Baldwin had said when he'd finally stopped laughing.

'True,' Naomi had said quietly. 'Any idiot can make a kid. It takes effort to be a father. Capacity to care. I never noticed that you had any of that, Terry.'

Terry had laughed again. 'You should get a job writing those stupid verses you get in greetings cards,' he'd said. 'Be about your intellectual level that would.'

Steel unlocked his car door and started the engine. He'd phone the hospital and check up on Sarah when he reached home, and then grab a bite to eat and get some shut eye and hope that by morning he might have something more of an idea about what Willis and Naomi and Alec should be looking for in the old files. And about what bothered him so much in Lisanne knowing Vic Griffin so many years before. And about that feeling he was certain Naomi shared, that Terry Baldwin had known him too.

TWENTY-ONE

Driving south, Gregory was exultant. He'd spent too long on the sidelines; too long out of action. He begrudged Nathan none of it, not his time, his energy or his care, but the restlessness had been growing. Gregory needed to be doing, not thinking about doing.

The first signs of spring had been a long way off in Scotland, but as he moved further south the blackthorn spread white stars on black hedgerows and the landscape flattened out. He took the coast road, rejoicing in his glimpses of the sea, and he thought about his boat, neglected for a lengthy winter spell, and it was as though Gregory could feel himself expanding again, filling up with spring and light and ocean and the readiness for action.

He did not for one moment speculate that Alec and Naomi would resent his presence. Might not need or welcome him. He hadn't called ahead to let them know he was on the way and, even if he had, even if Naomi had told him to turn back, Gregory would have ignored her. The fact was Gregory had decided to help, determined to become involved, and even if they had some reticence about that to begin with, he would have assumed he could win them round.

He paused at mid morning and called Nathan, checking that his friend was settled and everything was in order.

'Computer set up arrives this afternoon,' Nathan said. 'It's not quite what we're used to, but it'll do. Jackie is organizing the obfuscation software and she's brought a couple of associates on board that I've worked with before. It's starting to feel like old times.'

'You mean those old times when people took pot shots at us?' Gregory grinned.

'No. I'd as soon avoid that part. But you know what we talked about? Well, I've run a bit of that past Jackie. She's in favour. I think we might be able to start our own game.'

'You keep thinking on it,' Gregory told him. 'I'll be in touch tonight.'

He drove on. The sun came out and a brief blue sky brightened the afternoon. He planned to find a place to stay overnight and arrive in Ferrymouth the following morning, take a good look around and familiarize himself with the lay of the land before going to find Alec and Naomi.

He found a cliff top hotel just outside of Whitby and stayed the night, asking for a room with a sea view. He spent the early evening walking, the coastal path stretching the kinks out of his legs and back; he was uncomfortably aware that his body ached more readily these days than it had done once upon a time. That driving for long periods inflamed his right knee.

He ate in the almost empty dining room, reading a book on local shipping disasters that he'd found on a shelf in his room.

'I'll be leaving early,' he told reception. 'Will there be anyone on the desk before seven?'

Finding it was unlikely, he settled his bill, using a card in the name of Anthony Blake. Gregory slept well that night and by six in the morning was on the road again.

TWENTY-TWO

Sarah was dreaming. She ran across the field towards the barn, Jack's little body heavy in her arms. She tried to hold Jack tight but her right arm wouldn't grip and as the rain beat down on both of them, drenching her to the skin and stinging her face, she was afraid that Jack would just die of cold if she didn't find shelter soon. And each step she took towards the barn seemed more slippery than the last. Her feet were frozen and the wet earth sucked at her toes. When she looked up and peered through the torrential rain, the barn seemed as far off as it had ever been.

Desperately, Sarah struggled forward, but her little brother was a dead weight dragging her down and her feet could find no purchase in the mud. No matter how hard she fought, she could not seem to move forward.

In her dream, Sarah began to cry, desperately, anguished, her tears streaming down her face and on to Jack's tiny head.

Sarah woke, still sobbing. A soft voice spoke to her and someone held her hand and for a precious moment Sarah thought her mother was there. Then she opened her eyes and saw Trudi, one of the nurses who'd been looking after her, and the green walls and funny ceiling tiles, and she remembered where she was and that it couldn't be her mum who was talking to her.

'She's never coming back, is she?'

Trudi bent close, trying to catch the words. 'Oh Sarah, I am so, so sorry.'

Trudi held her hand and stroked her hair and Sarah wanted

her to keep on doing that but at the same time she wanted to pull away, to yell at Trudi that she wasn't her mum, that she wasn't Vic or Jack or anyone Sarah cared about.

She wished Joey were there. But Joey had to go. He wasn't allowed to stay. Sarah turned her face away from Trudi and buried it in the pillow and she wept until exhaustion won and she fell asleep again.

Sarah dreamed of rain.

TWENTY-THREE

Steel apologized for disturbing Maggie at work.

'It's OK,' she said. 'My boss knows what's going on. Did something urgent come up?'

She led Steel through to her office and offered him a seat, coffee. He sat down but declined the offer of a drink. 'Not urgent, no. But I wanted a word with you alone and that seems not to be something you manage very much.'

She laughed. 'Not unless I make a point of going out, no. Tel's a bit of a home bod and when he does need to go somewhere, yours truly is usually the taxi service. You try catching a bus from Ferrymouth after six o clock at night and you're stuffed.'

'I've seen you all at the bike project,' Steel said.

Maggie nodded. 'That's fine. I like to watch and I've got friendly with a few of the other parents who are in the same boat. Occasionally we give each other's kids lifts but we're coming from every which way so it's not the easiest thing to arrange. Tel and Joey love it, though, and the instructors are great.'

'I helped get it started,' Steel said. 'It's good to see how well it's turned out.'

'So why speak to me alone? Is something wrong?'

Steel shook his head, eager to ease the anxious look in Maggie's eyes. 'No, it's just there are some questions I'd like to ask and I don't want to make Joey feel more alienated or embarrassed than he already does.'

'Poor Joey,' Maggie said.

'He's lucky to have you and Tel.'

Maggie shrugged. 'To be honest, when Tel first made friends with him I was really against it. I knew about his father's reputation. In fact, I'd seen him in action.'

'Oh?'

'Tel's dad was home and we'd gone out for an hour to meet some friends in the Dog and Gun. Hughes showed up, very drunk, shouting and swearing about someone owing him money. Douggie removed him and it was all over very quickly, but I have to be honest. The man scared me. There was no sense of . . . control, I suppose. He simply didn't care who saw or what they thought of him or what the consequences might be.'

'I think he's not a man for whom consequence has been something worth considering,' Steel said. 'Few people have ever stood up to him and those that can't are not worth considering. Do you know Joey's mother?'

'Know her? No. I've met her maybe a half dozen times in the past three years or so. Tel and Joey became friends in their first year at secondary. As I said, I wasn't happy about it, but I thought I'd give the kid the benefit of the doubt as Tel was so obviously smitten . . . and I thought I'd also better make the effort with the parents. Well, Joey's mother, anyway. Everyone I talked to said she was so much in Hughes' shadow as to be practically invisible and I thought, I don't know, maybe I could be—' she laughed – 'I thought maybe I could help, I suppose.'

Steel nodded, understanding the impulse. She called Joey's dad 'Hughes', he noted, never using his first name. He figured it to be a measure of Maggie's contempt for the man.

'Parents' evening happened half way through the first term and I knew Joey's mum didn't drive, and the bus being non-existent I thought she might like a lift. So, I went round there, I knocked on the door and introduced myself.'

'Was her husband there?'

'No, but she looked as though she expected him to materialize out of nowhere any second. Anyway, she agreed to let me give her a lift. You know, I kept expecting to get a phone call or a message via Joey saying she'd changed her mind, but it didn't come. I got to her house and she was standing in the street. She practically fell into the car and I could see she was shaking, watching out of the window until we turned the corner like she was scared someone would see her and report back.'

Maggie paused, frowning. 'You know – well, my husband will tell you – I've never been one for standing in anyone's shadow, always done my own thing. I suppose I find it hard to understand how people get into that position.'

'You and Tel's father are . . .?'

Maggie smiled at him. 'Mal works away. When he's home we get on fine. We started out as friends and about five years into our marriage realized we'd drifted back to being friends. I suppose if one or other of us met someone else, it would be different. But we haven't, yet, and we're comfortable. Mal comes home every six weeks, stays home for two. I adapt my routine a bit and he spends a lot of time with Tel while he's home. But I've got no illusions; we stay married because there's no reason not to. No conflict, no issues. When Tel's a bit older I think we may well sell the house, split the proceeds and go our separate ways.'

'Sounds very civilized.'

Maggie shrugged. 'Not really. Probably just lazy, I think.'

'You were telling me about the parents' evening.'

'Yes, well, as you can imagine, I did all the talking. I tried asking her about Joey and how she thought he was settling at the new school. I said how pleased I was that Tel had found a really good friend – and she looked at me then like I was lying to her. But she hardly said a word all the way there. When we got to the school she stuck to me like glue, like she was terrified I'd suddenly disappear and she'd be stranded. And she was so worried about how long we'd be away.'

'Did her husband know she'd gone out with you?'

'Oh, I shouldn't think so. Not at the time anyway. I imagine he got to know. I can't see Marilyn ever managing to lie to him, not if he asked her a direct question.'

'And how did she interact with the staff?'

Maggie sighed. 'She didn't, not really. It was horrible. She was so much out of her depth she didn't know what to ask or who his teachers were or what she should say. I felt so guilty in the end, putting her through it. And it occurred to me after that she must really love her son in her own way. To risk the displeasure of that brute of a husband and to put herself through what must have felt like an evening of torture.'

Someone knocked on Maggie's door and reminded her she and her boss were leaving for a meeting in ten minutes.

'I won't keep you much longer,' Steel told her. 'After that?'

'I saw her occasionally, ran into her in town, that sort of thing. Joey became something of a fixture and then Sarah and Evie – though I've known Evie and her family since Tel started at nursery.'

'And they all got along. No jealousy?'

'Surprisingly little. Sarah and Evie became friends just after Sarah's family moved in. Tel and Evie were often part of the same social group – like I say, we've known them years. Joey kind of got absorbed into the crowd and when he and Sarah became an item, as they say, it didn't make a lot of difference. The four of them were very close. I suspect Evie has her eye on Tel, but so far he's not taking the bait.' She smiled a little sadly. 'Sarah is a lovely girl. I liked her mother very much and from what I saw of Vic he seemed pleasant too. Sarah certainly thought a lot of him.'

'One more question. Maybe two. How . . . close were Sarah and Joey? Their relationship—'

'You mean were they having sex?'

Steel nodded.

'Um, no. I don't think they'd got there yet. Joey is a bit of a slow burner, I think, and Sarah was definitely not ready. I know kids that age often boast about what they have and haven't done – often the latter, even when they say otherwise – but I don't think they'd got further than kissing. Lisanne was very worried when they got together. It was only because I like Joey so much that she sort of came round to the idea. But I can understand why she was so worried.'

She looked thoughtfully at Steel. 'Why all the questions? You can't think Joey had anything to do with this, and it's a bit far out even for Hughes. He strikes me as strictly a fists and bottles man.'

'No, I have no suspicions about Joey. His father – well, it seems unlikely, but we will be checking his whereabouts. It seems he does manage to hold down a job, though, and that he was definitely at work. My concerns are twofold. I bent the rules taking Tel and Joey to the hospital. I know you'd given permission for

Tel to go with me, but Joey . . . well. And we had a conversation on the way back that has me worried. Not about what Joey might do but about what might be done to him. I would like to help.'

Maggie snorted. 'That would be a first.'

'Apparently so.'

'And your final question?'

'I might well be needing an appropriate adult for Sarah. We'll have to do a formal statement at some point soon and there'll be a lot of official stuff going on. We can't track down any family, so I thought—'

'Be glad to. Just let me know what and when.'

Another knock at the door and Maggie rose. Steel followed her lead. 'Sorry,' she said. 'Got to go.'

Steel nodded. 'Thank you for your help,' he said. And your husband is a fool, he thought.

TWENTY-FOUR

He liked Ferrymouth as soon as he saw it. Gregory had a fondness for English market towns and this one, being on the estuary, carried through its streets that salt sea tang to which he was particularly partial.

Patrick had provided him with the name of the pub in which Naomi and Alec were staying, but he had not yet made contact with them, preferring first to check out the lay of the land.

He had lunch in a small café just off the market square. Fellow diners turned out to be journalists – some print, a few television – and Gregory realized he was assumed by the café owner to be one of the same. He settled down to listen, sipping his tea and eating his sandwiches while occupying himself with his phone.

From the conversation he discovered that an Inspector Steel was heading the investigation. That the Griffins were outsiders – arrived only three years before. The journalists had cottoned on to there being some mystery about where they had come from, and there was considerable frustration at the lack of developments.

'I've been told to head back tonight if nothing breaks.'

'Me, I'm apparently here for the long haul. My editor reckons it'll be big, when we finally get a handle on it.'

Gregory listened to their speculation. Talk of gang connections, violent husbands, links to a shooting at a farm two years before. He soon realized that they knew nothing.

Having finished his sandwiches, Gregory wandered round the small town on foot; one main road in, a good selection of shops. A primary school, library, town hall that, according to the notices on the board outside, doubled as a community theatre and concert space as well as accommodating play groups and pensioner's drop-in sessions. There also seemed to be a couple of churches – one obviously medieval – and a couple of chapels, one of which was now an antiques shop. He logged that fact for later, knowing that Naomi loved to collect small items of silver. It had occurred to him, suddenly, that she might not be best pleased about him turning up out of the blue. Gregory was pretty certain that Naomi liked him but he was also pretty certain that she didn't always approve of him. He figured some nice bit of silver would be an apt peace offering should she get on her high horse about the more unsuitable aspects of Gregory's life.

His slow perambulations took him down to the street where the shootings had taken place. He paused, fifty yards back from the crime scene tape. It was easy to see which house the Griffins had lived in from the police car parked outside. More officers going in and out of the Victorian church and the school building behind told him this was the centre of their operations. The Dog and Gun was a little way back in the direction from which he had come, but tucked off the main road and backing on to a narrow road and then open country.

Turning down the street at the back of the Dog, Gregory headed out of town. A signpost indicated a public footpath and he followed the directions over the stile, walking down towards the river. The scent of salt and mud was strong and, to Gregory at any rate, enticing and he stood for a while watching the gulls wheel and squawk and the boats floating at half tide. Facing back towards the town, he could make out the end of the row of red brick houses where the shooting had taken place and realized that the path forked, one fork leading to the stile he had crossed, the second following the line of the river back across the main road and, from the look of it, behind the houses.

So which way would I have gone in? he wondered. Where would I leave my car? He began to walk back, taking the second fork and crossing a very muddy field. The river arced around, here and there lying between shallow beaches and then disappearing between higher banks. He followed it over a second stile and across the road bridge, down the bank on the other side. He was at the other end of the police cordon now, with a good view of the house and the police car and the second line of tape. The path now split again, one branch continuing to follow the river and the second breaking off towards the rear of the red brick row. Passing by the end of this branch, Gregory saw another cordon and a bored looking officer standing outside a back gate. He followed the river path for a while, finding that after a few hundred yards it opened out into a picnic area complete with tables and benches and play equipment and a gravelled stand, room enough for three or four cars.

There was no police presence here.

Gregory stood and looked. A narrow road snaked off and joined a little road that he could see then rejoined the main carriageway, maybe a mile away. The flat land allowed him a clear view of cars moving in the distance.

'So, you parked up here,' he said. 'Went in on foot, round to the back of the house, and then got out the same way.' That, he thought, seemed about right.

Satisfied, Gregory retraced his steps back into Ferrymouth and went in search of a suitable gift for Naomi.

TWENTY-FIVE

'We had a phone call,' Sophie Willis said. 'Someone who claims to recognize Victor Griffin. Says his name was neither Victor nor Griffin when he knew him. Of course he prefers to remain anonymous.'

'Of course he does. Any idea where he made the call from? And who does he claim our Victor Griffin was?'

'He gave the name Anthony Bertram. We're chasing it up. The call came in from the Greater London area, but that's all we've got. There was another of interest, though. From someone claiming to be an old neighbour of Sarah and Thea. Left a call back number. You want to take that?'

'And what did they want?'

'Just to offer condolences, they said. That they had been fond of Thea and the little girl and wondered if there was anything they could do.'

'Another London number?'

'No,' Willis told him. 'The woman gave her name as Josette Harris, says she lived a few doors down and their kids used to play together. She now lives in Nottingham. Thought it might be worth you chasing up.'

Steel took the number and thanked Sophie. 'Anything else I should know about?'

'Not right now. I'll run the name Anthony Bertram past the Friedmans, see if it means anything. It's already being put through the system; we'll see if we get any hits.'

'Bet you a fiver we don't,' Steel said.

'You think it's just mischief making?'

'No, I think if Victor Griffin did have more than one identity then the odds are that Anthony Bertram is no more likely to be known to us than Victor Griffin was. If he's in our system it will be as someone else entirely.'

'Probably. But it's another possible twist to the tale.'

Steel had been on his way to visit Sarah when Willis's call had caught him on his way across the car park. He could glimpse the media crowd still outside the front entrance of the hospital. They had taken up residence on the circular green at the centre of the drop-off point and Steel could imagine the sense of running the gauntlet for anyone bringing visitors or attending Outpatients.

He slipped in through the back way as usual and made his way up to Sarah's room.

She was sitting in a chair by the window and playing a rather desultory game of cards with Stacy. He could tell that neither of them were really feeling distracted by the play. Steel sat down beside them.

'I'm going to get Joey and Tel over later,' he told her, and saw her eyes light at the prospect. 'Maggie's promised to drive them across after school.'

'Thank you,' Sarah said. 'I feel like I'm trapped in here, you know. I want to go home, but it's like I don't know where that is any more.'

She bit her lip and blinked back tears.

'Sarah, did you know a woman called Josette Harris?'

Sarah frowned and then nodded. 'Yeah, I remember her. She had two kids. I was friends with Tina at school. The other one was little. I can't remember his name.'

'She phoned the inquiry,' Steel said. 'She'd seen what happened on the news and wanted to call.'

Sarah shrugged. 'It was a long time ago,' she said. 'She was just a neighbour, really. It's nice of her though.'

'And did you ever meet your dad's sister, Madeleine?'

Sarah laid a card down on the table and shook her head. 'She got married. Dad said she'd betrayed the family. I think Mum met her, but she didn't live near us and we never saw her. Why?'

'Her name came up. Naomi, the police officer who helped you and your mum leave, she's helping us out with the inquiry. She mentioned her to us.'

'Mum liked her,' Sarah said. 'She was nice, but I worried about it all, you know. Mum was scared and Naomi kept telling her that it would be all right. That she'd make sure we were protected.'

'I know she did her best to make that happen,' Steel said.

'But it didn't work. Not in the end, did it? We just wanted to be safe. But nowhere was safe, not even here.'

'We will find out who did this,' Steel told her.

'So what? It won't make it better, will it?' She looked up from the card game and fixed him with such a desperate stare that Steel's heart sank. 'It won't make it right, will it?'

'No. I can't make it right,' he agreed. 'I can't do that.'

He sat and watched Sarah and Stacy play for a little longer, not sure how he should frame the next question. In the end he just asked. 'Sarah, does the name Anthony Bertram mean anything to you?'

A shake of the head followed by a frown. 'I don't think so. Why?'

'Just another name that came up. Did Vic have a middle name?'

'I don't think so. Why?'

'Because we're still trying to find out if he had any family. Victor Griffin is an unusual name, but if he had a middle name as well that might help us narrow things down even further.'

'He lived near Taunton,' Sarah said. 'I remembered that last night. When he and Mum met when she was at the festival, he lived near Taunton. He took us to the beach one day. It was a long beach and it was really windy and some people were riding on land yachts. I really, really wanted to have a go but they said I was too little. He knew one of them. I think he said it was a cousin or something. But I don't really know. Does that help?'

'It might,' he told her. 'Any little detail might. You don't remember the name of the place?'

Sarah shook her head. 'No. Just a lot of wind and sand and that. Mum laughed a lot that day. Vic could be really funny.'

She laid the cards down on the table, all pretence at playing ended. 'I think I'd like to sleep for a bit now,' she said.

Stacy helped her back to bed. Steel could see that she was still in a lot of discomfort. The rib would be very painful for a while, the doctors had told him. A section had been shattered and they'd removed all the fragments they could find, tidied it up. Steel, who'd once cracked two ribs and remembered how bloody painful that had been and how long it had taken before it ceased to hurt him when he laughed or coughed or moved suddenly, could only sympathize. 'I'll see you later,' he said. 'When Maggie gets here with Joey and Tel.'

She managed a small smile but Steel was struck by the sudden descent back into exhaustion and despair. Should he not have come? He had to ask questions. How could he avoid hurting her further?

There was no way he could.

Stacy came out into the corridor and he walked with her to the coffee machine. She bought two hot chocolates. 'You got any change?' she asked. 'I'm running out.'

He felt in his pocket and gave her what he had left. 'Keep a tally of anything you spend,' he said. 'I'll make sure you get reimbursed.'

She shrugged. 'Is it bad that I just want to go home now?'

'No. It's normal. Understandable. I'll see to it you get relieved by lunchtime. You need to take some time out.'

'No, it's all right.'

'Stacy, it's not all right. You need a break.' He sighed. 'OK, look, we'll compromise. You leave when Maggie and I bring the boys in tonight. I'll get someone to cover for you this evening and you can come back bright and early tomorrow.'

She nodded reluctantly, but he could see she was relieved.

He watched her as she carried the two cups of chocolate back to Sarah's room and then turned and walked back along the corridor, down the back stairs and into the car park. A man stood beside his car, waiting for him. At first Steel assumed he must be a journalist and his heart sank. He'd hoped to keep his visits here quiet. The next moment his heart was beating hard as, in sudden panic, he realized that the man was holding a gun.

TWENTY-SIX

Trinity Matthews had lived in the same street all her life. Her family had moved in when her mother was a little girl, and when Trinity had married she and her new husband had come to live with her then widowed grandmother.

She'd seen people come and go, seen the Baldwins take over from the Friths in her little neighbourhood, and she had no doubt she would see the Baldwins give way to someone else before she finally went to her rest. Trinity Matthews had lived too long and too well to be easily intimidated. Her mother was a God-fearing woman, as *her* mother had been before that, and Trinity was not of a mind to let the side down. Over time, she had become 'auntie' to half the street – much as previous generations of the Matthews women had done – and for the most part the dramas of life had passed her by, deferring to that status.

But she was, it had to be said, made a little uneasy by the man now sitting in her tiny living room.

'It must be a shock, Aunt Trinny,' Roddy Baldwin said. 'Hearing about our Thea like that. Seeing on the news about them dying.'

'Being *killed*, you mean. At least the little girl is going to be all right.'

'She's not so little any more, she must be a teenager by now. Thirteen, fourteen?'

She'd be fourteen, Trinny thought, but she held her peace. 'And what brings such an important man as yourself to my door today?'

'Important, am I? Some days, Trinny, I'm not so sure about that. My father, now, people listened up when he spoke. They listened up and they listened hard and they did what he told them.'

'And people don't take notice of you? Now you must find that hard.'

'Indeed I do. Trinny, why didn't you tell me you'd been in touch with our Thea?'

'Because I haven't been. She sent me a card for my birthday last year. That was all. I was very surprised she even remembered me.'

'But you were pleased.'

'Of course I was pleased. I was pleased when she and that little girl ran away. Pleased when that brother of yours was put inside, even if it wasn't for what he did to them. He deserved to be put inside for that.'

Roddy Baldwin nodded wisely. 'He wasn't a good husband to her,' he agreed. 'Violence has its place, I always say, but that should not be in the home.'

'I don't believe it has a place anywhere,' Trinny told him, and he nodded again. 'I can understand how a woman like you might think that,' he said.

She hoped he couldn't sense how much she was shaking inside.

'Do you still have the card?'

Trinny got up and removed the card from the sideboard drawer. Reluctantly, she handed it to him. Roddy studied it for a time. 'Roses,' he said. 'Very pretty. Did you keep the envelope?'

'And why would I do that?'

'And this is the only thing she ever sent you?'

'The only thing, yes. Look, I made no secret of this. I was

pleased. I told my friends, I told the ladies at the church. It wasn't a secret thing.'

Roddy handed the card back. 'Trinny,' he said. 'My father always said you were a good woman. A respectable woman.'

'One of the few women who'd said no to him,' Trinny told him boldly.

Roddy laughed. 'Yes, he told me that too. Trinny, I want you to get in touch with Sarah for me. Tell her that we are still her family and we're sorry for what happened to her and her mother.'

'And why don't you do that for yourself?'

Roddy laughed. 'Because the police don't view this family as a good influence, shall we say. I want you to convince her that – well, that we care.'

'And do you? Did you care when that brother of yours was beating seven shades out of her and Thea? I didn't see any sign of you caring then.'

'If I'd been here, I'd have done something. I promise you that. If our dad had known—'

'He knew. It was happening right under his nose.'

'He was a sick man. Sicker than anyone round here realized. We didn't want to make it public knowledge in case . . . you know, other people took advantage.'

Trinny narrowed her eyes and studied the man closely, like she'd have studied some strange insect that had landed on her prize roses. 'And what do you really want from her?' she asked, horrified at her own boldness but refusing to be intimidated. Roddy's father hadn't got the better of her, and she was damn sure the son wasn't about to.

Roddy laughed. 'Trinity, you are priceless,' he said. He hauled himself from the depths of Trinity's armchair. He was a tall man, looming over her as he came close. 'Just call the hospital,' he said. 'Get them to pass a message on. Ask that she calls you back. Tell her that her family is waiting for her. Waiting to make amends.'

Trinny watched as he let himself out and then sank down into the chair he had just vacated. Despite her bravado, her legs shook and her heart beat at twice its normal rhythm. But Trinity Matthews was not so intimidated that she had stopped thinking. 'And what do you really want?' she muttered thoughtfully. 'What little game are you still playing after all this time?'

TWENTY-SEVEN

'You're going to take me inside and up to Sarah Baldwin's room.'

'No. No I'm not. Are you the one who killed her family?'

The man laughed and gestured Steel to start moving.

He stood his ground. 'We're not going anywhere.'

'I could shoot you and just find her myself.'

'You could, but if you had any idea of where she was then you'd not have waited for me.'

'I know where she is. I also know there are two security doors and that each one needs a key code. Now you can either give me the codes or you can escort me inside. Up to you.'

'And I'm not doing either.'

'Fine, so I kill you and wait for a member of staff to come out. A nice little nurse, maybe. You think a nice little nurse would do as she's told?'

'So why not take that as your first option?'

Steel scrutinized the gunman carefully. He might sound cocky and self assured but Steel could detect a tiny tremor. An uncertainty that told him this was not the man's usual game. He was young, Steel thought. Early twenties, maybe, with sandy hair and a scattering of freckles and post-teenage spots.

'No,' he said. 'I don't think you shot Sarah's family. I think you're an also-ran that just got landed with the task of finishing the job. Am I right? Your friend the triple murderer flunked it. So, is he dead? Did he run? What happened to him? And where the hell did they find you? Scrape around the bottom of the barrel, did they?'

This is mad, Steel told himself. You don't provoke a man holding a gun. Not if you then want to walk away. But his major thought was to keep this man away from Sarah. His one other thought was to avoid getting shot – and he wasn't at all sure they were mutually applicable.

Across the car park a car door slammed and Steel could see a couple getting out and heading towards the hospital entrance. They were perhaps twenty yards away and for a second he considered calling out to them, trying to raise the alarm, but he abandoned the idea as soon as it occurred. What good would it do to involve others? He was aware that the gunman had seen them too. Abruptly, the man shifted his attention to the woman. The gun aimed in her direction now.

'Do we go inside, Inspector, or do I have to prove my intentions to you?'

'No.' Steel told him.

'So take me in, then.'

The firearm was shifted, pointing back at his chest. Steel turned, thinking fast. 'There are armed officers on Sarah's floor,' he said. 'You don't stand a chance of getting out of here, you know that?'

'Stop talking and move.'

Steel did as he was told, wishing he'd just been able to tell the truth. Yes, there were officers on Sarah's floor and one of them was armed, but they were right down at the far end of the corridor, at the back of the reception area watching for incursions via the main entrance. Stacy was the only one in Sarah's side room. But there were CCTV cameras inside, at the back entrance and on the stairs and at the junctions to the various corridors. There was the chance of someone picking up on what was going on.

If that didn't happen, then Steel was effectively on his own.

They made their way through the rear doors and into the utility area on the ground floor. There was no one around and the man behind him urged him on with a prod of the weapon into his back. Steel wondered what his chances would be if he turned on the man and tried to grab the gun. He thought about his conversation with Naomi about Terry Baldwin's arrest. He needed the equivalent of her wheelie bin. And he needed backup.

Slowly they started up the stairs. Two flights, two sets of security doors, then a long corridor and another key pad, Steel thought. But that was far too close to Sarah. He had no intention of letting this man get that far.

Each time they passed a camera, Steel looked up into the lens, tried to position his body so that anyone on the security team might understand that something was wrong, or even glimpse the gun at his back.

They passed through the first security door and mounted the next flight of steps. Steel knew that this was perhaps his one and only chance.

He opened the second security door and passed through. The man was close behind him. Steel swung around, slamming the door back against the threat. The gun fired, exploding deafeningly in the confined space. Steel staggered, aware he had been hit, pain blossoming in his arm. He thought about Sarah. She'd been shot and yet she'd managed to run on. Damn it, he wasn't about to be bested by a fourteen-year-old girl. The shooter was off balance now, caught between the door and the head of the stairs, and Steel seized the moment. He hurled himself forward, shoving at the gun with every ounce of strength and weight he had. His assailant fell; Steel somehow managed to grasp the handrail with his good hand, though his weight and momentum wrenched painfully at his shoulder and jerked pain through his entire body.

He collapsed on to the top step and watched as the gunman tumbled down the remaining stairs and lay still at the bottom.

Some portion of Steel's mind told him that the man was dead. That his neck, twisted so that the head lay at an impossible angle, looking back at Steel, was broken, but he didn't have the energy or the inclination to go and check. Instead, he groped in his pocket for his mobile phone and waited on the stairs for help to arrive.

TWENTY-EIGHT

B y the time Sophie Willis arrived the hospital was buzzing with rumour; Sophie could feel it seeping in through the car windows as she made her way down the drive. She drove past the lines of media gathered out front, trying not to look their way, and parked in the visitors' car park on the far side of the building. Getting out of the car she could see her colleagues in the other car park, and the crime scene tape separating Steel's vehicle and several spaces around it from the rest.

She crossed to speak to them, showing her ID to a constable she didn't know. A sergeant she did came to the taped barrier to meet her.

'Any CCTV?'

'Plenty. No one was actually monitoring that closely at the time, though. He walked your boss across this area and into the rear entrance with a gun at his back.'

'I imagine he's miffed,' Sophie commented.

'I imagine he is. You headed on in there?'

Sophie nodded.

'Well, there's nothing to tell him yet, but we've got our lot working with their security looking at the footage, so hopefully—'

'Was he alone?'

'So far as we can tell. Which strikes everyone as odd, though I suppose two people marching a police officer into a hospital at gunpoint might have attracted more notice. Maybe that's the reasoning?'

Sophie shrugged. 'Seems the media hordes are increasing in number,' she said, jerking her head towards the front entrance.

'It can only get worse,' her colleague said glumly. Sophie hid a smile. She made her way into the hospital via the side entrance, checking in with the officer on guard outside, and then through the Outpatients Department. There were, it seemed, police everywhere now. She had her ID checked three times before arriving at the ground floor office where Steel was getting patched up. His shirt and jacket had been cut away from his arm and replaced by dressings and tape. He looked *decidedly* miffed, Sophie thought, and a little sick.

'How you holding up?'

'I'm fine. The bullet went straight through my biceps, so no gym for a while.' He smiled. 'Could have been worse.'

'Could have been a lot worse. What the hell happened?'

'I don't know. He was there, waiting for me beside my car. I saw him, didn't think much of it, then saw the gun. He demanded I take him to Sarah. I tried to talk to him but it was obvious he wasn't going to back down. I thought we'd stand a better chance of being spotted by the security cameras inside the hospital and knew I'd have to find a way of dealing with him that, hopefully, didn't end up with me getting shot. It didn't quite work out that way, did it?'

He moved and winced.

'Have they given you painkillers?'

'Local anaesthetic for the stitches. The doctor's gone to sort me out a prescription.' He grimaced. 'I hope he gets a move on, I don't mind admitting the local's wearing off now and it bloody hurts.'

Sophie laughed and then apologized. 'I'm just relieved,' she said. 'When they said you'd been shot—'

Steel nodded. 'You been to see the body yet?'

'No. You want me to do that now?'

'Yes. See if they've managed to identify him. I'm going to wait for the doctor and then go up and see Sarah. Join me there, after. I'm going to need a lift home, I think.'

'You sure you should be talking to Sarah? She's going to be freaked out, seeing you like that.'

'She's going to be freaked out, as you put it, if I don't. She's probably heard all manner of stories by now. I want her to know it's been dealt with. She's going to be kept safe, no matter what.'

Willis nodded and took her leave. Steel watched her go and then slumped back in the chair and closed his eyes. There'd been a moment, just a split second really, when he had been certain of his own death. When he'd just known that this was it and the gun was going to fire and he was about to be hit.

Logic and reason told him that he couldn't possibly have been aware of that at the time. That he was superimposing narrative over memory. But he *knew* it was more than that. The world had decelerated, actions seemed many times slowed down; thoughts had elongated, blossomed, to fill the expanded gap.

The door opened and the doctor arrived with a prescription, a couple of pills, a bottle of water and a cheerful, 'This should do you for a while. Get your prescription filled at the pharmacy, then go home and get some rest.'

Steel thanked him and swallowed the tablets with a mouthful of water. It was very cold and he was suddenly aware that his throat felt parched and tight.

'Sit for a few minutes now,' the doctor advised. 'Wait until the pills kick in.' And Steel, both grateful and resentful, took his advice.

How the hell had Sarah Griffin managed? he wondered. Carrying her little brother and stumbling across that field in the pouring rain and with an injury far worse than his. He wasn't yet ready to make it down the corridor, never mind run across a ploughed field.

He closed his eyes again, fighting nausea this time, wanting more water to cool his throat but not sure his stomach could keep it down. His arm throbbed and the chill in the air had begun to trouble him. A nurse had given him a blanket and, a little sheepishly, he pulled it around his shoulders, over the torn shirt and remnants of the jacket they had cut away and the sling that held his arm tightly across his chest. Then, feeling rather sorry for himself and wearing the blanket like a yellow cloak, he got to his feet and began to make his way to Sarah's ward.

Sophie Willis crouched at the head of the stairs and peered down. The CSI team were getting ready to move the body, DI Martin supervising and, Sophie could see, generally getting in the way.

'Hey Joe,' she said. He looked up and smiled. 'Stay there, I'm coming up.'

Looking past him she could see the odd angle of the neck, the arm thrown out as though to halt the man's fall. The gun, fallen on to the bottom step.

'How's the boss man?'

Sophie got to her feet. 'Sore,' she said. She looked up at the bullet hole in the wall, close to the ceiling. 'That the one that got him?'

'So far as we know only one shot was fired, so yes, we can safely assume there are bits of DI Steel now permanently embedded in the hospital superstructure. You want a coffee? There's one of those dreaded machines down the hall.'

She nodded and followed him back through the glazed doors. She could imagine how Steel had rammed the door back against the gunman, then wrenched it open again and shoved him as hard and as fast as he could. She didn't know if she'd have had the nerve or the coordination. 'He was bloody lucky,' she said.

'He was.'

'Any identification yet?'

'No, the shooter had nothing in his pockets. We'll have to wait for fingerprints and hope he's in the system.'

'Which is likely, I'd guess.'

'I'm guessing so.'

They paused beside the vending machine and between them rustled up enough change for a couple of coffees. Sophie Willis had known Joe Martin far longer than she had known Steel and, despite his different approach and manner, she respected him pretty much equally. Unlike Steel, Martin actually liked dealing with the media, enjoyed the public appearances and what he had once called the 'performance aspect' of police work. At the time she had thought it an odd, uncomfortable phrase to apply to such a serious business and she knew it had earned him both censure and mockery from his colleagues – Steel included – but she had come to realize that actually, it could be a useful attitude.

It was certainly an attribute his colleagues exploited.

'You want to come and look at the CCTV footage? Some of it should have been collated by now.'

Sophie nodded. 'Then I've got to go up to Sarah's room. I told Steel I'd meet him up there and give him a lift home.'

'Where he needs to stay for the next day or two at least.'

'You know he won't.'

'I know it's unlikely. It might mar his superhero image.'

He led Sophie down the corridor and up a flight of stairs. This place is a maze, she thought.

Finally, he led her into a room filled with people, CCTV screens and a blur of assorted technology. She recognized and greeted a couple of her colleagues. Others, she guessed, were hospital staff or from other forces.

She watched as the technicians talked them through the montage of shots from various CCTV cameras. Camera two, in the car park, showed the first encounter, though Steel faced the gunman, who had his back to the camera so the weapon could not be seen. Camera four picked them up as they crossed the car park. Camera twelve in the stairwell, the first time the gun could be seen, Steel looking up into the camera, his face pale and mouth set in a straight line, hoping someone would take notice.

Camera thirteen as they turned on the first dog leg of the stairs and started up the next flight.

'Did no one notice anything?'

'Most of the attention was focused on the front entrance and the main reception areas,' someone told her. 'There are nearly forty cameras across the hospital campus and only three operators at any one time.'

Sophie turned her attention back to where camera fourteen picked up the final dramatic moments. Steel keying in the code, opening the door, then, as the gunman started through, his swift turn, slamming the door into the man's arm. The blast of the shot, Steel throwing his weight first back against the door, and then against the still armed man, catching him off balance and then hurtling him backwards. Sophie held her breath, watching as her boss all but followed his assailant's fall, making a grab for the handrail, then dropping down on to the top step, a look of utter relief on his face.

'I'd better get going,' she told Martin.

He nodded. 'Think you can find your way without a sat nav?'

'I'll manage. Catch you later.'

Sophie Willis slowly made her way back to the head of the stairs and from there found her way back up to Sarah's floor. What the hell was going on here? Sarah was a fourteen-year-old girl. She'd already had her family taken from her; what was all of this about? And would they try again?

TWENTY-NINE

Steel had spent some time with Sarah Griffin. The girl was utterly bewildered by what had happened. Shocked and scared all over again, she clung to Stacy's hand and Steel again wished he could find some family to comfort her, or at the very least bring her friends in again. He had forgotten that Maggie was to bring the boys to the hospital until a call came up to the ward from reception and he remembered that he had been supposed to meet them in the car park.

He made hurried arrangements for them to be escorted in and it was clear from the look on Maggie's face that their escort had filled her in on events on the way up.

She bundled Sarah into a warm embrace and reached out an arm to include Joey. Tel, on the other side of the bed, grabbed Sarah's hand. For a moment or two Steel watched the comfort and the crying and then gestured to Stacy that he wanted a word outside.

'I like the blanket,' she said. 'That your new superhero cloak, is it? Christ, boss, what the hell is going on here?'

'I don't know. My guess is that someone thinks she knows something or has seen something. Someone is determined to shut her up, but about what?'

'She and her mother ran away six years ago. Sure, Thea Baldwin knew what her husband was into, knew enough to get him put away, but this is all old news. I just don't see.'

Steel shrugged and then wished he hadn't. The aftermath was settling in now, something he supposed was a mix of shock and painkillers, and he badly wanted to sleep and forget everything for a while, though he felt he ought to go and talk to Naomi and Alec first. They'd have heard all kinds of rumours on the news and he owed it to them to give them a first-hand account.

He caught sight of Sophie Willis coming along the long corridor.

'Here's your lift,' Stacy said. 'You want me to say your good-byes for you?'

'Thanks. Look, I know we said we'd get someone in to cover for you tonight—'

'Don't worry. I can't leave her now. It wouldn't be fair.'

He nodded, gratefully. 'Talk to her about Vic,' Steel said. 'About anything she can remember her mother telling her about her step-father. Talk to her about—'

'Boss, go home. I know what questions to ask. Right now, though, I think she just needs hugs and comfort from her friends.'

Steel nodded again, then joined Sophie Willis. 'I saw you on the CCTV,' she said. 'It was . . . dramatic, I suppose, is the word. How are you feeling?'

'How do I look?'

'Like shit.'

'That would probably cover it. Take me back to the Dog and Gun, will you?'

'You sure?'

'I'm sure. But if I fall asleep in the car, leave me alone, will you?'

Sophie grinned at him. 'So long as you don't snore,' she said.

THIRTY

At the Dog and Gun pub Naomi and Alec skipped channels trying to get the latest updates on the rolling news and Alec used his phone to scan the Internet for further details.

Mostly, the reports just rehashed the few facts they had. That a further attempt to kill Sarah Griffin had been thwarted by a Detective Inspector who had been shot in the process. The gunman was reported dead, but there were no further details.

Alec's phone rang. It was Sophie telling him that she and Steel were heading back to the Dog.

'How is he?'

'Should be asleep in bed. As it is, he's asleep in my car. I feel like I should be doing what my sister does when her baby falls asleep: just driving round in circles for a bit. What I *am* going to do is take him home, then I'll come and fill you in, OK?'

Alec wanted to ask more, but Sophie ended the call and he had to remind himself that she was probably right. Steel had been hurt and his needs had to come above their wish for news.

They turned their attention, instead, back to the television. Douggie knocked on the bedroom door and Alec let him in.

'A friend of mine just called from the hospital,' he said. 'Reckoned they've got armed police moved in there now. Pity they didn't think of that before.'

'I think they had one officer there,' Alec said. 'But I assume they'd have been focusing on the main entrances. Who's your friend?'

'One of the porters. No one notices a porter.' Douggie winked. 'So if you want eyes and ears on the ground, as it were . . .'

Alec hid his smile. 'Thanks Douggie. DS Willis is on her way here. She'll probably be hungry.'

'Sophie is always hungry. Don't worry, I'll take care of it.'

Douggie departed. Alec could hear his heavy tread receding down the stairs.

'You think it's just revenge?' Naomi asked. She'd asked the same question a half dozen times in the past hour, but Alec didn't comment on the fact beyond saying, 'I still don't know. But I don't think so. It doesn't *feel* so, if you know what I mean. Terry Baldwin was a dickhead, a scrote. He beat his wife and child and he half killed his partner, but the thing is, it was all really direct. Really hands on.'

'Hard to be hands on when you're in prison.'

'True. But it was all kind of . . . simplistic, you know. Even the jobs he carried out, you'd never be able to accuse him of long-term, complex planning. They were all, hey, I've got nothing to do today, fancy robbing a shop/stealing a car/hitting the local building society?'

'True,' Naomi said. 'Strangely enough I think that's what made it work for him. No one knew what he had planned – because *he* never did. So no one could ever give him away. No, I know what you mean, this doesn't have the Terry Baldwin signature, but at the same time, Alec, if someone offered to get rid of his wife and kid in exchange for something Terry could provide, I can just see him doing that.'

'Me too,' Alec agreed. 'So the question is, after nearly seven years inside, what was it Terry Baldwin still had that was worth the trade?'

THIRTY-ONE

'There's a man at the bar, says he's a friend of yours. That someone called Patrick told him you was here. You want me to get rid of him?' Douggie asked.

Naomi frowned. 'Did he give a name?'

'Said he was called Gregory. Said you'd want to see him.'

'Gregory? What the hell is he doing here?'

'I can get rid,' Douggie said, interpreting her response as definitely negative.

I wouldn't like to see you try, Naomi thought. She shook her head. 'No, tell him we'll be down as soon as Alec gets out of the shower. Can you show him into the snug, Douggie? It's fine. I was just surprised, that's all.'

'He looks like a funny bugger,' Douggie said doubtfully. 'Ex copper, is he? Or ex military?'

Naomi smiled. 'Something like that,' she said.

Douggie departed, muttering something disapproving. He seemed to have become their self-appointed guardian, Naomi thought, not too sure how she felt about that.

Alec emerged from the shower a few minutes later and was given the news.

'Why would Patrick tell him we were here?'

'He and Gregory communicate most days, apparently. I suppose it came up in conversation or something. Anyway, he's here.'

'So we'd better go and find out why.' Alec sighed. 'And decide what we tell Steel about him.'

'As little as possible,' Naomi said. 'So far as Steel and Willis need to know, Gregory is just a friend.'

Gregory, pint glass in hand, was already installed in the snug when they came down. Seated in the corner, facing both the door from the bar and the one through which they entered from the rear of the pub.

'You're looking well,' he told Naomi. 'Douggie's left your drinks on the table. I don't think he likes me.'

'I'm sure you're used to that,' Naomi told him.

Gregory raised his glass, toasting ironically – though the action was lost on Naomi.

'So how's Nathan, and what brings you here?'

Gregory laughed. 'He's getting better. Sends his regards. As to why I'm here, well, I hear you have a mystery on your hands and I thought I might as well come and help out.' He laid something on the table in front of Naomi. 'Present,' he said. 'I'm not sure if it's a peace offering or a bribe, but . . . whatever.'

Curious, Naomi unwrapped the tissue and found a little box, heavily embossed, nestling inside.

'I found it at the antiques place up the road. Seemed right up your street.'

'It's beautiful,' she said, her fingers tracing the contours of the little object, examining the flowers and twining ribbons. She found the catch and the box lid sprang open. It closed again, with a satisfying click.

'So, does that get me a story?' Gregory asked. 'Who got shot and why, and what does that have to do with the pair of you?'

For the next hour Gregory listened as they told him about Thea Baldwin, who became Lisanne Griffin. About the dead child and the injured one, and about the new husband who seemed to have an even more opaque history than Thea herself.

'So, who was the primary target?' Gregory asked eventually. 'The woman or the man she shacked up with?'

'We're assuming Lisanne Griffin,' Alec said. 'But until we know more about Victor—'

Gregory nodded. 'I took a walk down by the river,' he said. 'I figure they must have come in the back way, along the footpath on the same side of the road as the house. There's a parking and picnic area about a quarter of a mile away. I figure the car was left there, the shooter came in, got out the same way.'

'That would fit with what is known,' Alec said. 'I've not heard anyone talk about the parking spot, though.'

'It's far enough along the river not to have figured in the initial search,' Gregory said. 'Might be worth mentioning.'

Alec nodded. 'I'm not sure what you can do to help,' he said. 'Did you know another attempt had been made on Sarah Griffin's life?'

'The girl? I heard something on the news.'

They filled him in on events, including how Steel had been shot; the would-be assassin was now dead.

'Does the shooter have a name?'

'Not that we know yet.'

Gregory nodded. 'Well, it strikes me this policeman of yours needs a bit of a helping hand. If someone is desperate enough to try to make a strike at the hospital, they will try again. Sure as God made little apples.'

'Probably,' Naomi agreed, 'but I don't see . . .'

Gregory drained his glass and set it down on the table. 'You know my motto: every good man needs a friendly psychopath watching his back for him. Consider your friend Steel's back well and truly watched.'

THIRTY-TWO

S teel slept. He woke briefly to take some more pills and then again because he was thirsty and thought he might want something to eat. He stood at the kitchen tap and refilled his glass three times, took more pills and then decided that all he really wanted was to get more sleep. Glancing at the clock on the mantelpiece as he made his way back to bed, he noticed it was three fifteen in the morning. The next time he was conscious of anything was when he heard Sophie Willis calling his name and his bedside clock told him it was a little after ten.

It took a moment to realize that she was standing in his bedroom doorway, leaning against the jamb, a look of great amusement on her pretty face. She'd braided her hair, he noticed, adding to himself that this usually meant trouble for someone. It was the equivalent of someone girding up their loins or getting into battle dress. It also meant she'd spent the night at her sister's place.

'I'll get the kettle on. I'll join you for breakfast too. Gracie never has anything more than cereal in the morning and I'm starved. I've left pills and water on your bedside cabinet,' she added, turning to leave.

'Thanks,' he croaked. His arm burned and his throat felt like the bottom of a parrot cage: shitty and dry. Painfully, Steel lifted his head and shoulders off the pillow and rolled on to his side, just enough to reach the pills and water. Then he lay back trying to summon the energy to move and listening to the sounds of Sophie Willis moving around his kitchen.

The smell of bacon finally roused him and he stumbled into the shower, remembering belatedly that he wasn't supposed to get the dressing on his arm wet.

She glanced over at him as he came through to the kitchen clad in sweat pants and a T-shirt and rubbing a towel half-heartedly over his mane of shaggy, light brown hair.

'Weren't you supposed to keep that dry?'

'I forgot. Would you mind—?'

She laughed. 'First-aid box still in that cupboard?'

Steel nodded. She set the bacon aside and crossed the kitchen, reaching into the cupboard for the first-aid box he kept there. 'Why do you keep this thing on the top shelf? Who the hell can reach that?'

'I can.'

'Yes, well some of us are not giants. Let me see. Does it hurt much?' She winced when he did as she pulled the plaster strapping free. 'Messy,' she said. 'But it looks clean.'

'I forgot you had a key,' he said.

'I forgot to give it back.' She grinned at him. 'We'll have tongues wagging.'

'I think I'll be the one flattered by the gossip.'

'Stop your flannel and eat your breakfast,' she told him. She brought tea and plates of egg, bacon and assorted accompaniments to the table. 'I can't find the ketchup.'

'I've probably run out.'

'Shame on you. So, are you up to work this morning?'

'I think so. Anything new?'

She chewed, swallowed and then nodded. 'We know who our man with the gun is. Got a hit on the fingerprints.'

'And?'

'And it leads right back to Terry Baldwin. His name is or was Ricky Lang. According to his record he had a bit of history, twoccing as a teen, and a couple of counts of ABH and one of GBH. I called our colleagues in the Met and talked to the arresting officer for his most serious offence. He reckoned Ricky Lang was strictly small time. He wanted to play with the big boys but frankly wasn't up to it. He is rumoured, however, to be another half brother of our Terry Baldwin.'

'Rumoured?'

'Like, everyone knew, but Lang's mother wouldn't say. Baldwin senior seems to have paid her regular money but when the CSA tried to get her to name the father she told them she didn't know, and stuck to it. After she stopped claiming benefits, they dropped her case. She worked part time, but it was, according to my contact, an open secret that Baldwin senior paid her rent and took care of most of her other bills. She, in turn, acted as a courier and when she was younger she paid her dues with sexual favours for one or another of Baldwin's friends. She left London for nobody knows where about ten years ago and Baldwin began to take more of an interest in Ricky Lang's career. Trouble was, as I said, he wasn't a particularly apt pupil.'

Steel nodded, remembering that the young man had seemed uncertain, nervous even. 'Trying to prove himself?'

'It's possible.'

'How old was he?'

'Twenty-three.'

'So, a kid brother to Terry Baldwin.'

'Yes. You finished with your plate? Want more tea?'

Steel replied yes to both. When she came back to the table she had several newspapers in her grasp and she laid them out in front of him. 'Guess who's famous?'

Steel groaned. He'd made the front page of two local papers and one national. The picture they had used was one that had been taken of him at the motorbike project. They'd been celebrating a grant made by a local charity which meant they could buy essential equipment and the local press had come along to capture the moment. Steel looked like a grinning wild man. His hair had needed the services of a comb and scissors and his beard would have looked at home on a member of ZZ Top. He'd intended to stay out of the photos on the night, had been kneeling in the mud mending a puncture only a few minutes before, but because he was one of the organizers they had dragged him into the pictures.

Sophie tapped the headline. '"Hero cop",' she said. 'Look, it says so in black and white.'

Steel groaned again. He skim-read the article, which gave a bare bones account of his adventures. 'Joe Martin is handling the media, I take it?'

'Don't knock it. He's doing a good job.'

'I know. He's got more patience than I have.' He tried stretching, realized belatedly it was a bad idea.

'Get into your work clothes and I'll tidy up here. Then I'm

going to take you with me to the Dog. Naomi and I have an appointment with Julia Tennant at the Winslow Trust. She's agreed to talk to us about Lisanne Griffin, but only if Naomi comes along. You can sit at a nice desk in the church hall and get on with tracking down the name Victor Griffin is supposed to have had before he became Victor Griffin, and if you want company you can wander over to the Dog and talk to Alec. He's still working his way through the old records.'

'Got my day all planned out, have you?'

'Well, someone has to,' she told him. 'And Stacy called from the hospital. Maggie and the boys stayed late and Sarah had a good night. She reckons Maggie got her to talk about Vic and about life before Vic. She's made notes and will courier them over. Stacy says she has no idea if there's anything useful in them but—'

'But anything is worth a look,' he agreed, and slouched off to his bedroom to get dressed.

THIRTY-THREE

The public face of the Winslow Trust was an old house with a rather ugly conference centre tagged on to the side. The house was built of rather drab grey stone, castellated and craggy. The conference wing of glass and concrete and steel tracked off at an odd angle from the left-hand side of the building. Sophie described the place to Naomi as they drove up the narrow, gravelled track towards it. 'God knows how they got planning permission,' she said. 'The old house isn't what you'd call pretty, but the new bit is a real excrescence.'

'I decided long ago that I didn't get modern architecture,' Naomi commented. 'No, that's not quite true. I can really admire plumbing and heating and rooms with big windows, but not the concrete and steel stuff.'

'Don't they call it "brutalism" or something? I dated an architecture student once. Didn't last. I think he required his girlfriends to have an admiration for Bauhaus. Looks like our host is waiting for us on the front step.'

She checked that Naomi was all right getting out of the car and then came round to take her arm and lead her towards the building and Julia Tennant. The woman took them inside and into a side room with a view of the garden.

'I've only got about a half hour,' she said. 'I'm really sorry, but I've got a train to catch then.'

'It's good of you to spare us the time,' Naomi said blandly.

'Well, to be truthful, I wasn't keen on the idea of talking to you at all, but—'

'This is a murder investigation,' Sophie remarked. 'A woman that your Trust helped has been killed.'

Julia laughed, mirthlessly. 'Many women die, are killed, every week,' she said. 'Men too, though they hardly ever get the reporting they deserve. Their deaths rarely make the headlines.'

Sophie shifted uncomfortably.

'But we're here about one particular woman,' Naomi said firmly. 'I tried to help Thea Baldwin and her child and your Trust took them to a place of safety. What we need to know now is who found them. How and why?'

'It happens,' Julia said. 'Sometimes no matter what we do their past catches up with them, and the results are rarely good.'

'There have been other deaths?'

'A few over the years. I suppose that's inevitable given the men and women we deal with. Those for whom all other options have run out. Some abusers can be unbelievably persistent. It's the idea that those they abuse are somehow property. You come between them and their property and you are the guilty party. For some it's almost a matter of – you can't call it a matter of honour, it's the opposite of that, but it's a matter of personal and absolute necessity that they either get their property back or make certain that no one else benefits from it.'

She paused, shrugged. 'I'm aware that sounds crude, but it's the closest explanation I can offer.'

'And that was the case with Thea Baldwin?' Sophie Willis asked.

'Well, I'd have thought Naomi here could answer that better than me. She knew the family.'

Naomi nodded. 'Property, yes. Terry Baldwin was quite as obsessive as that. He was lazy, impulsive, jealous. He might not

actually have wanted his wife and child, but the thought of them
having a life separate from him, that they might be able to take
control of their own lives . . . I think he'd have found that impossible to accept.'

'So you have your answer. I can't tell you much more. You
know how important confidentiality is to our clients; to the operation of the Trust?'

'I know that,' Naomi told her. 'And I was always terribly
careful not to overstep the mark and break your rules. But we
do need to know more. Sarah says that her mother found it really
hard to settle anywhere until she met Victor Griffin, and that the
Trust continued to help them all that time, finding them places
to live and finding Thea jobs. Is that normal?'

'There is no normal. Not really. Lisanne – Thea – well, she was
unusually unsettled for a very long time, I suppose. But you have
to understand, there is no central organization, not after we have
helped people get away from their abuser. What happens is that
Trust members make contact with their own circle of "friends"
– that's what we call our active volunteers. Some of those circles
overlap, some are completely separate. A woman like Thea Baldwin
would have been passed from friend to friend for a while, until it
was deemed enough distance had been put between her and her
husband. Each circle member typically knows only one member
of another circle. We keep contact to a minimum. It's usual for
each circle to know people who will accept short-term lets on flats
or who regularly employ casual workers. We help our clients create
new identities for themselves. And each will have a key worker,
though they are told only to contact them in real need. The idea
is not to have a chain; a trail for anyone to follow.'

Naomi nodded. 'And when Thea Baldwin wanted to go to
Bristol, do you know who organized that?'

'That would be confidential information.'

'Thea Baldwin is dead. Surely—'

'And there are others who are very much alive and whose well
being depends on silence.' Julia rose. 'I have a train to catch,'
she said. 'You'll have to forgive me, but I really must go.'

'We have to ask this,' Sophie said. 'But has there ever been
evidence of a breach in the organization? Of someone betraying—'

'Never,' Julia said firmly. 'We go to great lengths to protect those we help. Our security is tight and our people are vetted. Now, I really do have to go.'

Back in the car Naomi could feel Sophie seething with frustration.

'Well, that was a waste of time.'

'I didn't expect she would tell us much.'

'She didn't tell us anything.'

'Um, maybe not.' Naomi sighed. 'And I suppose we can't blame her for that. She has a responsibility to others.'

'Something bothering you?' Sophie asked.

'Probably nothing. It's just that when we talked to Julia she spoke about Thea Baldwin as Thea for most of the time and then, just once, she said Lisanne and then corrected herself.'

'And? I told her the name Thea Baldwin was living under.'

'I know.'

'But it bothers you?'

'Just a bit. It's like, if you've been used to knowing about someone by one name, it takes time for you to think of them as anything else.'

'There's no evidence she knew her as anything. No evidence she was ever directly involved with Thea Baldwin.'

'That is also true,' Naomi acknowledged. She shrugged her shoulders. 'I'm clutching at straws,' she said, but as they drove away she could not fully dismiss that sense of unease.

'Did you believe her when she said there'd never been a breach?'

'No more than you did. Oh, I'm sure it's been a rare occurrence and I'm sure they dealt with it, but I don't believe you can run something like this – well, this underground railway, without someone at least getting careless from time to time. Or doing something unintentionally that has consequences. She admitted there'd been deaths. That others had been found.'

'But you can also understand that she might not want to talk about it.'

'Not want to, yes. But she might have to eventually.' Naomi sighed. 'As I said, I'm clutching at straws, and Thea's death had nothing whatever to do with the Trust.'

'But you have a feeling.'

'I have a feeling I know something. I have a feeling that if I could actually see the files, I'd know what it was. I'd recognize it, you know.'

'Must be frustrating.'

Naomi nodded. 'Most of the time, I'm fine. I just get on with life. I'm happy and settled and I've come to terms with being blind, with the fact that everything has changed and there's not a bloody thing I can do about it. But just occasionally, you know?'

'I think I can guess. Bluntly, I hope I never have to find out. Sorry, maybe that didn't sound—'

Naomi laughed. 'It sounded like the way I used to feel,' she said. 'I'd see people overcoming problems and I'd think, wow, they are amazing. You know, like they were another species, or something. It was only after my accident I realized that they were amazing because life had fucked them over and left them with no option. You could either get bitter and twisted or you could figure out how to live.'

'And you chose.'

'I suppose I did. Though to be fair, at the start it was other people doing the choosing for me. My sister, Alec, other friends. They told me what to do when I needed telling and helped me when I wanted to decide for myself. And it sort of worked out.'

Sophie nodded. 'I hope it works out for Sarah,' she said. 'What happened to you, I guess, if I had to, I'd learn to deal with. What happened to Sarah – well, I'm not sure how I'd cope.'

'You just would,' Naomi told her. 'You would, because the only other choice is to lay down and die.'

THIRTY-FOUR

Back at Ferrymouth incident centre, Steel was catching up with calls. Twice, colleagues had attempted to contact the ex neighbour of Thea and Sarah Griffin who had left her new number and good wishes for Sarah's recovery. He finally managed to get through just before lunchtime, and introduced himself.

'How well did you know Thea Baldwin? I spoke to Sarah; she remembers you.'

'Does she? I'm glad about that. She was a lovely little girl.'

'And Thea? Did you get on with her too?'

There was a momentary hesitation. 'She was a nice woman, but that husband of hers . . . wouldn't allow anyone in the house and you never knew where you were with anything. I'd invite her for coffee or get chatting at the school gate, but if he was around, she'd clam up like . . . he didn't want her to be talking to anyone.'

'And Sarah? Was he as controlling of her?'

'Not in the same way, no. When he was there she had to be quiet and stay out of his way. We'd often see her out in the street. He'd told her to get out of the way, you know. She'd be out there for hours sometimes. All weathers.'

'And did you invite her in?'

Again that small hesitation. 'We did what we could. But he was . . . a difficult man. Not someone you'd want to cross.'

So, no, then, Steel thought. He frowned. When this old neighbour of Thea Baldwin's had got in touch, been so concerned about Sarah, he had assumed that the women had been close and that Sarah and her mother had been a major part of the lives of Josette Harris and her family. Otherwise, why go to the trouble of calling in? He was now getting very mixed messages. He tried a different set of questions.

'Did Thea Baldwin ever talk about having family? Parents? Siblings?'

'Not that I knew about. Except . . . there was a brother, I think. I seem to remember her talking about a brother.'

'But he never visited?'

She laughed then. 'No one visited. Not with Terry Baldwin around. You'd hear him. We were three doors down but we could still hear him. Shouting and screaming at her because he thought she'd spoken to someone he didn't think she should have. There'd be that little girl crying in the street and him shouting and her – Thea – screaming at him to stop. But he never did. Next day she'd be black and blue.'

'So you must have called the police?'

'And they'd have done what? Come knocking on my door? He'd have known then, wouldn't he?'

Steel let the silence lie this time, not quite trusting himself to break it. He thought about Joey, about the lack of help that left the boy so desperately isolated.

'Mrs Harris, why do you think anyone would want to kill Lisanne Griffin and her family?'

'Who? Oh, sorry, you mean Thea. I can't get used to her new name. Seeing her picture on the news, it was a right shock, I can tell you. I thought she was dead when she first went, you know. We all did. Thought he'd finally gone too far and then buried the body somewhere. Then someone said she'd been seen. With that policewoman who came round. Then we heard she'd made a statement. Put him away . . .'

'And so, do you have any ideas?'

'Well, it'll be him, won't it? Caught up with her.'

'Terry Baldwin is in prison,' Steel reminded her. Someone set a mug of coffee down on his desk and he nodded thanks, switching the phone to his other hand – and then back again when his biceps complained.

'Like that's going to stop him. He had family all over the shop. All he'd have to do is put out the call. You don't get away from the likes of Terry Baldwin and his lot.'

'Is that why you moved?' Steel asked. 'Mrs Harris, why exactly did you call us? It's clear to me that you and Thea Baldwin weren't what you'd call close.' He knew it sounded harsh. Knew maybe he was giving offence where none was due, but . . . today, he found he had little patience for the excuses of others.

Sounds of muffled outrage poured from the phone. Josette Harris let him know he had insulted her. 'I just called to ask after her. Poor kid.'

'The same poor kid you saw out on the street in all weathers and failed to help?'

'You don't know how it was.'

'So tell me.'

A stream of invective informed him that he was going to get little else.

Steel lowered the phone and picked up his coffee. There were some days, he thought, when you just wanted to despair.

He wandered through to the outer office, asked one of the constables who was following up on the supposed pseudonym for Victor

Griffin and was directed to another desk in the improvised incident room. Nothing, he was told, had come up in relation to the name of Anthony Bertram.

'Too much to hope for, I suppose,' Steel said.

He wandered off, unable to settle back at his desk. He thought about the 'auntie' Sarah had talked about and about the birthday card they had sent too. Sarah hadn't been able to remember her house number or real name – she was just Aunt Trinny – but Steel reckoned she was probably traceable – always supposing she hadn't moved.

He returned to the officer who had been doing the search for Anthony Bertram and explained what he wanted to do.

'Get hold of the voters' register for Terry Baldwin's old street. See if you can find this supposed aunt. Her name was Trinny; might have been Theresa, Trinity . . . I don't know. Just—'

'There's a call for you,' someone interrupted. 'Someone called Alec?'

Steel returned to his office. 'Hello, Alec. What can I do for you?'

'Do you have time to come across to the Dog? I think I may have found something.'

Nice if someone had, Steel thought. 'I'll be right over,' he said.

Terry Baldwin had a visitor. The visitor had supposedly come from his lawyer but one look at him told Terry otherwise.

The man was dressed for the part in a smart, charcoal grey suit, white shirt and a narrow silk tie and he had a briefcase, now laid out on the table in front of him. He appeared to be riffling through some papers.

Terry sat down opposite.

'So,' he said. 'And who the hell are you?'

'Maxwell,' the man said. 'I hear you had a visit from the constabulary. Your brother said you might be in need of a debrief.'

'In need of a what?'

'You might want to talk about it.'

'And why would I do that? They came to talk to me about my ex getting what she deserved. Not a lot more to say, is there?'

'And her husband. They tell you about him too?'

Terry dropped his gaze. 'I know about that. Yeah.'

'You don't sound happy.'

'Why should I be? What mad fucker decided that was part of the plan?'

'He married her. Well, as good as. No surprise he became collateral damage. You wanted it done, Terry.'

'No.' Abruptly, Terry leaned forward across the table. 'I wanted *her* done. That was the deal. No one told me she was shacked up with him.'

'What difference does it make to you? You wanted her dead; we told you we'd see to it. And in return . . .'

Terry fidgeted, all the bravado he had shown to Steel and Naomi now visibly absent. 'Yeah, but him. He's connected. He's—'

'He walked away from all that. Seems he preferred to be respectably employed. Married with a kid—'

'He wasn't married to her. I never let her have a divorce. She'd have had to show herself first, wouldn't she? The bitch never had the nerve.'

'She took his name. They had a kid. The world saw them as a loving, respectable couple.'

'So what happens now?'

'You keep your part of the deal.'

Terry could no longer meet Maxwell's eyes. 'That was before. Before I knew about him. It's a bigger risk now.' He turned back, leaned across the table, earnest now. 'Look, what I know, it's kept me safe all this time. In here. Kept all the other fuckers at arm's length. Why the hell should I let go of it now? It's insurance, that's what it is. I need assurances. I need—'

Maxwell rose and signalled to the guard that his consultation was over.

'Where are you going? I've not done talking.'

'I have done listening. Terry, get this. Your information gets less valuable by the day, and get this too. There's no such thing as safe.'

THIRTY-FIVE

'What am I looking at?' Steel asked as Alec handed him a press cutting with a photograph attached.

Alec pointed. 'Look, in the crowd at the back.'

'Victor Griffin,' Steel said. 'Do we have a real name?'

'For him, no. But we do for a good number of the other attendees, so someone somewhere will be able to put a name to the face.'

'If they're willing to tell us,' Steel said.

'Someone will be.'

Steel nodded absently and looked at the picture more closely. It was a press photo, taken at a funeral seven years before. 'How did it end up in the file?'

'This is the funeral of Terry Baldwin's father. So the pictures, alongside a lot of other random stuff, got scooped up and filed.' He pointed. 'Terry, Lisanne, Terry's brother Roddy, who became head of the family. This freckled kid here is Ricky Lang, the young man who shot you.'

Steel studied the face. He could tell, now it had been pointed out, that this was the same person – before he'd wielded a gun, shot Steel and finished up lying at the foot of the stairs with his neck broken.

'These three standing off to the side are representatives of the Tobias clan. If you remember, Terry beat one of the brothers so badly he never really recovered.'

'That was why his father sent him away.' Steel nodded. 'That must have been a tense meeting.'

'I'm guessing Roddy kept them well away from him. I'm still not clear in my own mind why the Tobias family would have let him get away with it, though. Why they'd be willing to grant an amnesty for him to go to the funeral. The only reason I can think of, apart from respect for Terry's dad, is that they actively wanted him there for some reason.'

'There's no record of them trying to get to him?'

'No. We do know that he went to the wake and that there was some direct discussion between him and the Tobiases. What was discussed, well . . .'

Steel nodded. 'And the people standing with Victor Griffin?'

'Or whoever he was. No, can't put names to any of them, I'm afraid. Naomi would have been able to, I think. Our best bet is to copy it to our colleagues who were involved and to the Met; they should be able to get a handle on it.'

Steel nodded. 'I'll get that done. Well done, Alec. It's a start at least. And it proves that Lisanne and Victor moved in the same circles. She didn't just meet him as a teenager and then happen to run into him again. He was always there – in the background, maybe, but not an unknown – and it certainly wasn't a coincidence when they met again.'

'Which begs the question,' Alec said. 'We've been assuming that the gunman was after Lisanne as his primary target. What if he wasn't?'

'Well, when we put a name to the face, we can base our speculation on something concrete,' Steel said.

His phone rang. Steel listened. 'I'll come right over,' he said. 'Developments?'

'We think we've found the Aunt Trinny that Sarah Griffin talked about,' he said. 'Maybe she'll be able to tell us something.'

THIRTY-SIX

That evening, Maggie drove Joey and Tel out to the bike project. To her surprise, Steel was there, accompanied by a man with dark hair who was almost as tall as the Inspector and a pretty woman who, Maggie realized, was blind.

'I didn't expect to see you here tonight. How's the arm?'

'I needed a break,' he told her frankly. 'I'm on the end of the phone should anyone want me and an hour here will clear my head.'

Maggie nodded. 'Any news?'

'Bits and pieces,' he said non-committally. His attempts to

speak with Trinity Matthews – Aunt Trinny – hadn't panned out so far and there'd been no reply, as yet, to queries about the photograph. He knew his frustration showed, even if Maggie didn't know the cause.

She smiled sympathetically.

'Maggie, this is Naomi Friedman and her husband, Alec.'

'Naomi?' Joey interrupted. 'You helped Sarah and her mum?'

The woman turned her head towards Joey. 'I tried, yes.'

'She liked you,' Joey said. He shuffled his feet awkwardly, evidently torn between wanting to ask Naomi questions and wanting to get on to the bikes.

'I'll get the boys sorted out,' Steel said. 'Maggie, maybe you and Naomi would like to get in the warm. Alec, you want to come with us?'

Maggie watched them go. 'I think the men are off with their port and cigars,' she said. 'While we ladies retire to the drawing room.'

She regretted that immediately, wondering if this Naomi woman would get the joke. To her relief, Naomi laughed. 'If the drawing room is warmer, then I'm quite happy about that.'

Maggie took her arm. 'It's this way,' she said. 'It's more of a hut, really. But there's a heater and there's a kettle and I've brought biscuits.'

'Sounds good. So, are the boys yours?'

'Only one of them. The other one, Joey, he's Sarah's boyfriend, or pretty much. To be honest I think that makes it sound too simple.'

'Oh? In what way?'

Maggie laughed. 'I suppose they both just need someone to hang on to. Especially now.'

'Was Sarah unhappy before?'

'Oh, goodness, no. Sorry, didn't mean to give that impression. Sarah was always a cheerful little soul and she genuinely loved Vic, I think. He was a nice man. Kind, you know? But there was still something like – missing, you know?'

'In what way?'

'OK, there's a bit of step up and the floor isn't what you'd call even. I came to the conclusion it was because she had so much in her past that was *verboten*. A whole pile of Christmases and birthdays and family that she couldn't talk about. It separated her out from the crowd.'

'And Joey?'

Maggie laughed. 'I'm guessing not much gets past you,' she said.

'Only things I actually have to see. The rest of me still works pretty well. Sorry, didn't mean that to sound so sharp.'

'That's OK,' Maggie said. 'Joey. Right. Well, Joey, bless him, has problems similar to the ones Sarah ran away from. Violent father. Only in Joey's case he's got a mother that can't or won't do anything about it. He finds it all very hard.'

Naomi nodded. Maggie had shown her to a seat and now she could hear her filling a kettle. So Vic was kind, she thought. That's what everyone said about him. But who was he?

Alec had told her about the photograph; Steel had notified colleagues and the picture had now been distributed to all relevant parties. And Alec had confessed that he'd photographed it on his smartphone and sent it to Gregory. Just on the off chance. He had been a tad sheepish about that but Naomi hadn't been surprised. Gregory had means and contacts that they didn't. She wondered what he was up to right now.

'Steel tells me he helped set this project up,' she said.

'That's right. Tell me, does anyone actually call him "Ryan"?'

'Probably his mother, and I suppose his sister. Did you know the Griffins well?'

'No. Only Sarah. I met them, of course, school things and community stuff, and we got on fine. Even went for a drink on the odd occasion. But it was all pretty casual. I liked them as far as it went. Evie's mother got to know Lisanne pretty well, I think. Evie is Sarah's best friend.'

Naomi nodded.

'But no one expected anything like this. Tea or coffee?'

The door opened and a couple more parent refugees came in. Maggie knew them and Naomi was introduced and it was explained that her husband had driven Steel out here because of his arm and that she'd come along for the ride. She was soon absorbed in the casual chat of people who knew one another only because of their respective kids. The deaths of the Griffins obviously emerged as a main topic of conversation and Naomi was asked if she knew anything, being a friend of DI Steel.

'Only that his arm hurts,' Naomi said, and was grateful that Maggie directed the conversation on to more general topics.

For the next hour she listened to the conversation and the roar of the bikes, her mind drifting back to the last time she had seen Thea Baldwin and her little girl, getting into a car with the woman from the Trust and driving away. Sarah had lifted a little gloved hand to wave. She'd been wearing red gloves, Naomi recalled. Red gloves and a blue raincoat and she'd been clutching a backpack and a small carrier bag of toys. Not much to carry with her off into the unknown.

The door opened again and Steel came in, announcing that they were all ready to go. 'Tel came off, fell in a puddle,' he said. 'He's fine but he's soaked through.'

Maggie groaned. 'Again. He's making a habit of it.'

She helped Naomi outside and handed her over to Alec. The roar of the bikes was much louder out here, two stroke engines spluttering their distinctive smoke.

'How's the arm?' she asked Steel.

'Hurts like hell, if I'm honest. I think I'm going to follow advice for once and get off home. Alec, would you mind giving me another lift? I can call someone from work or get a taxi if it's a problem.'

'It's no problem,' Alec told him. 'Just give me directions. Does it need the dressing doing?'

'I think I can manage, thanks. I'm at that point when I just want to sleep, you know?'

Naomi was very quiet as they drove away. When they'd said farewell to Steel Alec commented on it. 'What's on your mind? Apart from what a mess this is?'

'Victor Griffin,' she said. 'I've been trying to think who might have been at that funeral. Baldwin was a middle-ranking operator, never major league, but he'd been around long enough, involved for long enough that everyone would send a representative to pay their respects at the very least.'

Alec nodded. 'So it's a fair assumption that Victor Griffin would be from one of the major families or organizations. Someone had recorded a list of the big players there that day.

But most of those are in the parties closest to the grave. Vic Griffin was well back in the crowd. Of course, it's possible that he'd come to try and speak to Thea. That their relationship never really ended between her meeting him in the West Country and then getting back together with him in Bristol.'

'If that's the case, then she was far cleverer and far more secretive than I or Terry Baldwin gave her credit for. Unless, of course, that was where they made contact again. The funeral. If that was the last push she needed to shop her husband and make a break for it.'

'That would make sense,' Alec agreed. 'Timing-wise, it would make sense. You know what strikes me? Both Terry and Vic Griffin met Thea in the same location. Thea went to a festival when she was nineteen and met Victor, or whoever he was then. By the time she's twenty, she's met and got pregnant by and married Terry Baldwin, someone she's also met down there. Is it too much of a stretch to imagine the three of them were all together then? That Terry and Vic were both down in Somerset or Devon or wherever and Thea got involved with both of them and then Terry became the chosen one?'

'Not a stretch,' Naomi said. She thought for a moment. 'Thea was nineteen. Terry would have been twenty-two, twenty-three. What about Victor Griffin?'

'About the same age as Terry. Someone from his work said he was thirty-eight last birthday. Thea . . . Lisanne, would be about thirty-four, now, wouldn't she? So, an older friend, a minder?'

'All possible. But if the connection was made and maintained or even renewed at the funeral, it puts a slightly different complexion on things. It implies that Vic Griffin, nice though everyone agrees he was, wasn't quite the white-hat-wearing knight we assumed him to be.'

'Mixed metaphors aside, you're right. And when it comes down to it, I think the solution to all this depends upon us finding out who Victor really was. And what, apart from Terry Baldwin, he might have been running away from and why.'

THIRTY-SEVEN

G regory knew there was only so much he could do alone. He had seen Alec drop DI Steel at his flat, done a final check of the area and then driven away, guessing from the way the man moved so painfully that he'd be unlikely to go out again before the following morning. He'd found a place to stay about ten miles from Ferrymouth, checking first that it had a decent Wi-Fi connection and did a full English breakfast – Gregory had his priorities.

He had relayed the picture Alec had sent him to Nathan earlier and he contacted his friend now, asking for an update.

'Still working on it,' Nathan told him. 'We've identified about twenty people in the group and have a list of possible identities for about five more. Jackie's trying a different facial recognition package so we hope we'll get a few more hits, including our target. The picture quality isn't the best, you know.'

Gregory chuckled. 'Alec had to take pictures on his phone,' he said. 'He could hardly ask his policeman friend to do a high res copy.'

'No, I suppose not, but it does slow things down. I'll send you what we've got so far. It reads like a who's who of organized crime in that part of London.'

'High level?'

'No. Strictly porn, drugs and bank jobs. Not the sort of thing *we're* used to dealing with. The Baldwins are and were a long way down the food chain, which doesn't mean they aren't dangerous in their own way.'

Gregory filled Nathan in on events from his end and then opened his netbook and awaited Nathan's email.

Joey had made his way back home after a late supper at Maggie's. He expected his father to be at work by the time he got back and his mother to be still up watching the television. He was surprised, therefore, to find the house in darkness, the television off.

Joey paused just inside the front door. 'Mum.'

'Your mum ain't here.' The voice emerged from the living room doorway and a second later his father stepped through. He was in a mean mood, Joey could see that as soon as he saw his face. Joey took a step back towards the front door. 'Where's Mum?'

'She's not here.'

'What do you mean she's not here?' For a second, Joey's heart leapt. Did his father mean that she'd finally left? Had the nerve to get out?

That was replaced immediately by the thought that, if so, she'd not taken him with her.

'I told you. She's not here. Now where the hell have you been?'

'Out.'

'Out where?'

Joey didn't see the sense in lying. 'At the bike project. With Tel.' His father advanced and Joey took another step back. His father held something in his hand but in the darkness Joey couldn't quite make out what it was.

'I suppose that Maggie woman took you there.'

'Tel's mum. She gave us a lift, yes.'

'Your mum says you spend too much time round there. She says you think you're too good for us. That this Maggie is taking you away from her. That's what your mother says.'

Joey flinched. He didn't believe his father, and yet that was too close to what he knew his mother thought for it to be complete fiction. 'Mum knows I don't think that.'

'Don't you? Don't you really?'

Joey reached behind him, trying to get at the front door. His father was close enough now for him to smell the beer on his breath. There was another smell too that Joey couldn't immediately identify but he could see, even in the dimly lit hall, that his father's clothes were stained.

'Well let me tell you this, boy. You are going to stay away from that Maggie woman and you are going to stay away from that son of hers. And you are going to stay away from them because if you don't, then it's them that'll be sorry. You understand me?'

Joey backed away, but this last step wedged him right up against the door. 'Hurt Maggie and I'll kill you,' Joey said, but he could hear the fear in his own voice and knew his father could hear it too. His father just laughed at him, and then he raised his arm.

Joey dropped down to avoid the blow, but this time he couldn't run and he had nowhere to go. He cowered as the pain rained down, until he could no longer keep his arms raised up to protect his head. Until the world turned red and then a deeper black that swallowed him whole.

THIRTY-EIGHT

Terry Baldwin found out that his half brother was dead in a phone call from his older brother.

He listened in growing fury as Roddy outlined what had happened. 'His name's not been released yet, they only identified him earlier today and then told the family. But by tomorrow it'll be all across the news. I wanted you to hear it first.'

'Did you send him?' Even as he asked, Terry knew it was a stupid question, but he wasn't thinking right.

'What do you mean, did we send him? Fuck knows what he was doing there. Fuck knows what he thought he was trying to do. But we didn't have bugger all to do with it.'

Terry closed his eyes. He knew his calls were monitored and that his brother would have denied involvement anyway. He also knew from the tone of his brother's voice that Roddy was telling the truth. Roddy was baffled by the actions of their younger sibling.

'I want the bastard dead. You understand me? He killed our brother. I want—'

'Terry!' Roddy's voice was sharp. 'Shut the fuck up and listen to yourself. Look, I don't know what the hell he was into, but whatever it was, you and me, we leave well alone.'

Terry hung up on him. A rage was brewing that he could not contain. Roddy had agreed that Terry's wife should be dealt with. He'd known all about that, even if he'd not actually sanctioned it. They'd agreed; she was Terry's wife and it was Terry's choice, but the rest . . .

Furious, he thumped his fist into the wall, three, four times until the blood ran and he heard bones break. He felt his arms grabbed as the guards pulled him away. Better, Terry thought. Better than hitting something that didn't give a shit. He broke free, swung about and came out fighting, his ruined fist making contact with something that crunched satisfyingly beneath its weight. His other hand swinging and catching the second man a blow to the temple.

Dimly, he heard the alarm sound, felt himself grabbed again, held more tightly this time. Terry kicked out as he went down, making contact again. His head bashed against the concrete floor, stunning him for a moment, just adding to his rage. Terry Baldwin, a dervish of flailing limbs and blood that it took six to hold down and another two to pacify completely, was finally bundled into a cell and left to bleed.

THIRTY-NINE

Steel arrived at the incident room a little late that morning, having had to organize a lift in. He was greeted with the news that there was still no contact with Trinity Matthews but that Madeleine Jeffries, sister to Terry and Roddy Baldwin, had been in touch. She didn't want the local police coming to her home, but was willing to meet with Steel at a mutually agreed spot.

Steel called her.

'I'm willing to talk,' she said. 'Thea didn't deserve this, but I'm not having police coming to my door. I walked away a long, long time ago and I'm not getting involved. You understand.'

Steel was puzzled as to why she even wanted to talk to him. True, he had wanted to speak with her, to warn her of possible dangers should she be on Terry Baldwin's hit list – though he had never thought that truly likely – and to ask, perhaps, that she might be a support for Sarah. It seemed that Madeleine Jeffries had something else on her mind.

'Thea sent me something,' she said. 'I shoved it in a drawer and never thought much about it. To be honest, it's only because I liked Thea that I even kept the thing. What I really wanted to do was shove it in the bin.'

'What was it?'

Madeleine hesitated. 'Meet me,' she said.

'Where? You're a long way south. Ipswich, isn't it?'

She laughed. 'That was years ago.'

Trapping the phone between his shoulder and his cheek, Steel scribbled down her directions. He judged it to be a couple of hours' drive. Madeleine, he noted, had been very careful not to say where she'd be driving from.

'Sophie? I'm going to need taking somewhere.'

'Where are we going?'

'To meet Madeleine Jeffries.' He handed her the directions and was then interrupted by another phone call. This one was from the prison, telling him that Terry Baldwin had become very violent when his brother had told him about Steel's adventures at the hospital. 'He made specific threats,' the governor informed him. 'Threats to kill.'

Steel thanked him for the warning. 'He say anything else?'

'Nothing that made any sense. He injured four of my people before they managed to subdue him.'

Steel thanked him and rang off. He felt bad about the death of Ricky Lang, Terry's half brother, even though the young man had tried to shoot him. He had only been twenty-three; there had still been a chance he could have changed his life. Now there was none.

'Ready?' Sophie Willis asked. 'It's quite a distance.'

'I'm ready. I'll call Alec and Naomi on the way; let them know we'll be gone for a while. Let's just hope something useful comes from this meeting and it isn't just another wild goose chase.'

Steel could not remember ever being in Derbyshire before, though he assumed he must have driven through the Peak District on his way to somewhere else. Madeleine Jeffries' choice of rendezvous was a curious one. A picnic area high up in the peaks, deserted at this time of the year and overlooking a massive drop down into a steep valley. They had passed signs for Snake Pass a few miles before and seen heavy lorries trundling their way across the high road but apart from a few sheep, this spot she had chosen was isolated and utterly bereft of life.

'I'm assuming that's her,' Steel said. 'Seeing as it's the only other car.'

'Well, she's got a sense of the dramatic.'

They got out of their car and a woman vacated hers. She was alone, Steel noted, and not dressed for the location. Suit and heels suggested office rather than wilds, and only the big coat which she pulled on as she got out of the car implied that she was prepared for the wintry blasts funnelled down between the craggy hills.

'Madeleine Jeffries?'

'You know any other madwoman?' She smiled tightly. 'I almost didn't come. I was having second thoughts just sitting here.'

'I'm glad you're here.'

'I'm here for Thea. That's all.'

Steel nodded and followed Madeleine Jeffries over to one of the picnic tables. Willis stayed by the car. Madeleine had not even acknowledged her presence and Steel didn't want to push their luck. Madeleine Jeffries was about forty years old, he guessed. Neat hair, expensive coat, careful make-up, none of which hid the fact that she was deeply agitated.

'You wanted to tell me about Thea,' he said.

She opened her bag and removed cigarettes and lighter. Steel didn't rate her chances of getting anything to light in the howling wind but it seemed she needed something to do with her hands and fiddling with the lighter fulfilled that purpose. She seemed to be waiting for a cue before speaking and so he said, 'Sarah is doing well, considering. I wondered if you might like—'

'No. I've nothing against the child, but I made my choices long ago. She isn't part of my plans.'

'I understand,' he said.

'Do you?'

'Probably not.'

'Then don't presume.'

'Mrs Jeffries, what did you want to tell me? You've come all the way here, we've come all the way here, I'm sure we've both got better things to do than sit in the freezing cold playing games.'

She glared at him for a moment, then pointed her unlit cigarette towards his arm. 'Is that where he shot you?'

'Yes.'

'The news says you pushed him down the stairs, that he broke his neck.'

'He shot me, I pushed. There wasn't a lot else I could do. I'd be sorry for your loss, but I'm not sure you care.'

'You're right. I don't. At least, not as much as I should.'

She sighed, seeming almost to deflate, to release the anger. 'The only reason I contacted you was because of Trinny,' she said at last.

'Trinity Matthews. Sarah spoke about her. We've been trying to get in touch.'

'Well don't try any more. Leave her alone, she won't want to speak to you. Take it that anything I tell you comes from her too – you understand.'

'Sarah might like—'

'It doesn't matter what Sarah might like. Trinity still lives in the same street, still lives among my so-called family. Just leave her be.'

'You care about her?'

'She's the only bit of my own life I've kept in touch with, but don't read too much into that. She got a card from Thea and Sarah for her birthday last year. She didn't know where they were or even why they had suddenly decided to send it, but she was pretty happy not to have been forgotten.

'A few days ago Roddy, my brother, he calls on Trinny and starts asking questions about the card. Now she'd not made any secret about having it and he'd not asked before – bearing in mind that her birthday was last October. So, months ago. But anyway, he's asking about it and all but demanding that she calls the hospital, speaks to Sarah and reminds her what family she belongs to.'

'Did he threaten either of them?'

'No, but Trinny was a bit shaken by it. So she called me. Told me what had happened, gave me the heads up, if you like, just in case Roddy decided he wanted a word.' She laughed. 'I never told him where I live now, but I don't suppose that would make any difference. He'll have kept track, won't he? I didn't cover my tracks like Thea did, though fat lot of good that did her in the end.'

'Do you think Roddy wanted her dead?'

'I don't think Roddy gave a shit about her one way or another. So no. I don't think he had anything to do with it. Not directly anyway. But the fact that he might upset Trinny – well, that got to me a bit, I suppose. I don't know. It was a shock, hearing about Thea and everything. I decided I wanted to cut all ties now – you know, just in case.'

Her smile was weak. 'Sounds pathetic, doesn't it?'

Steel didn't commit himself. 'You said Lisanne . . . Thea left you something.'

'Sent me something. Just before she left she asked me to keep it for her. Said she'd ask me for it one day.'

'And? What was it? Did she ask for it back?'

'An envelope. I kept it, stuffed it in a drawer and forgot it was there, didn't even tell my husband.'

'Does he know you're here?'

'You're kidding, right? He's my life now, not them.'

She got up and walked back to her car, reached inside and handed Steel the envelope that had lain on the passenger seat. 'Take it,' she said. 'I'm going now and I won't be speaking to you again.'

'I can't promise to keep you out of this.'

'Yes. You can. You don't have to. I've done.'

Steel watched as she drove away.

FORTY

'**Y**ou are a mess.'

'So?' Terry's left eye was still swollen shut and a cut taped closed with butterfly sutures ran just above his eyebrow. His right cheek was heavily bruised and beneath his shirt his ribs were black and blue. He'd hurt several of the officers who had tried to restrain him; their colleagues had not been gentle with him.

'*So* that temper of yours, it'll get you killed one day.'

Terry leaned across the table to glare at Maxwell. He wasn't sure why the man had returned and it had crossed his mind that he should refuse to see him. One thing was for sure, Terry was in no mood for intimidation today.

'Who was the fucking idiot that sent my kid brother to do a job like that?'

'Why the fuck should I know?' Maxwell smiled at him. 'I'm on the other side of the law, remember.'

'Yeah, right. I want him dead. The policeman. I want him finished off.'

Maxwell's eyes flicked towards the guards. They were by the door, out of earshot, but Terry wasn't exactly being quiet.

'Terry, you've not kept the first part of your bargain,' Maxwell said. 'So what makes you think you can ask for favours?'

'Just get it done. After that—'

'Terry, my employers are beginning to wonder if you have anything to offer them, after all. They are getting impatient. I'm sure you don't want that?'

Terry looked away, paling beneath his bruises. 'I'll give you something on account,' he said. 'You got a pen?'

Maxwell extracted a pad and fountain pen from his briefcase and set them down on the table. He wrote the numbers Terry quoted, checked them back.

'Now fuck off,' Terry told him. He stood up, signalling that the interview was at an end. 'You'll get the rest after. Understand?'

Maxwell smiled at him. 'I'll be sure to pass on your regards,' he said, as the guard opened the door to the visiting room and Terry stalked away.

FORTY-ONE

Maggie called Steel just as they were on the outskirts of Ferrymouth, returning from their meeting with Madeleine Jeffries.

'It's Joey,' she said. 'He didn't turn up this morning, didn't go to school, and now he's not answering his phone.'

'When did you last hear from him?'

'When he left here to go home last night. Most days he goes to school with Tel. It's rare for him to miss, but it's been known to happen, so I didn't worry until Tel called me at lunchtime to say he'd not gone to school. We've tried to get in touch. Tel wanted to go round there, but—'

'Don't either of you do that. Look, we're almost back in town; we'll swing round that way and check up on things for you. I'm sure it's nothing.'

Maggie gave him the address and Steel passed it on to Sophie. 'We could get uniform to call in,' she said.

'We could, but . . . look, he's been let down time after time. I asked him to trust me, to let me help . . .'

Sophie shrugged. 'I'll go the back way into town,' she said. 'It'll be quicker.'

Ten minutes later Steel and Willis were standing outside the Hughes' house. The curtains were still drawn and there was no sign of life or movement.

'Doesn't look good,' Sophie commented.

Steel pushed the gate open and stepped into the paved front garden. The door needed painting, he thought, and, in contrast to most of the neighbouring houses, the place looked uncared for and drab. Steel rang the bell and then knocked on the door. Willis bent down and peered through the letterbox.

'Fuck,' she said. 'You up to kicking the door down?'

Moments later they were inside. Willis was calling for backup and an ambulance, and Steel knelt beside the prone figure of Joey, unconscious and cold and covered in his own blood.

The house was silent. Empty, Steel thought.

'He's alive,' he said. 'Just. Sophie, see if you can find a blanket or something. The ambulance is going to be easily twenty minutes getting here, even if it gets a straight run.'

She nodded. 'I'll try the bedrooms.'

'Joey.' Steel called the boy's name, but Joey was utterly unresponsive. Steel dared not move or even touch the boy for fear of doing him further injury. He lay still on the tiled hall floor and Steel thanked some random god that at least the central heating had kept him from freezing to death, though it was far from really warm in the house. How long had he been lying there? Steel wondered.

'Sir. You'd best come and take a look up here.'

Sophie Willis sounded scared and for an awful moment Steel wondered if he'd been wrong about the emptiness of the house. What if Hughes had been upstairs? He took the steps two at a time. Willis stood on the landing, a blanket in her hands. She was staring fixedly into one of the bedrooms, through a half open door. Steel followed her gaze. A woman he presumed must once have been Mrs Hughes lay across the bed, her face so swollen and pulped it was hardly recognizable as such. She was, very clearly, very dead.

Gently, he turned Willis away and took the blanket from her hands.

'Come downstairs,' he said. 'We can't do anything for her now. All we can do is help Joey.'

She nodded and followed him down the stairs. Steel covered the boy with the blanket and then sat down with his back against the wall. Willis stood in the doorway and used her mobile to update their colleagues, telling them that they now had a murder on their hands. It was only a few minutes but it seemed like a very long time until the sirens announced the arrival of their backup.

FORTY-TWO

Gregory's phone went to voicemail so Nathan sent what information he had directly to Alec. They knew the identity of Victor Griffin.

Alec read the email out to Naomi.

'His name is or was Marcus Karadzic.'

'What's that, Polish?'

'Don't know. Slovenian, maybe. But he was born in Luton, so . . . anyway, he's the youngest of three brothers known to have close associations with the Tobias family, so also known to the Baldwins. Of the three only one went into the family business, as it were. The eldest went off to university and is now living in Scotland as a photographer. Marcus did some travelling and then drifted around the West Country for a time, working as a casual labourer until getting a job with a charitable trust assisting in the resettlement of ex cons.'

'Really?' Naomi asked. 'That wouldn't be—'

'The Winslow Trust. Oh yes it would.'

'And he was back for Baldwin senior's funeral . . . talk about walking on both sides of the fence. What did he do for the Trust?'

'Well, he seems to have started as an office junior, or whatever you call it. They paid for him to go on various courses and he worked his way up. By the time he met Thea Baldwin again in Bristol he had left the Trust and worked for an agricultural supplies company, which went into receivership about four years ago, just before they moved up here, I suppose. His work record is good, pay is average, not even so much as a speeding ticket. Marcus seems to have lived an exemplary life except for one small incident.'

'And that would be?'

'He seems to have left the trust under a bit of a cloud. Nothing definite, and they even gave him a decent reference, but there were rumours about irregularities. Not financial, I don't think. At least, not directly. I managed to find something about computer records being altered. Marcus denied any wrongdoing, and whatever it was seems to have been covered up. He didn't work his notice, he just left, and nothing more was said.'

'See if you can dig anything else up. And contacts with his family?'

'Minimal, apparently.'

'But he turned up for the funeral.'

'According to this he also turned up for family weddings and christenings and his parent's anniversary bash. So he was part of the scene.' Alec skim-read in silence for a moment and then said, 'But this is interesting. Very interesting, in fact.'

'What?'

'Marcus's father might have been a bit of an also-ran, but his mother's maiden name was Vitelli.'

'As in Alphonso Vitelli?'

'Her father. That's a bit like being married to royalty, isn't it?'

'In certain circles, yes.' Naomi thought for a moment. Vitelli was not a name likely to be known to the general public, at least not in a criminal capacity. The family, on the surface, ran legitimate businesses in catering and hotels. Over the years these had prospered, as had their less legitimate business of money laundering, illegal gambling and protection.

'Do they know that Victor Griffin is one of theirs yet?' Naomi mused.

'That's the question, isn't it? But our next question is how we give Steel all of this information without having to tell him where it came from.'

Naomi shrugged. 'Tell him it's an old informant,' she said. 'And we can't possibly reveal our sources.'

FORTY-THREE

Roddy Baldwin was a dangerous man. A man that many people had reason to be afraid of. A man who exuded an aura of power and barely suppressed violence. Being such an expert he was well able to recognize the same traits in others and also to realize when he had been outclassed. The man sitting at his desk and drinking his whisky immediately impressed him as one such individual.

He stood in the open doorway to his study and for a split second considered calling upon his confederates in the next room. The man seated at his desk poured a second glass from Roddy's cut glass decanter and gestured to him to come and sit down. Roddy considered for a moment longer and then closed the study door and complied.

'How did you get in here?'

'I disabled your alarm system. I'm good at that kind of thing.'

Roddy took a sip of whisky. 'And I suppose it's no good asking who you are or who you work for?'

'The first question, no good at all. The second . . . well, you could say I freelance. You could also say this is *pro bono*. You know, like the free cases lawyers take when they think the client is worth it.'

Roddy considered his options. Something about the man told him that he was going to come out on top no matter what Roddy did. He noted also that the man had laid a gun on Roddy's antique blotter. His hand rested next to it.

'A Glock,' Roddy observed. 'Never much liked them, myself.'

'No, I understand you prefer a Walther. The PPK. I worry about their tendency to jam. The feed ramp is far too steep.'

Roddy sat back in his seat and nodded thoughtfully. 'So what do you want?'

'A few minutes of your time and the answers to a few questions. Don't worry, there are no wrong answers, no penalties. I just want the truth.'

'About what?'

'Did you arrange the killing of your sister-in-law and her family?'

'Why should I tell you?'

Gregory sighed. 'Because I'm asking. Because I suspect it's no skin off your nose if you give me a straight answer. If, however, I have to persuade you, then believe me: you are the amateur here. I, on the other hand, am not.'

'I have men within call.'

'Men you chose not to call because, I think, you realized that it would do you no good. I also understand that you are a man who fights your own battles. I understand that you look after your people, which is commendable. I understand, too, that unlike the rest of your clan you seem capable of maintaining a degree of self control, and that you don't make waves you can't ride.'

Roddy considered some more. The man across the desk seemed in no hurry. Roddy made up his mind.

'No,' he said. 'I had no reason to want Thea dead. I thought she was a fool getting involved with my brother. I didn't realize quite how much of a fool.'

'A fool?'

'My brother has what you'd call low impulse control. He was a violent husband. But I suppose you already know that.'

Gregory nodded. 'And did he want her dead?'

'Undoubtedly.'

'And he arranged it?'

Roddy was thoughtful. After a moment or so he seemed to

come to a decision. 'I don't want any further harm to come to my brother,' he said. 'He might be a fool and an embarrassment, but he's still my flesh and blood.'

'Not my decision. Not my business.' Gregory shifted in his seat; his fingers tapped the blotter next to the gun. 'But I do have places to be once I've ticked you off my list. And the man Thea ran off with?'

'She ran off alone, so far as I know.'

'All right. The man she was living with. The man who was also killed. I understand his name was Marcus Karadzic, even though he'd been living as Victor Griffin. Did Terry want him dead too?'

Gregory noted the slight flicker in Roddy's gaze when he mentioned Vic's real name. Was it recognition of the name or had he known who Victor really was? 'I'm told he had important friends. Family who might take exception to his being shot. You can't be happy about that?'

'Like you said; I ride the waves.'

'I'm sure you do. But it must be trying at times, having to clear up after the likes of Terry. I'm assuming he knew who Victor Griffin really was?'

Roddy looked into the pale blue eyes of the man across the desk and felt a sudden urge to tell him whatever he wanted, just as long as he went away. He sighed.

'Look,' he said, 'I have reason to believe that Terry wanted the hit on Thea, but that it wasn't his idea. Someone offered to do it in return for something Terry knew or had.'

'Like what?'

'Is the million dollar question. Terry isn't the sharpest knife in the box. He was always impulsive, always out for the easy option, but before Thea left and he got himself banged up he was boasting about some plan he had. Some dead cert. Frankly, we none of us took him seriously, but that doesn't mean that other people might not have done. Terry was so busy shooting his mouth off, someone might have assumed he had a reason to.'

'That's what you might call vague,' Gregory said. 'I hear you've been having trouble keeping all this together of late. That there have been challenges within the family?'

Roddy smiled. 'Goes with the territory,' he said.

'And Terry's brother. Ricky Lang?'

'Ricky wanted to think he was a big-time gangster when he was actually an inept kid who liked to be told what to do so long as the one telling him had a bigger gun.'

Gregory gestured that he should go on.

'I'd not seen Ricky or heard from him in a couple of years. He didn't think I took him seriously enough and, frankly, I'd rather someone else dealt with a loose cannon. I'd had enough of it with Terry.'

'So he went where?'

'Traded on his name, got in on a few jobs. I don't know where he spent the past six months. He didn't say, I didn't ask.'

'But there must have been rumours.'

Roddy sipped some more of his whisky and held out his glass for a refill. Gregory obliged. 'As you pointed out, there have been challenges. Power struggles. It's not affected our operations so much. The Baldwins have never been at the top of the tree; we found our niche a couple of generations ago and have been happy to stay put. But old names mean nothing these days. It's all new players moving in from central Europe and Russia.' He laughed, harshly. 'I sound like a UKIP advert. But Ricky wanted to be where the big boys played.'

'Whereas you were content with trickle-down economics.'

Roddy smiled. 'It may surprise you that I actually do under-stand the reference. Our father believed in the benefits of a decent education. And yes, that's a good way of putting it. Whoever happens to be at the top, they always need planners and foot soldiers and distributors. So long as you don't get greedy, there's plenty to go around.'

'And Terry? Was he content with that?'

'Terry didn't know how to be content. Terry is a fool.'

Gregory thought about this. 'So someone enticed Ricky Lang into trying to finish a job someone else had got wrong.'

'You don't think Ricky made the original hit?'

Gregory could tell that Roddy was genuinely intrigued. He shook his head. 'I'm told that when he pointed his gun at the policeman his hand shook so much he couldn't shoot straight. Whoever killed Lisanne and Victor Griffin got it right first time and with no hesitation. Even if they did only manage to wound the girl. But the question is, why is someone so keen on Sarah Griffin being dead?'

'Baldwin,' Roddy said. 'Not Griffin. She's still a Baldwin.'

Gregory shrugged. 'Whatever.' He studied Roddy Baldwin thoughtfully. 'You just thought of something, didn't you?'

Roddy shook his head. 'It's nothing,' he said. 'Just some random thing Terry said. Thea left and Terry did what he usually did and got blind drunk. He rambled on about Thea and how he wanted to "kill the bitch" and then started in on what he called his "whiny kid". How she'd overheard him say something . . . what, I don't know.'

Gregory nodded.

Roddy smiled suddenly. As their conversation had continued without mishap, so his confidence had slowly risen.

Gregory was about to disabuse him.

'Right,' Gregory said. 'I think you now have a decision to make.'

'What decision?' Roddy's lips curled in a sardonic smile. 'I don't have to decide anything.'

'A man should know why he is about to die,' Gregory told him. 'And I figure you have a lot of possible reasons. I'd like you to pick one for me. That seems only fair.'

Roddy stared at him in disbelief; then he began to laugh. 'Oh, you are priceless,' he said. 'Stupid and arrogant too, but priceless.'

'You've just added one more to your list of reasons,' Gregory told him.

'And you expect me to be scared? Try again.'

'The way I see it,' Gregory told him, 'is that the list goes something like this. I could kill you because you either permitted that family to be killed, arranged it or actively encouraged it.'

'None of my doing.'

'But you could have halted it. No? Not important enough for that?' He went on. 'Or I could kill you in revenge for any one of the bodies you've dumped in Savernake forest over the years.'

He saw Roddy frown.

'I do my research,' Gregory said. 'It's probably a little inconvenient, not being exactly on your doorstep, but I suppose Epping is probably knee deep in corpses by now, being as that was a favourite location for your father's generation. But it has the advantage of distance and of not having direct links with you and yours. So you could pick a name – I have a list to choose from, should you have forgotten any – and we could say that was the reason.'

Roddy shook his head. 'You're all talk.'

'Not me, no. But you're maybe wondering just who in your organization has been shooting their mouth off. Or, sorry, I think you added him to the list a couple of months ago, following an unrelated misdemeanour.'

Roddy's frown had deepened, creasing between his eyes and across his brow. He'd done playing. 'You know you'll not get out of here alive, don't you?'

'I think you're wrong,' Gregory said.

Roddy smiled. 'A lot of people have thought I was wrong. Usually I've proved otherwise. I'm still here; they, as you pointed out, are in the ground. And that gun of yours, it's less than useless to you, you know that? Shoot me and a dozen men will come running. Leave, and I've just got to shout and the same thing will happen.' He nodded towards the Glock. 'No suppressor. Your mistake, my friend.'

'I'm not your friend,' Gregory said. 'And this is not my only gun.'

When he left a few minutes later Roddy Baldwin lay on his back, looking up at the high ceiling of his study. He saw nothing. The hole at the front of his head was small and neat but the back of the skull was now little more than shattered bone surrounding empty space. What was left of his brain spread with his blood across the carpeted floor.

FORTY-FOUR

Maggie and Tel were at the hospital when Steel arrived. 'I should never have let him go home. Or I should have driven him there. I should—'

'Maggie, there is no way you could have known. It isn't your fault.'

Tel's face was white. 'Will he be OK?'

'I don't know, Tel. I honestly don't know.'

Joey was broken. No one yet knew the extent of the damage he had sustained. He had shown no sign of regaining consciousness.

'His mother?'

Steel shook his head. 'Dead when we arrived, dead before Joey got home, we think. The best guess is he walked in on his father either during or just after, and Hughes was still in a rage.'

There had been no sense of moderation in what had been done to Mrs Hughes. Her husband had beaten her with a nail bar. They had found it at the scene, still covered in her blood and hair. He'd kept hitting her until her face was pulp and her bones shattered. It was a small thing to be thankful for but the nail bar had been dropped on to the bedroom floor and not used to attack Joey. For that Hughes had employed fists and feet. That, Steel feared, might well have been enough.

'It's like someone spread a virus,' Maggie said. 'Like the whole place has been infected.'

'Does Sarah know?' Tel asked.

'Not yet. Maggie, it's a lot to ask but—'

'Of course I will. Poor little thing. She's going to be devastated all over again.'

The evening papers and news reports carried pictures of Ricky Lang and rehashed the story of the hospital shooting. Some also carried news of the murder of Marilyn Hughes and the attempted murder of her son, but this was way down the list; the murderer was known and public interest, though expected, would, according to the media, be focused on the section of the report that said Hughes was a dangerous man and should not be approached.

Tragic as this was, it lacked the mystery and speculation appeal that made it truly newsworthy.

The one major incident during that evening was a neighbour of the Griffins calling in to the incident centre with a printout from an Internet news site clutched in her hand. It was a picture of Ricky Lang.

'I told you,' she said. 'Or I told one of you anyway, about the two men Lisanne was arguing with? The two who kept knocking on her door? Well, he was one of them. I never really saw the other. But this was one of them.'

This was relayed to Steel as he stood in Sarah Griffin's room, watching Maggie do her best to comfort Sarah and Tel.

Stacy came to stand beside him. 'All this on top of everything else,' she said.

Steel nodded. He called up one of the news reports on his phone and sat down on the bed beside Sarah and Tel. 'Sarah,' he said, 'can you take a look at this picture and tell me if you've ever seen this man?'

She lifted her head from Maggie's embrace and clumsily wiped her eyes. She took the phone from Steel and looked at the picture of Ricky Lang. To Steel's surprise, she nodded her head. 'I think Vic might have worked with him or something,' she said. 'He called round one day and picked up some paperwork or something like that.'

'Can you remember when? Was that recently?'

'A couple of weeks ago, I think. Mum wasn't pleased. She said she didn't like him bringing work home. At least I think that's what she said.'

'Can you remember more precisely?'

Sarah stared at him. 'Is he the one?' she said. 'The one who shot my mum and Vic?'

'I don't think so,' Steel told her. 'But I think he was involved somehow.' He didn't think now was the time to tell Sarah that this young man who had called at her house was the one who had come to the hospital to try and kill her, nor that he was her dad's half brother. He also suspected Ricky had been there when her parents had died, that it was Ricky's voice she'd mistaken for her biological father's.

He could see she was trying to think but she finally shook her head. 'I didn't take much notice,' she said. 'He was only there for a few minutes. I think I thought it was work because Vic had put it in one of the folders he uses for his files. It had the works stamp on it.'

Steel thanked her. It was, he thought, yet another connection . . . but to what, he couldn't yet decide.

'Maggie, are you all right to stay for a while? I'll go and see what I can find out about Joey and I'll come straight back. Stacy, do you think we can smuggle takeaway pizza past that nurse on reception? I'm guessing we could all do with something.'

She smiled at him. 'I'll see what I can do,' she said. She followed Steel out into the hall. 'Isn't he the one that shot you?'

'Terry Baldwin's half brother, yes. It seems one of the neighbours recognized him as one of the two men hanging around in the days before the shooting. He was seen arguing with Lisanne and now it seems he actually visited the house.'

'But to see Victor Griffin.'

Steel nodded. 'Curiouser and curiouser,' he said.

On his way down to ask about Joey, Steel called Alec. He'd had two missed calls which events had made it hard for him to return. Alec told him they now knew the identity of Victor Griffin. Quickly, he summarized what they knew. Steel promised to come and see them later that evening. He told Alec about Joey.

'Douggie told us about it,' Alec said. 'He says it's no surprise, but—'

'But it's still a tragedy. I'll see you later, Alec. Good to know you still have useful contacts.'

Isn't it? Alec thought as he ended the call with Steel.

'What did he say?' Naomi asked.

'That he'll come over later and we'll exchange information. I'll put the news on and we'll see what the world has to say about all this. Then I suggest we go and get something to eat and then maybe take a walk.'

'Sounds good,' Naomi said.

They switched on the small portable in their bedroom and waited for the headlines. A plane crash in the Philippines and the latest political scandal pushed the news of Roddy Baldwin's death into third place. Shot in his study at his north London home, the reporter said. Discovered by his security, shot through the head.

Gregory, Naomi thought.

FORTY-FIVE

Sophie Willis met Steel on the stairs. She'd stayed in the waiting room on Joey's floor while he went up to see Sarah.

'Any news?'

'They've stabilized him enough to take him into surgery,' she told him. 'It's not looking good. That bastard. How could anyone do that to their wife and kid?'

He could see she had been crying. Steel touched her arm. 'We'll go looking for him,' he said.

'No we won't. Because if we did we'd kill the fucker.'

She laughed and poked gently at Steel's injured arm. 'Fine pair of vigilantes we'd make. Sorry, boss, I just can't get the image of that woman's face out of my head, you know?'

'I know.'

'So what now? We can't just hang around here, waiting.'

'Have the family liaison officers been organized?'

'What family? Who the hell is there to liaise with?' She sighed. 'Yes, Jennifer Stone. You know her?'

Steel nodded.

'And Phil Ackroyd is taking over at midnight. I know him slightly. He's come in from Kingsmere. He's a good man.'

'I've got Stacy organizing pizza in Sarah's room.'

'Don't think I could eat.'

'You need food. We all do. And company. Maggie and the boys are staying on for a while. Meantime, as I don't have to go down and enquire about Joey, I suggest we find a quiet spot and take a look at what Madeleine Jeffries gave us earlier. See what Thea Baldwin thought was so important she had to stash it at her sister-in-law's.'

'Shouldn't we take it to the incident room?'

'I'll get you to do that later. I know we said we'd wait, but that was before events overtook us. I'd like a look now.'

Deciding that the car would afford them the best level of privacy, Steel followed Stacy back down to the car park. He'd slipped the envelope into an evidence bag, intending to open it up when they returned to Ferrymouth, but he felt an odd sense of urgency now and he couldn't begin to guess what time they'd be able to get away from the hospital.

The envelope was standard brown manila, large enough to take an A4 sheet of paper folded into thirds. It had Madeleine's Ipswich address on the front, but looking at the gummed-down flap Steel decided that Madeleine had probably been telling the truth when she said she had never looked inside.

Steel laid it on the evidence bag and placed that on the car dashboard. He photographed it from all angles before taking it up again and looking apprehensively at Sophie.

'Ready?'

'You make it sound like it might explode.'

He carried a Swiss army knife in his pocket and he used the smallest blade to slit the envelope along its length, being careful to photograph the envelope again.

Inside was a single sheet of paper and two business cards.

'Naomi Blake, again,' Steel said. With gloved hands he turned it over. In neat script, Thea had written, 'If anything happens to me, tell her.'

He raised an eyebrow and looked at Sophie. 'What's the other one?'

'Looks like a solicitor. Maxwell, Clarke and Roper. She's written on the back of this one, too. "If anything happens to me, they know who did it." Did what? Killed her?'

'Perhaps. We know she was running scared. What's on the sheet of paper?'

Sophie slid the cards back into the envelope and unfolded the sheet. It was plain white copier paper, cheap and thin. On the top third was a list of numbers. Beneath that, Thea had written two names. Below that four more numbers. And taped beneath those was a key.

'She obviously expected Madeleine to open the letter,' Sophie commented.

'And probably expected her to understand what all this was about.'

'So, we have to talk to her again.'

Steel nodded. 'Won't be too hard. I took her number plate.

Whether she'll be willing to talk is another matter. Sophie, I think this needs to get to the incident room now. Could you do the honours?'

'Sure. I agree. You owe me pizza, though.'

'I thought you weren't hungry.'

'I've changed my mind.'

'And Sophie, I want a copy of all this taken to Alec and Naomi. They might recognize a name, have a theory about the numbers. We know Thea sent this to Madeleine around the time she disappeared, so it's in the time frame of their investigation.'

'Will do,' she said. 'I'll come back across and give you a lift home later.'

Steel nodded. He crossed back over the car park and into the hospital, thinking hard. The day's events had added a new dimension. Finding out who Victor Griffin really was, getting the letter Thea had sent, it all added layers to something that was already complex. Finding out that Ricky Lang had visited the Griffins at home and that Lisanne had not been pleased about it.

So had Victor Griffin or Marcus Karadzic, or whatever he called himself, been the one who had instituted the contact? Brought Ricky into play? Given away their location? Or had Ricky found them and made threats to tell?

And on another note, where the hell was Steve Hughes, and did he realize that he'd left his son alive?

FORTY-SIX

Steve Hughes hadn't gone far. He'd changed his clothes and put the blood-stained garments into a carrier bag, then left the house. He had some vague idea that he should remove evidence from the scene, then remembered he'd left the nail bar on the bedroom floor. He decided that it didn't matter anyway; the police, the neighbours, the blokes he drank with down the pub, his workmates, they'd all know he was the one. That he did it. And he found that he really didn't care.

His meandering eventually brought him to the street where

Sarah Griffin and her family had lived and Hughes walked for a while along the path beside the river. He dumped his bag of clothes in a bin in the picnic area, not really that bothered about who would find it, but deciding it was a nuisance to carry. Only then did he think about where he might go.

It had never really been in Hughes' nature to run from anything. He'd learnt early on in life that running seldom solved anything; it was nigh on impossible to run so hard or so fast that you could get away. He looked out across the muddy river, down towards where the old ferry had once taken people and their goods and chattels across to the other side; the other county. The other country, in a way. Wherever you went, he thought, you had to pay the ferryman. Nothing was free.

Had someone asked him at that moment why he had killed his wife and beaten his son so badly that he might well not survive, what would he have replied? Hughes found he had no preference one way or another about the boy. If he lived, who cared? If he died, ditto. Why he had done it? Well, it had happened, hadn't it? What was the use in asking stupid questions?

Someone had once told him, back in the days when they still took an interest in possible futures for Steve Hughes, that he had to acknowledge his guilt. Face up to it in order to make room for change to happen in his life.

Hughes had laughed in the man's face, and he would have laughed now. Truth was, Hughes felt no guilt. He felt no shame. He felt nothing, not even the need to run.

It was dark now, he could no longer see the river, and he thought about finding somewhere to stay for the night or about fetching his car and driving off. He walked back through town, along quiet streets. Everyone seemed to have gone home for the night, shut up in their bright rooms behind their thick curtains, living their safe little lives and watching endless soaps, just like his wife had done. He despised soaps, he despised the people who watched them. He passed the end of his own road. Police officers stood outside his door and all the lights were on. A white van marked 'Scientific Support' told him the forensic crew must be inside. He smiled; they'd have plenty to work through in there. He continued on to where, a couple of streets away, he had parked his car. Satisfied that no one had linked it to him and that there were no nasty police-shaped surprises waiting round the corner, Hughes got in and drove away.

But he didn't go far.

Hughes still had one more score to settle.

FORTY-SEVEN

'So why did you kill him in the end?' Nathan asked.

Gregory considered. 'I had a number of reasons lined up,' he said. 'In the end I'm not sure which of them won out. But the man was unpleasant and I doubt the world will miss him.'

'He'll leave a hole,' Nathan predicted. 'Nature and organized crime both abhor a vacuum.'

'True,' Gregory said. 'Nathan, can you find me anything more on Alphonso Vitelli?'

'Victor Griffin's grandfather. Yes, what are you looking for?'

'I'm not sure yet. I picked up some paperwork from Roddy Baldwin's office before I left. It looks as though he and the Vitellis had some sort of business arrangement planned. I've not had time for a proper read through yet but on the surface it looks like a property deal. It could be a front, of course.'

'Well, it's probably safe to assume that's now scuppered. Anything else?'

'Yes, it's being handled by a firm of solicitors. Maxwell, Clarke and Roper. See what you can dig up.'

'I'll get back to you as soon as. What are your plans now?'

'Head back to Ferrymouth and be on hand for whatever breaks. I have a feeling it's about to.'

Sophie Willis sat in the snug drinking coffee and eating a sandwich Douggie had prepared for her. It was, she thought, better than pizza. At her right hand was a glass of red wine that Douggie had insisted she have alongside her coffee. She was sorely tempted but thought it might be wiser to coerce Naomi into finishing it for her. She didn't want to hurt Douggie's feelings, but she didn't want to go to sleep either and Sophie felt that even a small glass of wine might be enough to finish her off.

Truth was, she was exhausted and really wanted her bed.

'The numbers could be bank accounts,' Alec said. 'Though the last four look more like phone numbers.'

'Tried that,' Sophie told him. 'Nothing.'

'They might need area codes,' Naomi suggested. 'It's possible that whoever originally wrote them down knew the area code but didn't memorize the numbers.'

Sophie shrugged. They had tossed ideas back and forth for a while now and this was the best they had come up with.

'The names,' Naomi said. 'Roddy Bishop and Karla Brunel. I really can't place them. I think you may be right about them, you know.'

'Aliases,' Sophie said. 'It sort of fits. I wondered if Roddy was Roddy Baldwin, but that doesn't really make sense, does it? Thea knew who they were, so she presumably thought Madeleine would know who they were too. But Madeleine didn't look at the letter.'

'So you'll be speaking to her again.'

'Oh yes, and I don't suppose she'll be best pleased.' Sophie stood up and stretched. 'She obviously thought a lot of you,' she told Naomi. 'You were her defence if anything happened to her. You must have made an impression.'

'Maybe. Or maybe she didn't have that many options left. I was one on a list of one. You heading back to the hospital?'

'Yes, pick the boss up, see what's happening with Joey Hughes. You ask me, they'll never catch up with the father. He'll be over the hills and far away.'

'I don't know,' Naomi said. 'If I had to put money on it, then my bet would be on his hanging around, seeing how it all plays out.'

'I don't think he's that stupid. Surely.'

'I don't think sense has anything to do with it. He'll want to see the reaction to what he's done.'

'Part of me hopes you're right. I'd like to see him caught, see him pay. Part of me hopes he was in so much of a hurry to get away that he got hit by a lorry and he's dying in a ditch somewhere.'

* * *

If the prison officials had been expecting a violent explosion when Terry Baldwin was told of his brother's death, then they were disappointed. This time, Terry did not lash out immediately. At first he seemed to shrink in on himself, become smaller and thinner, his face pale and his hands shaking.

'I want to call my lawyer.'

'What for? It's ten o'clock at night, no one's going to take your call at this time.'

'I want my fucking lawyer!'

The guard backed off as Terry, roused at last, sprang off the bed and advanced on him. This time he didn't get the first punch in. He was on the floor, on his face before he had taken the second step.

The door clanged shut and he was left alone to shout and rage.

Terry pounded his fists against the door until the blood ran. Roddy was dead, Ricky was dead. His whole damned family was being taken away from him.

The irony that he had been happy to see his wife and child shot dead was lost on him. Roddy and Ricky were blood and Terry, banged up though he might be, was out for revenge.

'Joey's still in surgery,' Steel told Sophie when she got back. 'I've saved you some pizza.'

The pizza was cold, but she ate it anyway, perched on the end of Sarah's bed. The side room was crowded with all the people: Maggie and Tel, Stacy, Sophie and Steel (who dominated the space on his own anyway). The night sister had put her head around the door earlier. Scowled at them and then left. Visiting time had been over for a long time. The lights were out in the main ward but Sarah's side ward was well away from anyone else, down a little corridor, and Stacy had assured them that so long as they didn't make a noise no one would bother too much.

And she would know, Sophie thought. She'd practically lived here since the night Sarah's family had been killed.

'When will we know if he's going to be all right?'

Sophie got the impression that Sarah must have asked the same question dozens of times, but was still hoping for a better answer.

'As soon as there's anything to tell, we'll be told,' Maggie said. She gripped the girl's hand tight and Sophie Willis could see the unwarranted guilt in the woman's eyes. Maggie would blame herself for a long time, Sophie thought, even though there was nothing she could have done.

'I'm going to take you home,' she told Steel, but it was a half-hearted offer.

'I'm going to sit downstairs for a while. See if anything happens. You go, I'll get a taxi.'

'No, I'll come down with you.'

Maggie didn't move. Tel had fallen asleep in a chair and Sarah too was fighting the urge to drop off. Stacy walked out with them. 'It's raining,' she commented as they passed the window on the way to the stairs. 'As hard as it was that night.'

Looking out, Steel could see that she was right. Rain pounded against the glass, flooding it. Hiding the world from view. He experienced a sudden vertigo, a sense of unreality as though this was all there was. This hospital, these people, marooned and cut off from some imaginary world. 'There's enough of us here,' he told Stacy. 'Go home, get some proper rest. I doubt we'll shift Tel and Maggie until morning.'

She nodded gratefully. 'Thanks. I will. I just need to get away for a bit. You know.'

She wanted to go home to prepare herself, Steel thought. To take some time out, so that she was ready for when she had to tell Sarah that Joey had died.

He looked at his watch. It was now almost two in the morning. Joey had been in surgery for hours and, like Stacy, Steel knew that every passing hour diminished his chances.

Tomorrow, he thought, might bring a change to the pursuit of Hughes. It might not just be one murder they sought him for; most likely it would be two.

FORTY-EIGHT

Gregory arrived at the Dog as Naomi and Alec were eating breakfast. He joined them for a cup of tea and helped himself to toast and jam.

'Roddy Baldwin,' Naomi said.

'What about him?'

'He's dead.'

'So I heard. It was on the news.'

Naomi stared hard in what she hoped was his direction. 'And did you have a hand in it?'

'Never confess to anything,' Gregory said. 'Have either of you heard of a bunch of lawyers called Maxwell, Clarke and Roper?'

'Don't change the subject,' Naomi said.

'Why?' Alec asked him.

'Because I came across their names on a document linking Roddy Baldwin to the Vitelli family. A business deal of some sort. Something about some property in Brighton, but somehow I don't see either the Baldwins or the Vitellis going into the housing business.'

'The Vitellis might,' Naomi said. 'They own a hotel chain and a string of restaurants and an events catering business. But I'm not finished with Roddy Baldwin.'

'Roddy Baldwin is no longer of this world,' Gregory told her. 'So I'm guessing he has finished with you, or any questions you might have wanted to ask him. And if you want to scowl at me properly, you need to move your head to the right about another ten degrees. Look, my methods are not your methods. We established that a long time ago. There are bigger fish to fry than what I might or might not have done with Roddy Baldwin. Nasty piece of work anyway.'

'And you're not?'

'I'm not *just* a nasty piece of work. That's the difference.'

'You were saying,' Alec interrupted. 'About this property deal.'

He glanced across at his wife. Naomi was fuming, but the truth was Gregory caught her off balance all the time. She knew she ought to hate everything about the man. The ex copper in her told her that she ought to have turned him in long ago. He was a killer, he was everything she had once worked to bring to book – but she also owed him, Alec thought. And he owed her. Lives had been saved because Naomi and Gregory had worked together, and so the bonds had been forged for good or ill and, in Alec's view, there was no sense making an issue of it.

Most of the time, Naomi realized that too, but Alec knew that she was sometimes still conflicted as the old Naomi and the woman she had become fought.

'You know about the Vitellis?'

Naomi sighed. She buttered her toast and then asked for the marmalade. 'I worked organized crime for the Met for a while. Secondment just before my accident. You know that. I met the Vitellis back then.'

'Met them?'

'Long story, but essentially the Vitellis had some artworks stolen. They were not best pleased. On the face of it, they are an important part of the business community: hotels, catering, they organize some really prestigious events . . . anyway, we were left with this issue: on the one hand we know they're a bunch of crooks; on the other hand we know they are an impressive and successful family business.

'Alphonso, the grandfather – the head of the family, even though he must be in his nineties by now – he had a sense of humour. Their property was recovered and they said they wanted to thank the police. They held a benefit event at this great big place they own up on the South Downs. All funds raised going to police charities.'

Gregory laughed. 'Stylish,' he said.

'And potentially embarrassing. Top brass managed to get out of attending but I was sent along with a chief constable who was on the point of retirement and therefore didn't care about potential embarrassment, and a few other disposable representatives. Alphonso Vitelli knew exactly what we were doing. Laughed like a drain.'

'And the benefit. Raised money, did it?'

'It was covered by *Hello!* magazine. One of the must-attend events of the season.'

'And you met this Vitelli?'

'Met the clan, drank the champagne, ate the canapés and enjoyed the music. I got to wear a posh frock – and feel totally underdressed. End of story.'

She frowned. 'It's just struck me. Victor Griffin . . . well, Marcus Karadzic. He might even have been there.'

Joey Hughes was out of surgery. On a high dependency unit, but he had survived the night.

Steel left the hospital at five in the morning and grabbed a couple of hours' sleep, then Sophie collected him again at nine. He had spent the past hour on the phone to his colleagues in the Metropolitan Police and was now a very irritated, very frustrated Detective Inspector.

Sophie set a mug of tea on his desk and sat down.

'Well?'

'Well, I've more or less been told to keep my nose out. They'll handle the Victor Griffin connection to the Vitellis and anything else that comes along on that side of things. They told me to lay off Terry Baldwin and that, essentially, we're relegated to gathering evidence at this end and handing it over to them for processing.'

'And their reasoning?'

'Is that Roddy Baldwin's death has opened the field and it's all looking to kick off. They don't want us provincial coppers getting in their way.'

He sighed and leaned back in his seat, closing his eyes. 'The one thing I did manage to get was confirmation of Madeleine Jeffries' address. It seems they have no real interest in her so we're free to go and interview her again. Providing, of course, that we play nice and share.'

'And they got her address from?'

'From the address book on Roddy Baldwin's desk. Along with half a dozen others. It seems she's moved about a bit in the past few years.'

'And taken Thea's letter with her every time. She must have known it was something really important. You move house, you have a clear out. She kept that all this time.'

Steel nodded. 'I've sent copies down to the Met, of course. I'm not sure how important they think it is. I get the feeling their main focus is keeping the lid on the pressure cooker right now.'

Sophie nodded. 'So we go and see Madeleine Jeffries.'

'Another long drive, I'm afraid.'

'Let me guess, back to where we met her before.'

'Give or take about ten miles, yes. Our colleagues in the Met are organizing a visit to Messrs Maxwell, Clarke and Roper and frankly, I wish them joy of it.'

'My, we are having a jaundiced morning.'

'We are. Yes. We are royally pissed off and suspect we are also going to be royally shafted when this mess is finally sorted out and our big brothers down in London get to take all the bloody credit.'

Maxwell, Clarke and Roper were a case study worthy of Harvard Law School, Gregory thought as he went through the information Nathan had obtained for him and added it to the little stash of documents he had taken from Roddy Baldwin. He wished he'd had more time to search Roddy's office, but he'd already spent far too long in the house; further risk was unacceptable. Someone would come knocking on their boss's door and he'd have to fight his way out. It wasn't so much that he worried about that aspect; Gregory knew himself capable. More that he was not of a mind to draw attention to himself.

He valued his invisibility. Over the years that was what had kept him alive.

He had Nathan on the phone now, checking facts.

'Did you ever see the film *The Princess Bride*?' Nathan asked.

'The Princess what?'

'Never mind. I love that film. Anyway, there's a character in it called the Dread Pirate Roberts, who's sailed the seas for decade upon decade, terrorizing anyone that crosses his path.'

'No one lives for that long. What's the catch?'

'Exactly! You see, it isn't the man that matters, it's the name. There have been generations of pirates called the Dread Pirate Roberts. When each one retires another takes on the name and the reputation.'

'And Maxwell and co?'

'Are a firm of solicitors who always happen to have a Maxwell and a Clarke as partners in the firm. Roper died ten years ago and doesn't seem to have been replaced, but the original, fully legitimate firm, was called Maxwell, Clarke and Roper. It has *gravitas*, so I suppose they kept the tradition.'

'So, what, do people change their names when they get the job?'

Nathan laughed. 'The official records have a half dozen Maxwells over the years. All fully accredited, all distant cousins, brothers, uncles – you get the picture.'

'But not one drop of blood shared between them.'

'Um, I can't tell you that. Not definitively. It did start out as a family business, but I've already managed to dig up one name change by deed poll, and as one of the previous Maxwells was definitely Asian, I'm guessing it's a *nom de guerre*.'

'And the Clarkes and Ropers?'

'There have been a few Clarkes. All gone now, but genuinely related. The last one retired five years ago, lives somewhere on the south coast and cultivates petunias, or something.' He paused for a moment. 'Sorry, begonias. I've had him checked out, and he looks clean.'

'Is that possible?'

'OK, so here's how it goes. Maxwell, Roper and Clarke have their main office in the same location it's been in for the past eighty years. It has kudos, reputation, respectability. Anyone needing to make a will or settle a dispute with their neighbour over the leylandii will be referred to one of a chain of smaller offices where a team of perfectly legitimate and well-trained associates look after them.'

'Nice,' Gregory said.

'The head office only handles the criminal side. Literally and figuratively. The successors to Mr Clarke – who are presently named Patel and Rhodes – handle the pre-court side. Again, they seem to be pretty much legit – how much they know about the Maxwells is, of course, a moot point. Because so many of their clients inevitably end up inside, on account of them being guilty and undefendable, the Maxwell part of the partnership is responsible for appeals so they have ready access to their clients, wherever they might be locked up.'

'Go on.'

'Well, currently there are two Maxwells and a couple of associates handling that. A father and son who changed their names about a decade ago – the son was still in his teens – from Meads to Maxwell. Maxwell senior was a barrister, but had a bit of a professional fall from grace and a wife who publicly humiliated him with a High Court judge, so you can see he might, legitimately, want a fresh start.'

'He was also in prime position to need a job offer,' Gregory said.

'I would think so. Anyway, that's the set up. I'm still trying to work out *who* set it up, but you now know a little more.'

'And do they have a conveyancing business?'

'Funny you ask. It's called Clarke and Roper, established in Hove about six years ago. Now has a second office, also in Hove. You're wondering if they're handling the Vitelli–Baldwin property deal.'

'Anything on that yet?'

'Not a lot. Sorry. We could do with another researcher. The only thing I know so far is what's in the public domain. The property is a town house, been empty for five years. It's very run down at present, but done up, and in that part of Brighton . . . I'll let you do the maths.'

'Which is all well and good but—'

'The Vitellis do buy up property like this all the time. It might be a false lead.'

'But do they involve the Baldwins?'

'That is a valid question. I don't know, Gregory, but it seems unlikely. Why would they? Unless there's something in the house that both families have an interest in.'

'Such as?'

'That I don't know.'

Agreeing to check in later, Gregory rang off and, not having anything better planned, decided he should go and keep an eye on Inspector Steel.

Naomi was restless that morning. Alec had been reading aloud old statements and court transcripts from the Baldwin trial and at first he just thought she was finding it upsetting, being reminded so much of the past.

'It isn't that,' she reassured him. 'I suppose it's Gregory.'

Alec set the transcripts aside. 'What about him?'

'Oh, I don't know. You do realize that he shot Roddy Baldwin?'

'I realize that he's shot or otherwise disposed of a lot of people.'

'And you're OK with that?'

'I'm not sure I understand.'

'I'd have thought it a simple enough question. Are you OK with him going round killing people?'

'Naomi, I don't think it would make any difference whatever

I thought. Gregory is a fact; what he is and what he does are facts. What I think about that is – well, irrelevant.'

'Is it? Is it really?'

Alec got up and came to sit beside her, taking her hands. 'What's this all about, love? Really about?'

She sighed and slumped back in her chair. 'I'm not sure I know,' she told him. 'I think it's just . . . being back, involved in an investigation. All right, on the periphery of it, but being involved with people like Steel and Sophie and being reminded of who I was—'

'Who you still are.'

'But I'm not, am I? Neither of us is and I don't just mean because we're older and water has flowed under the bridge, or any of the other crass clichés you might come up with.'

'Crass?'

'Sorry. I didn't mean that. I mean . . . When we both joined the force we'd got such a clear, clean idea of what our job was and why we were doing it. Didn't we?'

Alec shrugged. 'Probably.'

'It was all about doing the right thing, stopping the bad guys. Bringing people to justice.'

'And?'

'And I'm having to face the person I was, only a few years ago. I look at her and I know I've changed so much. And not because of the accident. Alec, we promised to do what was right and uphold the law without fear or favour and I really believed that. Really invested in it. You know? And I see people like Steel and Sophie and they are still so sure of where to draw the line. So sure of—' She broke off, not certain what she wanted to say.

'And you figure Gregory is the symbol of all that is opposite to them?'

'Yes! Well, no. I don't know, maybe.'

Alec squeezed her hands and then let go, instead slipped an arm around her shoulders. 'We're not that side of the line any more, love. You and me, we crossed over that line a very long time ago, scuffed it out and made a run for it. And that has nothing to do with Gregory.'

'Doesn't it?'

'No. He just . . . I don't know . . . made it easier to forget what we'd left behind. But Naomi, love, I've given this a lot of thought. For a while I felt utterly devastated by it, by having to recognize that there were no real right and wrong answers. I got very depressed and very miserable for a while. You know I did. Gregory saved lives. Gregory saved people we love. You and I, we protected him and Nathan. We made a decision and we now have to live with that. We stopped making simple moral judgements – and don't ask me when because I'm not sure now. Even that seems blurred around the edges.'

'You're telling me we're the same as him?'

'I'm saying that on some level we probably always were. If we hadn't been we'd have done everything we could to get him and Nathan locked up. But we didn't. We became complicit. No one forced us, not even circumstance. We made decisions and we took steps and, to put it crudely, love, we became the people we used to hunt.'

'God, that's depressing.'

'Is it? I'm not so sure.'

'Nothing is ever simple, is it?'

'Nothing ever was.' He kissed her hair and then her face. 'We just managed to fool ourselves that it might be.'

FORTY-NINE

Madeleine Jeffries was in her bedroom, packing. Her husband let them in. He looked worried and tired, Steel thought. Madeleine, on the other hand, was just furious.

'Going somewhere?'

'Away. None of your damned business.'

'You don't have a funeral to arrange, or anything?'

'They can chuck his remains to the dogs, for all I care.'

'Madeleine, did you really never look at the letter Thea sent you?'

'Why should I have done?'

'You kept it. You must have cared about her on some level.'

'I thought she had a raw deal. I thought—'

She sat down suddenly on the edge of the bed, the fight suddenly dissipating. 'That first year, after she left, I kept expecting a phone call, a letter, something to say that she'd be arriving to see me, or arranging to meet up. Then I started to think that maybe Terry had found her. That she and Sarah were dead already. Then I started to wonder if I should open the letter or take it to the police or something. After a while I just . . . well, not forgot about it, but I stopped thinking about it. Stopped thinking about them. Most of the time.'

'You were close to Thea?'

'I tried to be. I knew what Terry was. I knew her before Terry, you see.'

'You were friends before?'

'Oh, God. Yes.'

Her husband stood in the bedroom door. He came and sat down on the bed beside her. 'Maddie, love. You can't go on like this. You've got to talk.'

'There isn't much to tell. Maybe that's the trouble. There is so little to tell.'

They went downstairs, convened in the large kitchen, sitting around the table while Madeleine's husband made tea and offered biscuits.

'When did you meet?'

'Years ago. It was summer. I was twenty-three, same age as Terry. That was the mad thing about our family. All these kids knocking about. Maybe they were cousins, maybe they were half siblings. Half the time I don't think even our dad knew.'

'But you got on well?'

'Mostly, yes. The usual sibling rivalry, but nothing abnormal, especially considering how strange the set up was. Anyway, I'd just bought a car. It wasn't much and Dad would have paid for whatever I wanted, but even then I'd begun to pull away. I'd got a job, I'd saved and I'd done it myself.'

'How did he feel about that? Your father?'

Madeleine smiled, her eyes softening for a moment. 'Oh, I think he was proud. He encouraged us all to think. If we wanted to study, go to university, go abroad, he helped us do it. That was the daft thing about him. The crazy thing. Hard as nails so far as the rest of the world was concerned. You crossed him, you were dead. And his women, they were never more than flings. If they produced a kid, he didn't mind. The kids were his, sort of proved his manhood, I suppose. He'd use the mothers just as badly as he'd use anyone else. He never cared if they left him, just as long as they left the kid behind.'

'That sounds cruel,' Sophie commented.

Madeleine nodded. 'He was cruel. He was vicious. He was vindictive. But not with us and not with his wife.'

'Your mother.'

Madeleine nodded. 'She ruled the roost at home. There were five of us – the legitimate ones, I suppose you'd say. I was the only girl and so I was his princess.'

'And when you left?'

'He wished me well and told me not to come back. I'd chosen my path, he said, and I was welcome to do that. But once I'd chosen, I couldn't change my mind. He hated ditherers.' She laughed, harshly. 'Decisiveness, that was what he valued. Trouble was, Terry thought he was being decisive when all he was doing was being a prat.'

'And you were all together. When?'

'Me, Terry, Roddy and Marcus, we all drove down to Somerset.'

'Marcus? He went with you?'

She nodded. 'We'd known one another for ever. Literally all our lives. Roddy and Marcus were about the same age; they were supposed to be keeping an eye on us. We dropped Roddy off somewhere on the way. I forget exactly where. He was like our dad, a girl in every town. The rest of us carried on to the festival.'

'And you met Thea.'

'Yes. She was nineteen, very pretty, down with a group of friends, but by the time the weekend was over, they went home and she stayed on. I'd got a couple of weeks' holiday booked from work and she came with us. We wandered round Somerset, went down into Cornwall. It was a lovely couple of weeks. Then I had to get back to work and Thea, Terry and Marcus stayed on.'

'How long for?' Steel asked.

'I don't know. A couple more weeks, I think. Then Terry came back.'

'Without Thea.'

'That time. Yes. He said she'd hooked up with Marcus and he was staying on for a while. That she'd found a job in a hotel . . . I think. It was summer, there would have been a fair amount of casual work around, I suppose.'

A hotel, Steel thought. Weren't Marcus's wider family, the Vitellis, in the hotel business? Was there a link there too?

'And then?'

'And then I don't know.'

'She met me,' Madeleine's husband said.

'I'd got a new job in a school reception. Brian worked there and it all happened a bit quickly after that. By Christmas we'd moved in together, but I'd moved away from London anyway after the summer. Taken this new job, found a bedsit.'

'So you'd not seen Terry or Marcus?'

'Terry a couple of times. Marcus, no. I didn't go back until the following summer when I went to a family wedding and I told our father that I was leaving for good. Terry wasn't pleased. No one else was bothered but Terry had this sort of proprietorial air, you know. Even within the family.'

'And you heard from Thea?'

'Not for a while. I got postcards for a bit, the odd phone call. She sounded happy. I saw Marcus at the wedding and he told me it hadn't worked out. He had to come back to London and she'd stayed in Somerset. They'd kept seeing one another for a while, but . . . long-distance romances are hard.'

Steel nodded, considering his next question. Sophie got there first.

'So Thea was nineteen when you all met. It was a couple of years after that when she hooked up with Terry.'

'He brought her back to London the summer after the family wedding. The summer after I left, yes. She was pregnant.'

'Did you renew your contact with her?'

Madeleine glanced away. 'We'd sort of kept in touch,' she said. 'Terry didn't like it, but at first Thea didn't care. It was only after Sarah was born that he really started to wear her down. Even so, she stuck it for another seven years, didn't she, stupid little—'

'And in the meantime, your father died and you got on with your life.'

She nodded.

'And Marcus?'

'I had Christmas and birthday cards. Nothing more. I left, they cut me off. Same difference.'

'But you kept in touch with Trinny?' Sophie reminded her.

For the first time, Madeleine smiled properly. 'Aunt Trinny,' she said. 'We lived in the big house at the end of the road and she was in the middle of the terrace. Terry moved Thea in three doors down.'

'And do you remember someone called Josette Harris?'

Madeleine laughed harshly. 'That bitch. I remember her. Why?'

'Because she called the incident room asking about Sarah, said she was a friend.'

'A friend? You have to be kidding me. She was Roddy's bit on the side. Rumour was Terry wasn't above . . . anyway, she was no friend. Thea hated her guts.'

So maybe she was fishing on behalf of someone else, Steel thought. 'You were telling us about Trinny.'

'She and Mum were friends. Dad tried it on with her but she wasn't having anything to do with it. I think he respected her in an odd kind of way. When Mum was dying she was in and out of our house like family. Sat with her for hours. Mum was terrified of going into hospital, dying away from her family, and Dad said that he would never let that happen. And he never did. He paid for nurses, but Mum liked to have Trinny there. So, I kept in touch and she tried to keep an eye on Thea because I asked her to.'

Steel nodded. He doubted Madeleine could tell him much more. 'You were packing,' he said.

'Yes. We're going away for a while. Brian's school think it's a family bereavement.'

'Well, I suppose it is. In a way,' Steel said. 'Madeleine, I'd like a phone number, just in case I need to contact you again.'

'Why would you? I've told you all I know.' But she gave him one anyway and he entered it into his phone.

'Just one more thing,' Willis said as they were about to leave. 'Did Marcus ever use an alias?'

'What, a false name? Oh, all the time. It was a game to him. He'd got false ID in all sorts of names. Mostly, I think, just because it amused him. Just because he could.'

'And did one of them happen to be Anthony Bertram?'

She shrugged. 'Might have been. He had a thing about the name Tony for a while. He hated the name Marcus.'

'And what about these?' Steel spread the copies of the A4 sheet, with the taped key and the business cards, out on the table.

'Looks like a locker key,' Brian said.

'That's pretty much what we thought. Do the names or numbers mean anything to you? Roddy Bishop and Karla Brunel? Did Roddy ever use a different name?'

'I don't think so. Not that I remember.' Madeleine shook her head. 'The business card. Maxwell and the rest. I think they were the solicitors our dad used, but I don't really remember.'

Steel nodded. 'Call me if you think of anything,' he said.

As they drove away Sophie asked him, 'How much of that do you think was true?'

'In broad terms, I think most of it. I also think she was more fond of Marcus, aka Victor Griffin, than she'd like her husband to think. And I suspect she had an inkling of what the names and numbers might be, but she's so busy denying her past that she won't let herself think about it.'

'Sounds convoluted.'

'Probably is.' Steel conceded. 'But it makes a few connections clearer at any rate and it raises the question again: did Marcus and Thea keep in touch all that time?'

'I'd bet on it,' Sophie said.

FIFTY

Steel and Sophie checked in at the hospital. There'd been a press conference at noon – which Steel was relieved not to have handled, though he did feature as the subject of questions. Links were being made to Roddy Baldwin and the two deaths in Ferrymouth and Steel was curious as to how that had come about. The Griffins might have been a mystery, but no one had suggested that the name Baldwin was relevant.

Questions had been asked too about Joey Hughes and his mother. Absence of anything useful or new to report had led to some odd little stories about the growth of rural crime.

Steel shook his head as he listened to the radio.

'Don't fret, boss. They'll get bored soon enough and bugger off home. I imagine they're jockeying for position down in London right now. Roddy Baldwin is bigger news.'

'And once the link is fully established? That Lisanne Griffin was his one time sister-in-law? That Ricky Lang was a half brother? I'm surprised no one's come up with that one yet.'

'Oh, there's time,' Sophie said cheerfully. 'I reckon that'll be on the six o'clock.'

Sarah was in poor spirits. Stacy was back. Maggie had gone into work for a few hours and taken Tel with her so they could get something to eat and a change of clothes.

There was no encouraging news about Joey. Steel stood in the reception of the high dependency unit and looked through the glass. The doctor he had been waiting for came and stood beside him. 'Any change?'

'None, I'm afraid.'

'His chances?'

The doctor hesitated. 'Poor, at best,' he said. 'But every hour is a bonus. Every day an even bigger one.'

'Will there be brain damage?'

'I can't tell you that, not yet.'

Steel left, depressed and frustrated. Sophie was waiting for him beside the car. 'No news on Hughes,' she said. 'A few possible sightings, but nothing conclusive. The neighbour who recognized Ricky Lang as one of the men that called on the Griffins has tried to write a list of days and times she spotted them, but—'

Steel nodded. 'Everyone wants to be useful,' he said. 'But the truth is, it's all ground to a shuddering halt, hasn't it?'

'We could pay another visit to Terry Baldwin.'

'We could. Our colleagues at the Met would really love that. If nothing useful has broken in the meantime I'll call the prison, see what we can arrange. But not today. I think you've done enough driving and I've had enough of being driven. I want to talk to Naomi and Alec and then see what we can do with that list of names and numbers.'

Sophie smiled. 'You do know a dozen people are working that angle already, don't you?'

'And what else am I going to do? Sit about and twiddle my thumbs?' He thumped down into the passenger seat and closed his eyes. 'I feel like someone's slamming doors in my face,' he said. 'I've got three shot dead and one battered to death and one who probably won't survive the next few hours, and I'm getting absolutely nowhere. And the bastards putting the biggest block on me are those supposed to be on the same side.'

'They're scared of a turf war. Who wouldn't be? Someone has to replace Roddy Baldwin, and while the Vitellis and the Baldwins are busy accusing one another of murder it'll be like a powder keg.'

'Drive me to the Dog,' he said. 'Then you go and check in with the incident room. I'll join you as soon as I've had a word with the Friedmans.'

Sarah had drifted off to sleep. She'd had so little the night before and exhaustion finally overcame anxiety. Stacy watched her for a while and then decided she needed to stretch her legs for a bit. She wandered out into the corridor and looked through the window down into the car park below. The overnight rain had cleared and given way to a clear and blustery day. She leaned her head against the glass, thinking about her family and her kid sister, not much older than Sarah. About Joey and the probability that he wouldn't survive. She closed her eyes.

'Stacy?' Sarah came out into the hall. 'I wondered where you were.'

'Sorry, Sarah. I thought you were asleep.'

'Can we walk down to the coffee machine?'

'I don't see why not.' Steel had left her more change. 'You want a hot chocolate?'

'I think so, yeah.'

'Did something wake you up?'

Sarah nodded. 'I had this weird dream,' she said. 'It was kind of like I was remembering too. You ever have dreams like that?'

'Sometimes. Are your feet cold? Where are the slipper socks Maggie brought for you?'

'I'm OK. I'll put them on in a minute. I wish I could go and live with Maggie. What do you think will happen when . . . when I get out of here?'

'I don't know, love. I really don't. But wherever you end up staying you know that Maggie and Tel will keep in touch. They love you, you know that?'

'And Joey,' Sarah said softly. 'Him too.'

Oh Christ, Stacy thought. 'Him too,' she said. 'And me if you want me to.'

'Thanks. I'd like that.' She wiped her eyes, tears never very far away. Stacy put an arm round her shoulders and hugged her. 'So, what was your dream about, then?'

They walked slowly towards the vending machine. I've practically worn a furrow in this corridor, Stacy thought.

'I was dreaming that I was just a little kid again, before we ran away from my dad. He was in the other room, downstairs. He'd told me to go away, so I had. He was always telling me to get out of his way. Sometimes he'd just turf me out of the house. Mum wasn't home, but I don't know where she was. I'd gone into the kitchen to get a drink when I heard him come downstairs and let someone in.'

'You remember who?'

'Not really, no. The voice sounded kind of familiar, like family, but it . . . I don't know. Dreams are like that though, aren't they?'

'They are. Yes. You said this was more like a memory?'

Sarah nodded. 'Yes, but it's all kind of confused, you know. They were talking about something, planning something, I think. Some kind of theft. My dad said that the man should go.'

Stacy fed coins into the vending machine and bought them both chocolate. The flimsy cups were hot as she carried them back to Stacy's room.

'The man went and I looked out of the kitchen window – which was silly, because the kitchen was at the back and he'd gone out of the front door. But he heard me. My dad, I mean. He heard me and he came into the kitchen yelling and threatening and I hid under the table because I couldn't get out of the back door.'

'Did it upset you? The dream?'

Sarah perched on the side of the bed and Stacy put the chocolate cups down. 'Careful, it's very hot.'

'Sort of,' she said. 'I used to dream about him all the time. I used to dream real things about him. Memories all mixed up with bad things in my dreams. Mum used to tell me that the things I dreamed never happened. She used to tell me it was all imagination.'

'And what do you think? Do you think you dreamed of real things?'

Sarah hesitated before she replied. 'I used to believe her,' she said. 'She'd kind of made me believe that when I dreamed about him it was just because I was worried, you know. But I keep thinking about it now. I keep wondering. It was like she wanted me to think I couldn't remember anything right. That everything about him was different to what I thought.'

'But he was violent. You know that.'

'She never tried to tell me that he wasn't. It was the things he argued about, not with her but with other people. No one takes much notice of little kids. If he saw me he'd tell me to get out. Sometimes I just hid in the other room. Sometimes I listened near the windows.'

'Can you remember any of those things?'

'I don't know. Maybe I just think I remember, you know?'

Stacy nodded. 'I could get you some paper and you could try to write things down,' she said.

Sarah thought about it and then nodded. 'I suppose it's something to do,' she said.

FIFTY-ONE

Steel arrived at the Dog just after four. He discovered that they had a visitor already. The man sitting with them in the snug was a little older than the Friedmans, with close-cropped sandy hair and pale eyes. His face was lined and tanned, suggesting a life spent outside. They introduced him as Gregory and Steel got the impression that Naomi was not totally comfortable with Steel meeting him. From the paper-work spread out on the table and the computer set up on a nearby stool, Steel guessed that this might be the informant they had mentioned. He was a little reticent of speaking in front of this stranger. Gregory, Steel noted, said very little. He was watchful, wary even. Steel wondered about him but he departed soon after Steel arrived, and Alec lost no time in telling him what they had discovered since they had spoken last.

'We know that Marcus Karadzic worked for the Winslow Trust,' Alec said.

'Did he now?'

'What we don't know is why he left or even why he went to work for them in the first place. He had no need to. Unless he was trying to emulate Madeleine Jeffries and break away from the family business.'

Steel listened while they told him what they knew about Maxwell, Clarke and Roper and their various levels of business. It chimed with what Madeleine Jeffries had told him earlier that day.

'And we've turned up something interesting about a possible business deal between the Vitellis and the Baldwins,' Naomi added. 'It seems they both have an interest in a property in Brighton. The fact that they are working together on some project or other is suggestive, don't you think?'

'And you have this information from where?'

'Sorry, can't tell you,' Alec said.

Alec handed Steel a copy of the paperwork Gregory had removed from Roddy Baldwin's study. Steel flicked through it, puzzled. The significance dawning. 'Where did you get this?'

'I said, I can't tell you.'

'That's very close to obstruction, Alec.'

'Giving you information is *assistance*, not obstruction,' Alec said. 'Steel, take what's on offer. Check it out. You want to solve this. The rest is all academic.'

'Is it?'

Alec ignored the question. 'The house is apparently semi derelict, but potentially worth a hell of a lot. But I wonder if that was the only motive. It's worth looking at, surely?'

Steel nodded. 'Perhaps,' he agreed.

'Anything on the list of numbers yet?' Naomi asked.

'Not yet, but we're working on it. Alec, Naomi, your friend Gregory—'

'Is just a friend,' Naomi told him.

Dissatisfied, Steel made his way back to the incident room carrying the papers that the Friedmans had given him. Once there he asked one of the team to check out the Land Registry for the Brighton house.

Sophie came over to give him an update and found him pensive.

'Something wrong?'

'Only that the Friedmans seem to have access to better intelligence than we do.'

'Ah.'

'Ah what?'

Sophie looked a little shame faced. 'I kind of checked them out a bit,' she said. 'I was curious, you know. I could understand Naomi having to leave the force, obviously. But Alec . . . I remembered hearing something about him. Some kind of disciplinary stuff.'

'Oh?'

'No, it was all dismissed, but he's got connections in some odd places. He's been brought in as consultant a couple of times before this, but when I tried poking about I hit a bit of a wall.'

'What kind of wall?'

'The kind that says I don't have clearance,' she said. 'I can dump the stuff I found to your computer, if you like.'

'Do that,' Steel said. Another door slammed in his face, he thought. He indicated the paperwork on his desk. 'This lot just came from them,' he said. 'Sophie, I want you to go through it with me, then we'll see what needs further attention. These are all copies and I'm not sure I can ever prove it, but I suspect the originals were all obtained from Roddy Baldwin.'

'Interesting.' She eyed the small stack of paper warily. 'How?'

'One of their contacts. I sort of met him today. At least I think I did.'

'Sounds like the man who wasn't there,' Sophie laughed. 'You know, the nursery rhyme. You don't think he had anything to do with Roddy Baldwin's death?'

Steel shrugged, not entirely sure he was ready to know that just now. 'So what do you have to tell me?' he asked.

'Well, a few interesting bits. Our colleagues in Nottingham tracked down Josette Harris, the woman who called wanting news on Sarah?'

'And who Madeleine Jeffries is sure was involved with Roddy, and possibly Terry.' Steel nodded. 'And?'

'And nothing. She denies hearing from Terry in years, says she was nothing to him anyway, and stuck to her story about being friends with Thea.'

Steel nodded. He had expected nothing else.

'Then there's the financial records for the Griffins. All very normal: the only money going into Lisanne's account was her wages from the surgery and child benefit for the kids. Victor Griffin had an account too; his wages went in, and there's the odd small payment in cash and cheques, but nothing suspicious. Apparently he did a bit of IT support on the side. Then they had a joint account for housekeeping and bills. They both paid into that each month. They seem very organized,' she added. 'Wish I was. But there's one anomaly. When they moved here, they bought the house for cash.'

'Are you sure?'

'Certain. One of our lot traipsed around local estate agents finding out who'd sold the place. They remembered the Griffins, especially with recent events bringing it all back to mind. Stow and Walton,' she added, checking her notes. 'They went back through their records and the Griffins definitely bought for cash. They did a BACS transfer, but get this: there's an IBAN number attached to the code the money came from. It wasn't from a British bank.'

Steel sat forward. 'And the estate agents, they didn't think that odd?'

'I imagine they were just thinking about the sale. They thought they remembered that the Griffins had sold a house abroad and just moved back to the UK; all the transactions were smooth, so . . .'

Steel nodded. 'So where did the money come from? How much was the sale for?'

'A hundred and fifty thousand pounds. It had been on the

market for a bit less than that, and that's top end for round here three or four years ago. The housing market's taken a right battering and Ferrymouth isn't exactly commuter belt. Apparently there were other couples after it, but the Griffins offered cash. Above the asking price. I don't imagine the vendors hesitated for long.'

Steel nodded. 'Our view of the Griffins is subtly changing, isn't it?' he said. 'Sophie, I want you to go and tackle the Winslow Trust again; see if Naomi wants to go along for the ride. I don't care who you talk to, or how long you have to spend on their doorstep, but I want detail on what Victor Griffin, aka Marcus Karadzic, did for them and why he was dismissed.'

News came in from the hospital a little after that. It wasn't good. Joey was showing no signs of improvement; if anything his condition had destabilized. Steel called Stacy, warning her that there might be more bad news to break.

'Maggie and Tel are here,' she said. 'Maggie made Tel bring some homework in, which, actually, I now think was inspired. Sarah's helping Tel with his French comprehension and they're both managing to escape into normality for a while.'

'She's an unusual woman,' Steel said. Her husband is definitely a bloody fool, he thought. 'I'll be along later. You want someone to relieve you?'

'Tonight would be nice. I'm missing my bed and the cat thinks I've left home.'

Steel promised he would sort something out and rang off.

There had been a few more sightings of a man that might be Hughes, but nothing more than that. The irony of it is, Steel thought, that there are more police in Ferrymouth than the place has seen in probably the past thirty years and none of us have got time to look for one murderer because we're too busy looking for another.

He decided he would shift his priorities. Instinct told him that the Griffin case was falling from his grasp, the field of play getting steadily larger and more remote from his patch. Hughes, on the other hand – always supposing he hadn't run – was a known quantity, a local who could be recognized.

That settled, Steel took himself off to speak once more to Lisanne's neighbours, in the probably vain hope that, now Ricky Lang had been identified, someone might remember something more about the other man who had called on the Griffins in the days before their murder.

FIFTY-TWO

G regory returned to the Dog in time for dinner. 'I've brought you a phone number,' he said. 'Did Steel want to know who I was?'

'We told him you were a friend,' Alec said. 'I doubt he's satisfied, he's too good a policeman to be satisfied with any of this. But it'll have to do.'

'What number?' Naomi asked.

'The private line of Mr Alphonso Vitelli. I pulled a few strings,' he added. 'The rumour is the Vitellis are being blamed for Baldwin's death. They in their turn are making accusations about double dealing. They don't yet seem to realize that Victor Griffin was one of theirs. The Met don't appear to have passed the message on.'

'But Roddy Baldwin knew. Terry knew. And it's standard practice to inform next of kin.'

'Interesting, yes? I'm beginning to think that Roddy Baldwin had more fingers in this pie than we first thought. And talking about pie . . .'

Gregory looked up expectantly as Douggie and one of his bar staff came into the snug carrying trays.

'I assumed you'd show up,' Douggie told Gregory sternly. 'So I served up an extra plate.'

Gregory thanked him solemnly, told him it looked good. Douggie seemed mollified if not exactly approving. 'Everything all right?' he asked Alec.

'It's all fine, thanks, Douggie. You've made us very welcome.'

The look the landlord shot Gregory brought that into a bit of doubt.

'And so, this number,' Naomi said when the landlord had gone. 'Why should I call Alphonso Vitelli?'

'Because he should know what happened to his grandson,' Gregory said. 'Because it's time all sides knew where they stand. Because, I'm guessing, the Vitellis hold the rest of the cards in play. Because you met the man and he'll remember you.'

Naomi shook her head. 'Why would he? It was years ago. I was just one of the makeweights sent to an event. I was a nobody.'

'He'll remember,' Gregory predicted. 'Not many cops came to his parties and I'll bet there were none as pretty as Naomi Blake.'

'Gregory!'

Alec laughed at her response. 'Are you flirting with my wife?'

'I don't flirt,' he said. 'But you'll admit I have a point?'

They ate in silence for a few minutes while Naomi thought about it. They had spoken briefly to Steel earlier and Naomi, unable really to back off, had called an old friend in the Met and asked a few direct questions about the state of play down there. It wasn't that she doubted Steel's intention to pass their information on, just that she wasn't sure if he'd frame it with sufficient urgency. She was told it was looking tense, that it felt as if everyone was holding their breath.

'I'll call him,' she said. 'But I don't know what good it will do. What should I say?'

For a while they discussed it, knowing that even if they got directly through to old Alphonso he was unlikely to take the call himself. In the final analysis they decided to go with Gregory's original suggestion. Just after seven fifteen Naomi called the number he had obtained from Nathan.

'Tell him,' Naomi said, 'that we met once, about seven years ago, at a charity ball. That my name was then Naomi Blake and that I'd just been made detective inspector. Tell him I know what happened to his grandson, Marcus Karadzic. That I'm sorry to say that Marcus is now dead.'

At Gregory's insistence she left his number and not hers.

'So,' she said. 'What now?'

'Now we wait. They'll check you out, see if you're worth contacting, and when they realize you are someone will call back.'

FIFTY-THREE

The following morning Steel called at the hospital before going to the incident room.

Sarah was trying hard to be upbeat. Stacy had been down to the unit which housed Joey and he seemed to have rallied a little.

'He's going to be all right,' Sarah told Steel with as much conviction as she could muster.

'I hope so,' he said. 'I really do.'

She seemed to have lost a lot of weight, he thought, despite Stacy feeding her hot chocolate and pizza and anything else she could tempt the girl with. Dark circles were a permanent feature beneath her eyes and her hair, always carefully maintained in the pictures he had seen of her, looked unkempt and dull.

'You need some fresh air.' He smiled at her, trying to sound positive and normal.

'I need everything to be a week ago,' she said. 'And for us all to be somewhere else.'

He checked in with the high dependency unit. Yes, Joey had seemed a little better, but the change was not sufficient for any real optimism.

'All we can do is wait,' Steel was told. They asked him again if Joey had other family, and Steel was forced to tell them that he still didn't know. There had been nothing at the house that did not relate just to Hughes and Joey's mother. No family photographs, no Christmas cards with a convenient address written on the back. Neither Maggie nor Sarah could recall Joey talking about trips to aunts or uncles or grandparents, or even mentioning them in passing. Joey had been as cut off from his family's past as Sarah had from hers. Steel guessed that this was another thing that had drawn them to one another.

Returning to the incident room, he found that Sophie had news for him. The Land Registry search had been fruitful.

'The house had been through a lot of changes,' she told him, 'But about ten years ago it was rented by the Winslow Trust. The building was sold shortly after to Mr Thomas Vitelli and Mr Roddy Baldwin – who became the Trust's new landlords. It was in a poor state even then, but the Trust used the bottom two floors as offices and sublet the middle one to students. The small suite of rooms on the top floor – well, it looks as though they used it as emergency accommodation from time to time. And guess who worked there?'

'Marcus Karadzic. Our man Victor Griffin.'

She nodded. 'A warrant has been served – the Trust lease ran out and they didn't renew. It's been empty since, boarded up and left – so there'll be a search of the place later this morning with a bit of luck. Sounds like they are waiting for structural engineers to go in and declare the place safe first.'

'Good.' Steel nodded. Maybe things were moving. 'You're off to the Trust this morning?'

'Yes, taking Naomi. I'm picking her up in half an hour. That Julia woman talked mainly to her last time. She barely looked at me.'

He went through to his office and dragged the phone across the desk. His arm was hurting this morning, burning and stinging, and he suspected a slight infection. Maybe he'd call on Dr Pauley later, get the medic to patch him up properly. It wasn't easy to manage one handed. He called Vic Griffin's old employers; something Sophie had told him the day before had been nagging at his mind. She'd said that Vic Griffin did some IT stuff on the side. What did he do and how good was he?

He spoke to the manager of the agricultural supply company Vic Griffin had worked for, and was then handed over to a couple of Vic's colleagues. By the time he had finished his conversations, he had his answer. Vic Griffin was very good indeed. He'd single-handedly redesigned the ordering system at work, streamlining the process and updating their spreadsheets and databases so that anyone in the company could access straightforward menus with a couple of key strokes.

'He saved us a lot of time and a considerable amount of money,' Steel was told.

He'd been the go-to guy when anyone wanted computers installed, viruses dealt with, advice on what to buy.

'He knew all about stocks and shares and online trading,' he was told. 'You know, all that financial stuff. He did something . . . what did he call it . . . day trading? Does that sound right? He was a real tech head.'

Steel returned the landline phone to its cradle and sat back, staring at it, not entirely sure how this latest snippet of information fitted in with everything else.

He wondered what Sophie would learn from the Trust this time and what would happen once police finally got into the Brighton house.

Naomi was not in a fit frame of mind to go with DS Sophie Willis that morning, but she could not think of a good reason to say no. They had still had no response from the Vitellis and had almost given up hope. To be honest, she'd been of a mind to resist Gregory's persuasion – it seemed like an outrageous and foolish thing to do; something akin to poking an uncaged tiger with a stick – but now she had committed, she was impatient to play the end game.

'Penny for them,' Sophie said.

'Sorry. Not very good company, am I?'

'That's all right, but you do seem a bit out of sorts.'

Naomi smiled. She supposed she was. 'Apart from anything else, I'm thinking this trip is a waste of time,' she confessed. 'I get the feeling that the Trust want to keep us very much at arm's length, and we can't even guarantee that there'll be anyone in charge that we can talk to, turning up unannounced.'

'True,' Sophie agreed, 'but announcing ourselves didn't do us any favours last time, did it? Personally, I think we'll end up having to get a warrant for their personnel files, but who knows?'

'And what exactly are we asking anyway?'

'How long Marcus Karadzic worked for them and why he was dismissed.' She glanced at Naomi, unable to resist a little dig. 'I don't suppose this mysterious informant of yours would be able to tell us that, would he?'

Naomi's mouth twitched in a slight smile. 'Given time, probably.'

'Who is he, then?'

'A friend. Just a friend.'

Sophie laughed; she hadn't expected a straight answer. 'You and Alec have had a busy couple of years,' she said. 'I got curious and looked you both up.'

'I don't imagine you found a lot of detail,' Naomi said.

'No, you're right there.'

Sophie glanced sideways at her again, wondering if patience and persistence would earn her more information. She decided they would not.

'Any news on the Hughes case?' Naomi asked and Sophie Willis allowed herself to be led on to neutral ground.

'Nothing yet. Sightings that were probably the local milkman. You ask me, he's long gone. Steel seems to think he'll hang around.'

'I wouldn't be surprised,' Naomi said. 'He'll want to see how everyone behaves, what reaction he's got. I don't know that you can expect him to do the sensible thing.'

'Well, we're here,' Sophie said. 'Here we go.'

'Into battle?' Naomi smiled at Sophie's tone. 'And the boy, Joey. Any news?'

'Nothing good. But Steel has shoved more resources into catching Hughes. If he's still around, we'll get him for what he did.'

As it happened, there was a conference on in the ugly steel and glass centre and so Julia Tennant was present – and not best pleased to see them again. She showed them into the same room and told a woman at reception that she was not to be disturbed.

'What do you want?'

Naomi spoke first. 'Information. Hopefully you can give it to us without our having to go and apply for a warrant. If it got out that the Winslow Trust was obstructing a murder inquiry it wouldn't play very well in the media, would it?'

Sophie was a little startled that Naomi had taken the lead. Julia was furious. 'Is that a threat?' she asked. 'If so, then it's very ill judged. You are here, I believe, as a civilian. You have no authority—'

'I don't,' Naomi agreed. 'Neither do I have to be polite and circumspect, as my friend here does. And I'm also deeply resentful that you weren't straight with us last time we were here.'

'In what way? I answered your questions. I—'

'Did you know that Victor Griffin had worked for you in the past? True, you might have known him then by his real name—'

'Which was what? If he'd changed his name, how on earth was I supposed to recognize it?'

'Because I suspect you already knew. I suspect that when Dr Pauley was asked to give Lisanne an interview you – or whoever her friend was within the organization (you do refer to your contacts as "friends", don't you?) – would have checked out the man she was living with. No one would want a scandal. No one would want to take the risk that a woman you'd been protecting had shacked up with a violent man, one with a record, one that was unacceptable.'

'We don't control people's lives,' Julia said. 'We don't do in-depth background checks of those they choose to live with after we've got them away.'

'But you do some checking?' Sophie interrupted.

'Yes. We look for criminal records, anything obvious. Nothing came up for Victor Griffin.'

'Then perhaps you could check it out now. Victor Griffin, a man you'd have known as Marcus Karadzic, worked for you about ten years ago, we think for about three years. From our information, he was dismissed from his job. We'd like to know why.'

'I can't just—'

'I think you can,' Naomi said. 'And while you're checking, perhaps you could see if he ever had access to this location.' She took a slip of paper from her pocket on which was written the address of the house in Brighton. 'Police are waiting to search it,' she added.

'Waiting?' Julia looked at the piece of paper and Sophie saw a flash of recognition in her eyes. 'The Trust rented this place for a while. It was too expensive to keep on. What are they waiting for?'

'Apparently it's structurally unsound,' Sophie said. 'Structural engineers are assessing it before they let our colleagues enter. Did Marcus Karadzic work there?'

Julia shook her head. 'I have no idea,' she said.

'But you can go and find out?'

She hesitated and then seemed to make up her mind. 'I'll see what I can do,' she said. 'Then you go. Come back again and I'll be the one raising the media storm when I accuse you of harassment.'

Naomi received a phone call from Alec on the way back. Gregory had called. The meeting would take place that evening, at the Dog. Alphonso Vitelli was sending a representative to hear what she had to say.

A second phone call came through to Sophie's phone. She was driving and her phone was on a hands free cradle. 'Steel,' she said. She pressed the speakerphone button. 'Boss?'

'They've gone into the Brighton house,' he said. 'There's a sub basement that's been blocked off behind a false wall. They're focusing the search there. Any luck your end?'

'Some, yes. Marcus Karadzic started as a general assistant; by the time he'd left he was working on their IT, creating databases and looking after their financial resources. He couldn't actually touch any of the money himself, or so Julia Tennant reckons, but it looks as though he was sacked for trying.'

'So, not such a white hat after all,' Steel commented. 'And if he tried it once—'

'He may well have done it again, and against a less forgiving target,' Sophie agreed.

FIFTY-FOUR

B y the time they returned to Ferrymouth there was a little more information. The police search team had entered the sub basement and found another false wall, beyond which was a set of old school-style lockers. Three were locked and the locks appeared to be of the kind that the key in Thea's letter might fit. It seemed likely that anything hidden there would have been left by the man who became Victor Griffin.

Steel paced impatiently waiting for more information as Sophie reprised what had happened when they met Julia Tennant this time around.

'If the Baldwins or the Vitellis knew there was something hidden there, why didn't they just look?' Sophie asked.

'I wondered the same thing. Apparently the place is a death trap. It took the engineers three hours to make it safe this morning. And anyone searching would have had to be aware that the basement was there, and that sections had been walled off. Apparently it had been done when the Trust rented it – I'd speculate that Vic had had a hand in it – but there was still a way in via a service hatch. You'd have to know it was there, and you'd have to be small enough to get through.'

'Not Vic, then. He was a solid lump of a man.'

'No, but *Thea* might have been slight enough to get inside. She must have left whatever's down there just before she ran, perhaps thinking that as her family owned the building it would be safe in its hiding place indefinitely.'

Steel nodded. 'But now we're just going to have to wait.'

Gregory was waiting for Naomi at the Dog, sitting with Alec in the snug.

'So, the meeting is on, then?'

'It's on. We're just waiting for the call,' Gregory said.

'Where are we meeting?'

'When I did my little scout around I found a place by the river. Parking and picnic spot, by the looks of it. No one around this time of year. It's open and you can see anything coming for miles. It's less likely that anyone will get jumpy.'

'Not here, then?'

'Too many curious eyes,' Gregory told her. 'This way is better. When we get the call you and I will walk up there while Alec goes to fetch Steel.'

'You're involving Steel?'

'It's better that way,' Alec said. 'Makes it sort of official.'

'And the Vitellis know that?'

'They know,' Gregory said calmly. 'We all want answers, don't we? They see as well as I do that this saves time and could prevent a few repercussions later on.'

'Repercussions?'

Gregory shrugged. 'There are times when you don't need witnesses and times when you do,' he said.

Gregory's phone rang. He listened. 'This is it,' he said.

Steel hadn't been sure what to think when Alec had come to fetch him but something in Alec's manner told him not to ask too much until they were outside. Walking along the river path, Alec filled him in on what they had done.

'You're certifiable. The pair of you. You know that?'

Alec shrugged. 'It just seemed to us that the number of available witnesses to what actually happened when Thea Baldwin left is diminishing rather rapidly. There are clear indications, now, of something going on between the Baldwins and the Vitellis, and there have been enough deaths.'

'And what do you hope to gain by this?'

'The truth,' Alec said. 'What actually happened. Why Thea and Vic were killed; maybe even who was really responsible.'

'You think the Vitellis organized the hit?'

Alec shook his head. 'Actually, no. My money's on Roddy Baldwin.'

A strong, damp wind blew across the estuary as they rounded the bend beside the river and came upon the picnic ground. A black car was parked up and beside it stood two men. A third, in a wheelchair, sat close by, his chair wheeled up to a picnic bench. The old man in the chair, dressed in a thick, dark coat, woollen scarf and grey fedora, was talking to Naomi. The man called Gregory stood nearby.

Alec and Steel halted as one of the men stepped forward from the car.

'Let him search you,' Gregory instructed. 'He needs to feel he's doing his job.'

Reluctantly Alec raised his arms and was patted down. To Steel's surprise, when it was his turn the man treated his wounded arm gently. He looked at Gregory, who shrugged. 'I expect he knows how much bullet wounds hurt,' he said.

They walked over to where Naomi sat. 'This is Alphonso Vitelli,' she said. 'He would like to know how his grandson died.'

This is surreal, Steel thought, but he sat down on the other bench, facing this old man with his paper-thin skin stretched tight over an over-large skull. 'What do you want to know?' he said.

The old man had grown cold and his bodyguard had helped him back to his car. The second man came over and sat down beside Steel and the others.

'Mr Vitelli has authorized me to give you certain information,' he said, 'on the understanding that Mr Vitelli and his family only discovered these pertinent facts over the past few days. Mr Vitelli and his family had no involvement in the events I am about to disclose and concerning which I have prepared a statement. Mr Vitelli would also like you to know that he is concerned for the welfare of his great granddaughter, Sarah. His legal team will be contacting the local social services tomorrow with a view to Mr Vitelli taking over her guardianship.'

Steel frowned. 'Mr Vitelli is a known—'

The man held up a hand. 'Mr Vitelli has a clean record,' he said. 'He is a respectable business man with the means and wherewithal to take care of his great grandchild.'

'And he had nothing to do with her stepfather's death, I suppose.'

'Nothing whatsoever. Be assured that Mr Vitelli was at a loss to know the whereabouts of Marcus Karadzic. Our enquiries over the past few days have assured us that the man responsible for his death was Roderick Baldwin.'

'And you can prove that, I suppose? What about this business deal between Baldwin and the Vitelli family? The property in Brighton—'

'That the police are currently searching? Ten years ago, Mr Baldwin expressed an interest in broadening out his business portfolio. He came to Mr Vitelli's son, Mr Thomas Vitelli, and asked advice. They came to an agreement. A business agreement. The Vitellis often invest in property; it is possible that Marcus had recommended the building to his cousin as a potential investment. We believe he was working there at the time. Before he changed his name, he was in regular contact with his family.'

'Marcus and Thea,' Naomi said.

'Were unwise.'

'In what way?'

'They fell in love. They separated, but it seems that they remained in love. According to our enquiries – and you will find details of all of this in the statement – some seven years ago, Mr Marcus Karadzic was enticed, shall we say, into assisting Terry Baldwin in a criminal act. Terry had the connections, Marcus had the skill. He'd already tried to defraud the Winslow Trust and failed, and been sacked for his trouble, but Terry believed that a second attempt at theft would be successful. The consequence was that, acting on information received from Terry Baldwin, Marcus . . . misappropriated a substantial amount of money.'

'Where from?'

The lawyer smiled. 'In the main from the Baldwin family,' he said. 'The Baldwins realized that Marcus was involved, so he had to disappear, assume a new identity. At that point, Roddy Baldwin had no idea that his own brother had also been involved; Terry believed he'd got away with it. What Terry *didn't* know was that Marcus had taken Thea into his confidence and the two of them had planned for her to join him, once they were sure they were out of the Baldwins' reach. Terry never found out, until Marcus and Thea were dead, that his ex wife hadn't just run away – she'd run into Marcus's arms. Recently, it seems, Roddy Baldwin finally tracked Marcus down, despite all of their efforts to hide, and found him with Thea. He sent representatives to try and . . . *persuade* them to return what they had taken. It seems that they told Roddy Baldwin about his brother's involvement and told him, correctly as it happens, that Terry had access to half the funds. Roddy seems to have fooled Terry into believing that a third party was willing to kill his wife and child, and, shall we say, facilitate Terry's removal from prison, if he provided details of the accounts holding the stolen money.'

'Oh, come on, even Terry isn't that stupid! He's doing an eighteen-year stretch.'

'Because of evidence that his own wife handed over. Evidence that she *might* have fabricated, a lawyer could argue.'

'So Terry Baldwin believed something could be done because that's what he wanted to be true,' Steel said. 'Incidentally, there's a flaw to your boss's plan to adopt Sarah. Victor Griffin wasn't Sarah's biological father. He had no legal rights.'

'Victor Griffin loved Sarah like his own child. That is one thing that everyone agrees upon, I believe. His last act was to try to save the life of his children. And Mr Vitelli has very good legal counsel.'

'What happened to Thea and Marcus's half of the money?' Naomi asked. 'Is it in the basement of that house?'

The lawyer shook his head. 'I doubt it,' he said. 'Marcus Karadzic seems to have moved it into offshore accounts. They dipped into those funds only on rare occasions. They were patient and careful. It seems that he wanted to do this one job, just so that they could escape from Terry Baldwin and his family.'

'He tried to defraud the Winslow Trust,' Naomi objected.

'The Trust brought no charges.' He stood up and laid an envelope on the picnic table. 'You should find all you need in there,' he said.

They watched him walk back to the car and Naomi shivered. The wind had grown colder and threatened rain and she had been sitting still for too long. The black car drove away; she heard the crunch of gravel beneath its wheels and then it was gone.

FIFTY-FIVE

J oey Hughes gave up his fight for life at eight o'clock that evening. Irregular as it might have been, Maggie had managed to get permission to sit with him and she was there, holding his hand, when he died. And now she didn't seem to know how to stop crying.

She had wept with Sarah and with Tel and with Stacy, and then cried some more when she spoke to Steel.

'I can come over,' he said.

'Thank you. I appreciate the offer. I just want to go home now. I think Tel and I just need to retreat for a while. Sarah is sleeping and Stacy is with her.'

'You've been brilliant,' Steel said. 'I'm very grateful.'

Maggie drove back to her home. Tel fell asleep in the passenger

seat and she was reminded of how, as a little kid, he used to do
that all the time and she used to carry him into the house and
lay him down in his little bed. And she cried some more because
that time was now long past and because for Joey it had never
happened.

It was after midnight and she wished she'd thought to leave
a light on. It always felt so miserable, getting back to a dark and
empty house.

Maggie felt the tears start to flow again. Impatiently she wiped
her eyes with the heels of her hands and then reached to shake
Tel into reluctant wakefulness.

'Hey, love. We're home. Time to move.'

He stumbled from the car, dazed and a little confused.

'You go up and get into bed and I'll bring you a cuppa. I need
some tea and five minutes before I turn in, I think.'

He nodded. 'Yeah. Thanks.'

Maggie let them both in and watched as Tel made his way
up the stairs. She hoped that he'd be able to sleep. That he'd
just be able to let go and forget for a while. She shed her coat
and kicked off her shoes, leaving them in the hall, and then
made her way to the kitchen. The first thing she noticed was a
draught where there had been none before. The second, as she
flicked on the kitchen light, was that the glass in the back door
had been broken. The third, hard on the heels of the second,
was that Steve Hughes was standing there, and that he held a
knife.

Maggie knew she was supposed to be scared. Instead of that,
she realized she was just mad. A slow rage that had built over
the past days seemed to bubble within her now. She could hear
Tel upstairs, flopping down on his bed, taking off his shoes. The
image of Joey Hughes lying in the hospital bed, dying even while
she watched over him; that was all she could see. It obscured
her vision of the man with the knife. There was no way he was
going to do to her son what he had done to his own.

Slowly, deliberately, eyes fixed on the man with the knife who
had invaded her domain, Maggie reached behind her and closed
the kitchen door.

Hughes laughed. 'You think that will help? I'll deal with you
and then with him.' He waved the knife in her direction. 'This

is all down to you,' he said. 'You came along and turned the boy against us. All down to you.'

Maggie said nothing in reply. Hughes had begun to move. The kitchen table stood between them. The knife had been taken from her own block. *That*, she thought, was just a step too far. He broke into her home, lay in wait and threatened her with her own damned knife!

Maggie consciously allowed the rage to grow, revelling in it, coaxing it into life. Tears forgotten, Maggie knew that now it was all about just staying alive. She grabbed a storage jar from the kitchen counter and threw it towards Hughes. It went wide. She threw another, moving away from him, towards the back door. She saw in his eyes that he expected her to run. The third jar actually hit its target, bouncing off the arm that held the knife. She could see the block he had taken it from out of her reach on the far side of the kitchen, but now he had shifted it was out of *his* reach too.

With a yell of sheer fury, Maggie grabbed the edge of the table and, throwing her whole weight behind it, drove forwards, pushing it towards Hughes. She took him by surprise. This was a man who expected to win. Who didn't expect anyone to fight back.

She trapped him momentarily against the kitchen cupboards, the table edge hard against the top of his legs. She shoved it harder and to her satisfaction Hughes yelled in pain.

Up in the room above, she heard Tel move. Heard him call.

'No!' Maggie yelled at Hughes. 'Never again, you hear me? Never again.'

She could reach the knife block now and she grabbed at it, pulling free the twin to the one Hughes held in his hand. She shoved the table again but he pushed back hard and for a moment Maggie staggered, her footing lost.

Hughes all but leapt across the room. Maggie dropped down, scrabbling away. As he turned, she pushed upward and towards him, knife gripped tight in her hand, and came up behind him.

Now, Maggie thought. It has to be now. She could hear Tel's feet on the stairs.

She plunged the knife deep into Hughes' back. 'You bastard. Bastard. Fucking bastard!'

Hughes groaned and then lay still.

'Mum.' The kitchen door was thrown open.

Maggie looked up.

Tel stood in the doorway, gazing in horror at the scene.

EPILOGUE

They drove home the next day, Alec and Naomi, leaving the aftermath behind them.

Steel had told them about Maggie and Hughes. He had died on her kitchen floor. A lucky strike, Steel said. Through his back and upward into his liver. He'd bled out. Maggie was in shock, but rage was still carrying her through and she told anyone who would listen that he deserved it.

Steel, Naomi thought, probably agreed. She knew that she did.

Joey Hughes' funeral would, Steel said, be in a week or so. He'd let them know; but Naomi knew they wouldn't go.

Sarah had been told that she had a step family who wanted to take care of her. Naomi was pretty certain that Alphonso Vitelli would get his way and somehow she couldn't manage to regret that. It was better, she thought, than being alone. Though, if she needed to escape, she would have the financial means – Lisanne and Victor's stashed fortune had been discovered, hidden in six overseas bank accounts. They'd used aliases to hide the money – Roddy Bishop and Karla Brunel. The legal process of identifying Sarah as the rightful owner of the money would be long and drawn out, but Naomi was hopeful that the money would eventually make its way to the bereaved teenager. She thought she might mention it to Gregory – just in case.

'Are you OK?' Alec asked her. 'We should be home in about an hour.'

'I'm fine,' she said. 'I was just thinking about what you said the other day, about us having crossed the line.'

'And?'

'And I can't seem to feel angry about it any more. It's just what is. I can't change it, just do my best with it, you know?'

He reached out and clasped her hand. 'I know.'

'Did Steel ever say what was in the basement? I meant to ask.'

Alec laughed. 'Nothing,' he said. 'Nothing important. At least not from a criminal point of view. It seems that Lisanne Griffin

– well, Thea as she was then – left a few possessions behind. Cards and bits of jewellery and a letter to her daughter. Just personal stuff.'

'One day I'll find that amusing,' Naomi said. 'But not yet.'

'No,' he agreed. 'Not yet.'

Maybe that was her payment for the ferryman, Naomi thought absently. You left something behind when you crossed the river.

'I want to go home,' she said. 'I want to close the door and shut the world out and I want to stay there until I've got cabin fever.'

'We'll have to go shopping first and collect the dog from Mari's place. There's no milk or bread. Then we can hide for as long as you like.'

I'd like that, Naomi thought. She closed her eyes and, lulled by the motion of the car, drifted into sleep.